PIANO
in the Dark

ED J. THOMPSON

Piano in the Dark

ISBN: 978-1-7923-2102-3

Printed in the USA.

To Stephanie and Karis:

This one's for you.

Prologue

S andy turned quickly and ducked into the storage closet. He felt bad, but there was just no way that he was going to listen to Edna Jones talk about her daughter today. He had heard it all a million times before. For some unknown reason, Sister Jones seemed to think that he and her daughter, Britney, were a match made in heaven. Actually, nothing could be further from the truth. Nothing against Britney; she was always a nice girl and he was very sorry to hear that she had been unable to find a good man. However, this was starting to border on outright harassment. Usually Sandy would just listen politely and smile appropriately while Sister Jones talked and then break away at the first available opportunity. She was known in the church as one of the resident prophets because she had supposedly accurately prophesied several future events, all based upon things she had seen in dreams. Truth be told, however, although she might hear from God in her sleep, she somehow still lacked any ability whatsoever to read social cues during her waking hours. Sandy waited a few minutes in the darkened closet until he was certain she was gone, and then he sheepishly exited.

Sandy walked quickly because he didn't want to be late for the staff meeting, another reason why he really didn't want to talk to Sister Jones. Reverend Glenn hated tardiness and he had a habit of always looking anxiously at his watch whenever anyone walked into the small conference room late. There was a regularly scheduled staff meeting every Monday afternoon at 1:00 p.m. Although there were twenty-five full-time employees at Mount Moriah Missionary Baptist Church, only professional staff attended the staff meetings. Unfortunately, that included Sandy, who was the minister of music at the church. Besides Reverend Dennis Glenn, who was the senior pastor, and Sandy, regular attendees included Assistant Pastor Willie Graham, Youth Pastor Marcus Grimes and church trustees Sabrina Watkins, Deacon Bobby Sykes, and Millie Evans. All six of them were already seated at the conference room table when Sandy walked into the room.

Reverend Glenn, who had taken his place at the head of the table with his back to the door, quickly glanced at his watch and frowned as Sandy hurried past him, but didn't say anything. Sandy whispered, "Sorry," and took his seat at the opposite end of the table.

Mount Moriah Baptist Church was the largest black church in Syracuse, New York, with approximately two thousand members. Even though the church was located in the heart of the poverty-stricken Syracuse south side, the interior of Mount Moriah was beautiful. The building itself had a very modern design with an entirely-brick interior which incorporated several stained-glass windows. Inside was a five-hundred-seat sanctuary, including a large balcony. Office space was located on the second floor, although only Pastor Glenn and Pastor Graham had their own offices. Everyone else just had a desk in a small cubicle. There was also a small kitchen, a break room, a conference room, two bathrooms, and a small waiting room for visitors.

The exterior of the building, however, was anything but grand. There was a chain-link fence around the entire perimeter of the building except for the front entrance. The main parking lots were located inside of the fenced-in area behind the church and were protected by exterior lighting. Directly across the street in front was an overgrown open lot that was littered with debris.

Reverend Dennis Glenn had been the pastor of the church for just ten years. Before that, Sandy's father, the Reverend Stephenson Coleman, Sr., had been the senior pastor for almost twenty years. He had a massive heart attack and died suddenly one Sunday night after having preached two sermons earlier in the day. The church's board of trustees had conducted a statewide search for a new pastor and eventually settled on Reverend Glenn, who was originally from nearby Rochester, New York. Many people left the church when he first arrived, but the church managed to survive the short-lived exodus and was having consistent growth ever since that time.

Reverend Glenn started the meeting the same way that he began every meeting, with the question, "So what did everyone think of the message yesterday?" Sandy, for one, always hated that question because it seemed like Reverend Glenn was not seeking an honest critique of his sermon, but rather was just soliciting compliments from everyone. Almost on cue, Sister Millie chimed right in.

"Pastor, I thought it was really powerful. I really did. Romans 8 has always been one of my favorite chapters in the Bible and I really believe that it is more important than ever that we understand what it means to be righteous in Christ and not to be consumed with guilt and condemnation. People are just too quick to judge others these days, I always say. Like any one of us are perfect. What I mean is that I thought that you really made the point well and I think a lot of people got blessed yesterday. I just really want

7

to thank you for that, Pastor. I have to say that my spirit man rejoiced greatly within me for the rest of the day. Praise God!"

Reverend Glenn chuckled to himself and coyly asked, "Anyone else?"

Deacon Sykes responded, "That was a good one, Pastor. We didn't have to worry about anyone going to sleep. The people know when God is speaking to them."

"Amen," Millie offered, "that is so true."

"Did you see all the people who responded to the altar call?" Deacon Sykes continued, referring to the appeal for salvation that Pastor Glenn routinely made at the end of all his sermons.

"According to the report," Reverend Glenn proudly read, "looks like there were fifteen people in the first service and twenty-six people in the second service."

Sabrina Watkins, who worked in the business office, promptly spoke up. "Surprisingly, the collection was up yesterday too. Normally, offering is down a little in the fall because of football season and because a lot of our older members stay home because it's so cold in the mornings now. It's always a good sign that the message really ministered to people's hearts when the numbers are good."

"I just felt that the Holy Spirit was prompting me all week to remind people that they didn't have to live in bondage to sin any longer. Where the Spirit is, there is liberty. That is why I had the choir sing 'Loosed and Free ,'" Reverend Glenn stated.

Millie added, "Like I said before, it was really powerful! I love to hear you sing that song, Sandy. Reminded me of your father. It was truly anointed." She was looking at Sandy, smiling and tearing up at the same time.

"Thank you," replied Sandy, trying to sound sincere.

He hated to be drawn into the discussion. He had always thought that it was wrong somehow to praise people too much for doing what God supposedly had told them to do. He felt like it took the focus off Jesus and onto the person. However, he also understood that it was important to encourage people to be obedient to the Spirit of God. Ministry was hard work, and everyone needed to be encouraged from time to time. It was easy to grow weary. His father had taught him that.

Looking at his watch, Reverend Glenn said, "Well praise God, but we should probably move along so that you all can get back to work."

No one spoke much after that besides Reverend Glenn. He was not a bad person, a little awkward maybe. However, he certainly was a hard worker. Typically, Reverend Glenn was the first one at the church on Sunday morning and the last one to leave in the afternoon. That Sandy had no special affinity for him was due, in part, to the fact that neither one of them were particularly outgoing. Sandy's father loved being with people and almost craved their attention. In contrast, Reverend Glenn appeared to be playing the role of the reluctant servant leader. He was always just a little too aloof for Sandy's liking.

It took Reverend Glenn about fifty-five minutes to get through the entire agenda, most of which pertained to the upcoming holiday services. Thanksgiving and Christmas, along with Easter, Mother's Day and Father's Day, were the highlights of the church's yearly calendar. Each one of these services required new music and additional rehearsal time. Sandy was always completely drained when one of them was all over, but the feeling of accomplishment from a job well done felt good at the same time. Reverend Glenn liked to talk about the importance of preparation and thinking big and he took this opportunity to remind everyone, yet again, of the need to stay connected to the people in the congregation in order to anticipate their needs.

"Remember we're in the business of loving people," Reverend Glenn said.

Sandy was never sure exactly what any of that meant practically, but it sounded good. He could not have been more relieved when the meeting was finally over. He had been feeling a little fatigued the last couple of days and he prayed to himself as he walked out of the conference room that he was not coming down with something. The last thing that he needed was to get sick. He had yet to work out the arrangements for the new song that he wanted the worship team to learn and he was hoping to start teaching it at practice on Wednesday night. He also needed to prepare for choir rehearsal on Thursday night. Sandy was generally not one to do things at the last minute. He had a type A personality and had a hard time sitting still. As he walked to his office he realized how much his neck and back muscles were aching and now he was getting concerned that he might have caught the flu bug that was going around. He hadn't gotten a flu shot in years because the last time he did he came down with the flu.

After the meeting ended, the day dragged on mercilessly. Sandy's throat was starting to hurt and he had a mild headache too. He wanted to take some zinc tablets to head off this cold, but there were none left in his desk and no one else had any. He probably should have just gone home early, but he could not make up his mind about it. He did manage to get a couple of minor things done, although he never had a chance to work on the new song. For one thing, he helped two of the guys bring some new furniture upstairs which took longer than he had anticipated. In addition, his sister, Tanya, called him, and he was on the phone with her for nearly an hour. Tanya lived about three hours away in Buffalo, New York, and it seemed that she was always in crisis. But she rarely called so he didn't want to cut her short. She had just needed to vent a little, and all he did was listen. He left the church at exactly five o'clock and he determined that no matter how bad he felt tomorrow morning that he would come in early to work on the song.

Sandy lived in a one-bedroom apartment in the town of Liverpool, just a few miles north of Syracuse. He had lived in the Lakefront Apartments for about five years. The "lake front" they were named after was Onondaga Lake, which, ironically, was several miles from his complex and there was no view of the lake. The apartment complex was composed of fifty-five units, and Sandy's apartment was on the second floor in the back. Most people who lived there were young couples just starting out so it was mostly a quiet place, although it could get a little rowdy at times. Sandy mostly kept to himself and really didn't know any of the other residents in his building. On occasion, he spoke briefly to the guy who lived in the apartment just below him, but that was only when they ran int ach other by chance and he was forced into being neighborly. T last thing that he wanted was to have to contend with having vis tors on a regular basis.

It took about twenty minutes for him to drive home from work. Fortunately, there were no delays and traffic had been light for that time of day. His cat, Mel, greeted him when he opened the front door to his apartment. Sandy was not really a cat person, but he loved Mel. He found him last year in the parking lot adjacent to his building on one of those winter mornings when the temperature outside was well below zero degrees. He simply didn't have the heart to leave the poor thing there to freeze to death and decided to bring the cat inside and to try to find the owner. It didn't have a collar, but was a very friendly male cat. Later that day, he put up some signs around the apartment complex, including in both laundry rooms about the cat and after two weeks with no response, Sandy realized that he was now the proud owner of a ten-pound, mostly-white Persian cat with a thick flowing plume of a tail. He was shocked when he took the cat to the veterinary clinic and found out how much everything cost. When the receptionist asked what the cat's name was, he only hesitated slightly before he told her that it was Melchizedek, "Mel" for short. The name just popped into his head, probably because he had just seen it in the scripture verses that he had been reading the night before.

He locked his door and petted Mel for a moment, set his things down, and looked in the fridge for just a moment before closing it. He couldn't bring himself to eat anything, his stomach was too upset. He made himself a cup of tea with honey and took some syrupy cold medicine that he found in the back of the medicine cabinet. Other than that, all that he could do was lay on the couch and try not to move. In spite of how tired he felt, Sandy somehow managed to stay up until ten o'clock, the time that he usually went to bed.

Most nights he would typically watch the local news in bed and then read for an hour or so until he was tired enough to go to sleep. Mel usually slept with him on the end of the bed. On this night, however, Sandy never even turned on the television in his bedroom. Instead, he just turned off the light and he immediately fell into a deep sleep. He never heard someone enter the apartment, walk into his bedroom, or get into bed. He never heard Mel drop to the floor and leave the room. In fact, he never heard anything all night. Not even the snoring coming from the naked man sleeping next to him.

Chapter 1

Sandy loved waking up next to Tony. It always made him feel safe, like shelter in a storm. On average, Tony would sleep over twice a week. They had been dating for about a year. They had met at the mall, of all places. Sandy loved to shop, so he loved the mall. Fortunately, he only lived about ten minutes from Destiny U.S.A., one of the largest malls in the United States. On the other hand, Tony hated shopping and rarely went to the mall. They met when Tony was shopping in Macy's for a birthday present for his sister and, assuming that Sandy was a store employee, asked for assistance as Sandy walked by. After telling him he didn't work there, Sandy offered to help anyway. There was no missing that Tony was a smooth operator with his classic good looks and outgoing personality. Together the two selected a nice sweater for Tony's sister, Annette. Afterward, Tony asked if he could show his appreciation by treating Sandy to coffee or something and Sandy readily agreed. They ended up going to one of the bars in the new section of the mall. Anthony Moreno was a lawyer who worked for Syracuse Legal Aid. He was not cocky, just confident, which Sandy found very appealing. They immediately hit it off and Sandy had never laughed so much. The chemistry between them was electric and they ended up talking for over two hours before Tony glanced at his watch and announced that he had to go. They exchanged phone numbers and shook hands goodbye.

"Good morning sunshine!" Tony proclaimed before kissing Sandy passionately on the lips.

"When did you get here?" Sandy asked. "I never heard you come in."

"Around midnight," Tony responded.

"Why so late?" Sandy questioned.

"I had to work late on that brief I told you about. And I'm still so far behind. This is crazy. This is the thing I hate most about appellate work. It takes me forever to write the actual brief because it takes so long to read through a trial transcript."

"You should have woken me up," Sandy muttered.

"I didn't want to wake you. You looked so cute," Tony teased.

"Too bad for you, I would have made it worth it to you."

"Now you tell me. It's not too late now, is it?" Tony asked.

"Actually, it is," Sandy said playfully, turning away.

"Please," Tony begged.

"No."

"Pretty please," he begged again.

Now face to face, the two stared longingly into each other's eyes for several seconds before Sandy rolled Tony onto his back and ducked his head under the covers. Tony smiled.

Thirty minutes later, Sandy was preparing breakfast while Tony was in the bathroom. Tony loved his coffee in the morning and now the apartment smelled of it. Sandy remembered that he needed to hurry because he had so much to do today, but he also cherished every moment that he could spend with Tony. To be clear, while he didn't think he was in love with Tony, he had never met anyone quite so sweet and kind. Tony was thirty-four years old, just five years older than Sandy. He was five-foot, ten inches tall with a muscular build, dark hair, and dark eyes. Syracuse is full of handsome Italian American men, so Tony didn't necessarily stand out from the crowd; but he had a way of making people feel special, as if he really understood them. As Tony appeared and sat down at the kitchen table, Mel scurried away. Clearly, Mel was not as impressed with Tony as Sandy was because he always ran away whenever Tony came around.

Sandy poured a cup of coffee and placed it on the table in front of Tony.

"Thanks," Tony said.

"You want eggs?" Sandy asked.

"Yes, please," Tony responded without making eye contact.

Tony loved Sandy's eggs. It was his mother's recipe. Everyone thought there was a secret ingredient in them that makes them so good, but it's actually a combination of the right kind of skillet and the correct level of heat, which needs to be on high when the eggs are dropped. Sandy gave half to Tony and put the rest on his own plate. He gave Tony the bottle of hot sauce before sitting down.

"You sick?" Tony asked. "There's a bunch of cold medicine on the bathroom sink."

"It's weird," Sandy responded. "I had a bad headache yesterday, so I took some cold medicine before I went to bed. I really can't afford to get sick right now. Pastor wants new songs for the holidays, and most of the people in the choir can't even remember the old ones from one Sunday to the next."

"Your problem is that you run yourself into the ground for those people," Tony proclaimed. "You always try to do too much. It is probably all just catching up to you."

"Well, I can't help it. I just want everything to be right," Sandy said.

"Good eggs," mumbled Tony with his mouth full.

Just then Sandy jumped to his feet and ran down the hall and around the corner to the bathroom. Tony immediately followed and watched from the doorway as Sandy vomited his guts into the toilet.

"Gross… You okay?" Tony asked when Sandy finally stopped dry heaving.

"I don't know," Sandy whispered.

"Well, I guess that settles it. Superman needs to go back to bed. No work for you today."

"I really can't," Sandy insisted. "You don't understand."

"Yes, I do," Tony replied. "You're trying to kill yourself. I'll clean up here and call the church for you. Now, go please!" He pointed his finger in the direction of the bedroom.

Sandy did as he was told. To his utter surprise, he felt even worse at that point than he had the day before. He slowly climbed back into bed and put a pillow over his face because the light in the room was hurting his eyes. Again, he fell asleep almost immediately. He woke up alone in the apartment about four hours later. He looked at the alarm clock and could not believe that it was almost noon. He went into the bathroom to find that it had been thoroughly cleaned. Tony had also washed the breakfast dishes and cleaned up the mess. The only thing on the table was a piece of paper. Sandy picked it up. It read:

> Sandy baby: I hope that you are feeling a little
> better. I called into work for you and told them
> that you are sick and won't be coming in today.
> You really need to take it easy. I will check in on

you later. Also, I will never speak to you again if
I find out that you went to work today anyway.
And I'm not kidding. Luv, Tony

Sandy smiled to himself. He then picked up his cell phone
and left a voice mail message for Shonda Jackson, one of his lead
vocalists, that he was sick and wouldn't be at rehearsal tonight.
After making himself another cup of tea, he turned on the TV, got
a blanket and pillow from the hall closet, and laid down on the
sofa. Soon he was asleep again.

He awoke to the sound of knocking. For a second he had no
idea where he was or what that sound was. Then he heard it again,
and he came to himself enough to realize that someone was at
the door.

"Who is it?" he yelled.

"Sandy, it's Mom," was the quick response.

"Oh, Lord," he whispered. "Verna Louise!"

Sandy and his sisters often referred to their mother by her full
Christian name when she wasn't around. While it was not exactly
a term of endearment, they meant no disrespect. Similarly, they
had gotten into the habit of referring to their father as "Reverend
Coleman," or "Rev" when speaking to each other. Down deep,
Sandy, Whitney, and Tanya loved their mother very much. It was
just that Verna Louise was a force of nature, and it was very hard
not to get swept away when she was in full effect, which was most
of the time. Sandy sprang to his feet and tried to clear his head. He
took a deep breath and opened the door.

There she was in all her glory. She was dressed as if she had
just come from a state dinner at the White House with the coat,
dress, shoes, hair, and nails all done to perfection. Normally Sandy
would have complimented her on her appearance right away to

get on her good side, but he just didn't have the strength today to strictly follow all the established rules engagement. Besides, Verna Louise already looked agitated.

"Mom, what are you doing here?" he asked with a puzzled look on his face.

"They called me and told me that you were very sick," she promptly responded.

"Who called you?" He wondered aloud.

"You know, Reverend Glenn's daughter, the one who answers the phone at the church. She called this morning and said that some strange guy called and said that something was going on with you. They're all worried about you. What was I supposed to think? They were concerned that you were in the hospital or something. Can I come in, please?"

"Oh, sorry. Come in," he said and stepped aside. Verna walked quickly past him and immediately started looking around the apartment.

Sandy thought to himself that he could kill Rachel Glenn about now.

Irritated, he asked, "Mom, what are you looking for?"

"Nothing," she replied sharply. Then redirecting her focus to the primary target, she took aim, "What is going on, Sandy?"

"Nothing's going on," he protested. "I just have some kind of a virus or something. That's all. I will be fine."

She stared directly into his eyes for a second before completely looking him over from head to toe. She seemed unconvinced. In one swift motion, she stepped toward him and put her hand on his forehead, and then on the right side of his face, and then under his t-shirt. Verna prided herself on her ability to take care of her family and she always overreacted when any of her children showed any sign of illness or distress. For that very reason, all three of them learned very early on to never ever let their mother see any sign of true weakness, physical or otherwise—that is, not unless they wanted Verna to make their pain her own and completely upstage them.

"You have a fever! Why didn't you call me?" she asked in disbelief.

"I don't know. Maybe I was too sick to call."

"I could have come over earlier. Maybe brought you some soup or something."

"I don't want any soup," was his abrupt reply.

Just then his phone started ringing. Sandy picked it up off the coffee table and answered it. It was Tony checking in. Sandy told him immediately that his mother was there and that he would call back in a few minutes. He hung up.

Verna immediately asked, "Who was that?"

"Mom, please."

"Was it Troy?" She dryly inquired.

"You know that is not his name." Sandy was becoming more irritated.

"So, I gather you're still with him then?" she sighed.

"Yes, we're still together. I don't know why you just can't be happy for me. I finally found somebody who really cares about me."

"Happy for you?" she repeated. "I don't even know him."

"And whose choice is that?" he barked.

"Look, Sandy, I didn't come all the way over here to fight with you again. I really don't know why you have to bite my head off all of the time. You're getting to be just as bad as your sisters. I was just worried about you so I dropped everything to come see about my baby. You should have called me, you know. You are my only begotten son. Please don't try to make me feel guilty just because I worry about you."

"As you can see, I'm fine, Mom. I'll be like new tomorrow, you'll see. You really don't need to worry. Dad always said that worrying is a sin anyway."

"Your father was never a mother!" she stated emphatically. "He is not the one who carried you for nine months, or the one who took care of you when you were a baby. Let me tell you, men will never do like women. Only God and mothers truly understand the hearts of children."

"What scripture is that from again?" He rolled his eyes.

"You have to read between the lines," she maintained. "Where was Joseph when they were crucifying his son Jesus on the cross? We know that his mother was right there."

"I don't know. Maybe he had to work," Sandy answered sarcastically.

Rolling her eyes now, she continued, "All I know is that his mother was right there with him the whole time, feeling every lash. Because that is what we women do."

"Why are you all dressed up anyway?" He needed to change the subject.

"I'm going to dinner with the ladies from my prayer group."

"Then look, I don't want you to get sick..."

"You're just trying to get rid of me, but I don't want to get caught in that traffic on Route 81 by the mall. I should probably go. How was your birthday? I called you on Tuesday. Are you sure that you don't need anything?"

"My birthday was good, and I'm sure," he said, trying to sound confident.

"And you will call me if you do need something, right?"

"You know I will."

She whispered, "Sandy, you know that I just love you with all of my heart."

"Yes, I know."

He walked her to the door and opened it. She cupped his face in her hands and looked deeply into her son's eyes. She said, "Promise me you will take care of yourself."

"I promise."

"I'm not sure I believe you." She mumbled as she turned away.

As soon as he closed the door, Sandy grabbed his phone and called Tony back. When he answered he said that he was with a client and would call later. Sandy got up, took a shower, and made himself some clear broth. He felt a little better, but was too afraid to try to eat anything heavier. He and Mel just watched TV in the living room for the rest of the evening. Tony called around ten o'clock. and said that he was still at the office. He sounded tired, but he was pretty sure that he was not coming down with the same virus that Sandy had. They managed to talk for a few minutes before saying goodnight, which was rather typical for them. Like most millennial couples, they were both very busy in their individual careers and their time together was severely limited.

Chapter 2

T he adage that Sunday is the most segregated day of the week is true. The reason for this is because most Christians choose to worship with people who look just like they do, meaning with people of the same race or ethnicity. It's uncommon to find many churches in the United States that look anything like the heavenly church, that is, multicultural. There are probably twenty-five or so churches on the south side of Syracuse, all of which are within a five-mile radius of each other, and most of them are considered "black churches" because African American pastors lead them and majority of the members of the congregations are African American or minority. Denominational affiliation varies, but Mount Moriah Missionary Baptist Church is the largest of them. It is unclear when Mount Moriah was first organized because early church records are almost nonexistent. Unofficially, it is believed that a minister named Isaiah Carter, who had relocated with his family from the state of Georgia in search of employment, started the church in 1923. The church struggled over the years and changed locations three or four times within the city. On occasion, there had been strife and disputes within the congregation, most of which were based upon perceived petty offenses rather than theological disagreement. When Sandy's father, became the pastor of Mount Moriah in 1985, membership was at approximately two hundred families.

Isaac Stephenson Coleman was not the typical preacher's kid (or "PK" for short). Sandy felt no added pressure being the pastor's son, in spite of the fact that many children who have one or more parent in the ministry rebel at some point and run afoul of the church the first chance that they get. This is most likely because they feel like they are always under the microscope of public scrutiny and therefore cannot be themselves. Interestingly, most of these prodigals typically find their way back to the church as adults. But Sandy had always loved the church, especially the music.

It was also obvious very early on that he was gifted musically. He started to tinker around with his mother's old piano when he was just four years old; by the time he was six he could play every song that the choir sang in church. Because he never had a piano lesson in his life, he played by ear, meaning that he didn't know how to read music.

He also had a very good singing voice, but Sandy didn't really consider himself a vocalist, probably because his father had such an amazing voice. Reverend Coleman had always hoped to become a professional singer and his vocal talent contributed mightily to the growth of Mount Moriah under his tenure. The truth is that most congregants preferred to hear him sing more than they wanted to hear him preach. His sister Tanya also inherited a nice singing voice.

However, it was on the piano where Sandy had no match. Eventually it got to the point that whenever Revered Coleman was invited to minister at a church out of town, he would bring Sandy along to play for him. The two of them together could bring an entire congregation to its knees.

One of Sandy's favorite things to do was to play the piano in the sanctuary at Mount Moriah in the dark. It started when he was young and had to wait after service for his parents to go home. Sometimes they waited for hours. Tanya and Whitney usually spent their time playing with friends or, later on, in pursuit of boys. In contrast, Sandy would venture into the sanctuary to play the piano until Verna called for him. The lights in the church were normally turned off by one of the ushers as soon as the last person had left the sanctuary, and because he didn't know how to turn them back on, he learned how to find his way to the piano in the darkened church. It was fun for him and he grew to prefer the darkness because it allowed him to lose himself in the music. Sometimes he even forgot where he was or where the music ended and where he began. He considered this his own special time with God. Over the years, he would sneak into the sanctuary to play whenever he was sad or troubled about something. He always felt better when he left.

Much of Sandy's angst-ridden youth had to do with his relationship with his father. Reverend Coleman didn't always understand or consider his son, whom he thought was too much of a mama's boy. Although they were in perfect harmony as Sandy started to play the piano when Reverend Coleman was closing in on the climax of one of his sermons, at home the two rarely interacted together. For one thing, Sandy hated sports, and his father was a sports junkie who especially loved the New York Giants and the New York Knicks. Secondly, Reverend Coleman was moody and particular at home, which meant that he usually took every opportunity to criticize his son. He was always much more gracious with his daughters, who were more likely to misbehave than Sandy ever was.

As a late bloomer, Sandy was unaware of his sexuality for most of his junior high and high school years. He was never particularly interested in girls or boys in that way, nor did he ever have any crushes on any celebrities, male or female. He was quite popular with the girls at Mount Moriah, however, and even went out on a couple of so-called dates. He had kissed a couple of girls too, or rather, they kissed him. But he always believed that the girls were interested in him only because his father was the pastor, so he never took them seriously. For the most part, he remained guarded.

Although he had a couple of male friends at school, he was busy at the church several nights a week and every weekend, so he only saw them at school. One night after choir rehearsal, however, one of the young men in the choir rubbed against him provocatively and Sandy instinctively pushed him away. Nothing like that had ever happened before and he was mostly just annoyed. It never occurred to him to tell anyone about it.

In hindsight, Sandy had a crush on his drama teacher in high school, although he honestly didn't recognize it for what it was. He was never much interested in anything at Liverpool High school except graduating. However, Mr. Davidson, an English teacher, approached him one day in the cafeteria and said that he had heard Sandy could sing and that he was in dire need of a male with a strong voice for the spring play. He was in his mid-forties with dark hair and dark eyes. Sandy was not interested, but he reluctantly agreed to audition because he immediately liked Mr. Davidson. He ended up getting one of the leads in the school's production of "Hair Spray" and, to his surprise, really enjoyed the experience. He especially liked the special attention he received from Mr. Davidson, who was married with two small children. Overall, it was a very positive experience, and the entire Coleman clan came to opening night, including his father.

Sandy's first sexual experience occurred in college. To the dismay of his father, Sandy enrolled at Morrisville State College, a small two-year school about an hour southeast of Syracuse. Reverend Coleman wanted him to go to a Community College and major in music. Instead, Sandy majored in business because he thought that it might be a gateway to the real world and getting out of Syracuse. He lived in a single room in one of the dorms on campus. One morning he noticed one of the white guys on his floor coming out of the shower. Sandy had seen him before but didn't know him. He was tall and handsome with a nice smile. Apparently, Sandy must have stared a second or two too long at the naked guy before discretely looking away, because soon after, the guy started talking to him whenever their paths crossed in the hall or on the campus. Sandy was embarrassed by what he had done and reminded himself to be careful not to violate social rules of etiquette while in the bathroom again. The last thing he needed was to get a reputation of being some kind of a pervert. However, one week later around midnight, the guy appeared at Sandy's door. For some reason, he let him in and an hour later Sandy lost his virginity.

His name was Clay Mathers and he was from some small town on Long Island, New York, that Sandy had never heard of. He experimented sexually with Clay on many late nights during that first semester. Sadly, Clay, who was enrolled in the equine program at the college, suffered a serious injury stemming from a fall from a horse and suddenly left school in December. In hindsight, it was probably for the best that the affair ended. Sandy completed the year, but always felt a little uneasy on campus. He decided not to return the following year.

Still, the whole Clay thing really rocked Sandy's world. The truth is that he was caught completely off guard. His sexuality had never been an issue for him before, because he never saw himself as a gay man. He had just assumed that his life would be normal like everyone else's and that his future would one day include a family of his own as a husband and a father. After all, one of his sisters was married and the other one already had a kid. Now he was not quite sure what to think, and it wasn't like he could ask someone about it. There was no one. Obviously, he knew that what he was doing with Clay was dangerous. He was also very much aware of the fact that Clay was probably just using him. Nevertheless, to his surprise, he couldn't help himself. He never said no when Clay came calling, nor was he remorseful afterward.

Throughout the second semester, Sandy tried to pretend that Clay never happened, and he told himself the whole thing meant nothing. However, it was undeniable that something had been awakened in him that he never knew was there before. He found himself looking at guys more and more, even at the church. Sandy also discovered that he seemed to have a special attraction for white guys.

If that wasn't odd enough, he never considered the moral or spiritual implications associated with his feelings, or otherwise asked himself what God thought about his behavior. Rather, his preoccupation was that someone would find out and that he would eventually have to face his father. Sandy was aware of the position of the church that homosexuality is a sin and "an abomination," but he himself never really considered the matter or cared one way or the other.

His father had always said that homosexuals were "confused," but he never explained exactly what he meant by that. For most of his career, Reverend Coleman just preached Jesus as set forth in the four gospels in the Bible. He simply lacked the depth of knowledge or sophistication to address some of the weightier theological issues. His gift was that he was a master motivator and he rarely ventured too far from his strength. He also rarely did any counseling for individual church members, leaving those responsibilities to the deacons.

As for his mother, Sandy realized that there was at least the likelihood that she already had her suspicions about his sexuality. Although Sandy hated to admit it, Verna Louise always understood him better than anyone else. When he was growing up, she often knew what he wanted before he knew it himself. There had been numerous times over the years when he would come home from school, only to find that she was preparing the exact thing for dinner that he had been craving all day. Similarly, there were the occasions when she gave him the perfect birthday or Christmas gift that he had never thought to ask for. While he appreciated her efforts, he still often felt she was suffocating him because she respected no boundaries with him. For instance, shortly after he returned to live at home after his first year in college, he discovered one day that Verna Louise had opened mail that was addressed to him. When confronted, she explained that she had opened the letter because the return address on the envelope indicated that the U.S. Army had sent it and she feared that he had enlisted. Things like that infuriated him and made him resentful toward her.

Sandy never consciously planned to come out to his mother when he did. He just kind of blurted it out in the heat of the moment after dinner at her house one night. For some unknown reason, there came a point when Verna became obsessed with the idea that it was time for him to start thinking about settling down. She was always raising the subject and, true to form, simply refused to let it go. On one such occasion when she not-so-innocently asked him, yet again, how much longer she was going to have to wait for grandchildren from her only son, he mercilessly exclaimed,

"I'll have to discuss it with my boyfriend and get back to you!"

At the time, he hadn't met Tony yet and wasn't involved with anyone. He knew it was wrong and mean as soon as he said it; however, he told himself that she had it coming. While it wasn't his intention to hurt her, the truth is that, on some level, he knew that she needed to know.

In response, Verna Louise was clearly startled by the outburst, but she managed to gather herself and matter-of-factly replied, "Oh, I don't think so. The devil is a lie." She then calmly got up from her chair and walked away.

Sandy, on the other hand, was shaking to his core. He trusted his mother, but he also knew that she would never accept this about him. He now faced being rejected by the one person who loved him the most. Behind her hard demeanor, she only pretended to be tough. Sandy immediately followed her. She was in the kitchen standing next to the sink putting the dishes in order.

"Mom, can we talk?" he begged.

"What do you what to talk about?" she asked without looking in his direction.

"I'm really sorry," was his sincere response. "You didn't deserve that."

"I don't understand. Are you telling the truth? I don't even think you know what you're saying." She sounded as if she was on the verge of tears.

"Look, it's not the end of the world." He knew that he needed to be clearer. "I'm still the same person."

"What happened to you?" she asked and stared into his eyes.

"Mom, nothing happened to me. I'm not broken. This is just the way God made me."

"No, it isn't. Is it my fault?" she asked with tears in her eyes. "Did I do something? You can tell me." Her breathing was heavy, and she looked desperate.

"No, you didn't do anything. Mom, this isn't about you. Please understand that. I don't know what it means either, but I need to be honest with you, even if I'm not honest with myself. This is really hard for me and I'm doing my best to figure it all out. All I need you to do is give me some time and not act like you hate me. If you hate me for being me, then I won't have anyone."

He could tell that she was offended and was trying to figure out what he had said.

"Now you are really talking foolish," Verna cried out. "You will always have me. Don't you know that? Hate you? Are you kidding? Is that how you see me? I would gladly die for you."

She fought to maintain her composure.

"I know that, Mom. That is why I don't want to disappoint you. I'm sorry."

"You are my sweet boy. My blood! Mine! Sandy, maybe you just need to talk to someone. A counselor or somebody. But don't worry. You better believe that your mother will always take care of you."

"You still don't understand, Mom. I don't need you to take care of me. I just need you to love me," he proclaimed.

"I do love you," was her quiet response.

He didn't know what to say, so he said nothing. The silence was stifling. His heart was beating so hard. They both stood, lost in space, for several seconds.

She finally said, "It will be okay, Sandy. You'll see. We both need time... But if you ever tell your father any of this, then you're on your own. Hear me? Just give me some heads-up before you do it, though so I have time to move out of the country," she joked.

They both smirked, but neither one laughed outright.

Chapter 3

S andy woke up still feeling a little crappy. He had missed two days of work because of this virus and he was starting to panic. Other than the time he had a root canal done on one of his teeth and it got infected, he could not recall the last time that he had missed both rehearsals in a week. His birthday was last Tuesday, and he had still attended practice that night instead of going out to celebrate with Tony. The choir practiced on Tuesdays, and the ten-member worship team rehearsed on Thursdays. The two groups sang on alternating Sundays, unless there were five Sundays in a month when special arrangements had to be made. Sandy went to Thursday night rehearsal, even though he hadn't been in the office that day. He was glad to be back and there was much that needed to be addressed. After rehearsal, he went up to his desk to check his messages. Because the church offices were closed on Fridays, he would not be back to work until Monday. It appeared that his desk was not the way that he had left it. It looked to him like someone had been sitting there and had moved some of his stuff around, which slightly annoyed him. There were two messages; both from choir members letting him know that they would not be at rehearsal. He erased the messages and headed home.

Sandy was not exactly hiding his relationship with Tony from the world. They normally texted each other several times during the day and planned to get together when it was convenient for both. Sandy worked every Sunday, and Tony complained about it all the time. He usually slept over at Sandy's apartment on Saturday nights and was sound asleep when Sandy left for work early Sunday morning. He was always gone by the time Sandy returned home around three in the afternoon.

Tony also hated the fact that Sandy was still closeted. He obviously had a very different relationship with his family than Sandy had with his. For one thing, Tony's family was a lot more open with each other and they had always been supportive of Ton'y choices and lifestyle. Sandy had met most of Tony's family and many of his friends, who were mostly gay. Tony's world was foreign to him and he was not always comfortable in it, however, he couldn't help but notice that Tony always seemed to be so proud to be with him, which made him feel valued. It's fair to say that he was a little jealous of the fact that Tony seemed to know exactly who he was, whereas Sandy didn't have a clue about who he was or what he ultimately wanted in life. This was one of the reasons he still hadn't disclosed his sexuality to anyone other than Verna, who apparently took it upon herself to tell his sisters. However, neither Whitney nor Tanya had ever asked him directly about it, which was the way that he wanted it. Tony thought that the whole thing was absurd. He sarcastically once asked,

"Could anything be more cliché than a gay choir director?"

Sandy was not sure how much his strained relationship with his father affected his sexuality. It was possible that it hadn't a thing to do with his attractions at all. Ironically, Mount Moriah is the place in the Bible where Abraham, the father of the Jewish nation, offered his son Isaac as a sacrifice. Sandy often felt as though Reverend Coleman had sacrificed him for some unknown reason. However, focusing on the root cause of sexual orientation was a futile exercise, in his opinion. The bottom line was that for the good, bad, or otherwise, Reverend Coleman was the only father that he would ever have, and Sandy loved him. The rest of it no longer mattered.

One thing that did matter, however, is that Tony had a habit of disregarding his feelings the same way that his father had done, and Sandy could not help but wonder if one of the reasons that he was so attracted to Tony in the first place was that Tony reminded him of Reverend Coleman on some level. Tony liked to do that lawyer thing where he flatly refuses to credit any other opinion other than his own. Moreover, he never apologized or even acknowledged the offense and usually the moment just faded away as if it never happened.

The truth was that Sandy had no idea where his relationship with Tony was going. The sex was good, but Sandy's desire for Tony went well beyond the physical. A part of him wanted Tony all the time. Sandy didn't know if this was true love, and he really couldn't care less at this point. Nor did he want to examine their relationship too closely and risk reading too much into things. One undeniable truth is that his first thought in the morning was of Tony, as well as his last thought each night.

Similarly, whenever he had a bad day, it was Tony's voice that he yearned to hear. It felt good to have someone, but he also recognized that it didn't necessarily feel right all the time. Somehow, he innately understood that all human relationships are tenuous, and that tomorrow is not promised to anyone. On that front, Tony told him that he loved him both early and often in the relationship. As a result, it didn't always ring true to Sandy when he heard it. Tony could be quite the charmer and Sandy knew it. He also knew that he was in a vicarious position because Tony held all the cards in the relationship.

Chapter 4

There were two Sunday morning services at Mount Moriah Missionary Baptist Church. They were at 9:00 a.m. and at 11:30 a.m. The second service was usually full, except on winter days when the weather was too snowy or cold. Sandy was usually at the church by 7:00 a.m. He needed the time to go over the songs with whichever of the groups was singing that day. It always amazed him that no matter how good they had rehearsed during the week, there were always a few people who could not remember the words to the song, let alone their parts. Usually the worship team was a little better in this regard than the people in the choir, but Sandy had learned from experience that it was best to have at least one run through of the song list—regardless of who was singing—just to make sure.

The primary difference between the worship team and the choir is that the choir typically sang the bigger, more traditional gospel songs, whereas the worship team did the more contemporary spiritual love songs. Generally, the older congregants at Mount Moriah preferred the choir, and the young people liked the worship music. Sandy considered himself a worshipper at heart, so he leaned more toward intimate worship, which he sometimes jokingly referred to as "Jesus unplugged."

Sandy's approach and style were also very different from his father's in that he wanted no part of "performing" for the congregation. He hated slick productions or when the focus of the music was on someone other than the God that people supposedly came to exalt. He never wanted any of the singers to get too carried away or to think too highly of their own talent. To him, true worship isn't a type or style of music, or even a feeling. He had discovered early on that worship is actually a place where people can go that has been reserved just for them and God. As the instrumentalist, he felt as though his job was to simply usher people to that place, and thus into the presence of the Lord.

The order of service was the same every week. With everyone seated, and the choir or worship team in place on the elevated platform, one of the deacons or deaconesses or prayer leaders walked up to the platform and began the service with a small exhortation to welcome visitors and encourage everyone to "enter into His presence." After that, Sandy and his team would sing three songs, followed by the collection being taken up, and then a sermon by Reverend Glenn or another minister. On average, a typical sermon was about thirty minutes long, always followed by an altar call, during which people were invited to come forward and to give their lives to Christ. The service always ended the same way that it began, with another deacon or minister encouraging the people to remember what was just taught and giving a prayerful benediction.

Sandy preferred not to sit through the sermon twice. Usually after the offering plates were prayed over in the first service, he would stop playing the piano and go to the serving room where coffee, donuts, and fruit were available, only to return to the sanctuary when the speaker was winding down the message. He also used the time to tweak any one of the songs if needed. On this day, there wasn't anything major that needed altering so Sandy just chatted with some of the people who were standing around eating their breakfast until it was time for him to go back to his seat.

As a practical matter, the first service acted as a dry run and the second service was always better. Sandy never understood why anyone would go to the early service if they could attend the later one. Reverend Glenn was always better the second time around too. He was a very good speaker for the most part. Substantively, he was probably better than Sandy's father had been in terms of clarity and depth, but Reverend Glenn could not sing like Reverend Coleman. Baptists generally like to "feel the spirit," and nothing moved a congregation more than the right song. For that reason, his father always made sure that Sandy knew beforehand what his message would be about, as well as his choice for the closing song. In contrast, Sandy rarely knew what Reverend Glenn was planning to preach, and they were seldom on the same page.

Considering that Sandy had been out sick and rehearsals had been impacted, worship went well for both services that day. He arose from the piano after finishing for the second time and took a seat on the front row as Revered Glenn approached the pulpit. After offering some perfunctory praises to God, Reverend Glenn announced that the title of the message for today was "Sin in the Camp." He began by reminding the congregation of the story of Moses and the Ten Commandments in the Old Testament. He recounted how God sent Moses to deliver the Israelites and forced the Egyptian pharaoh to set the slaves free. He further explained how God had separated the Red Sea for them and provided them with a daily supply of food and water before bringing them to a place of safety. Nevertheless, when Moses left them there for a short time to spend time alone with God and to receive the Ten Commandments, he returned only to find they had turned completely away from God and were again serving idols. Then

Reverend Glenn looked down at his Bible and began to read three verses from the book of Exodus:

> So it was, as soon as he came near the camp, that he saw the calf and the dancing. So, Moses' anger became hot, and he cast the tablets out of his hands and broke them at the foot of the mountain (Exodus 32:19).

> And the Lord said to Moses, "Whoever has sinned against Me, I will blot him out of My book… (Exodus 32:33).

> So the Lord plagued the people because of what they did with the calf which Aaron made. (Exodus 32:35).

Looking up and directly at the congregation, Reverend Glenn began to speak in his big, booming voice about how the United States used to be a Christian nation, but how that was no longer the case.

"Immorality has become chic," he said, "and what would have been shocking to the conscience just some twenty years ago, is now being called good and accepted as normal. This is true in Washington, it is true in our state and city governments and, sadly, it is true in our churches. Sin is in the camp, I tell you."

There was an echo of "Amen" from the congregation.

He went on to talk about how, even with all our modern advances and conveniences, life is still getting harder. He expounded:

"Corruption is everywhere," he declared. "We are losing the fight against drugs and street violence. Bombings are becoming more and more common. Incidents of police brutality are occurring every day, and pornography and offenses against women are laughed at or ignored. I ask you, are we really any better off than before?"

Now beginning to find his stride, he continued, "And if that was not enough, gay marriage is now the law of the land!"

Some people in the congregation gasp audibly as if they had been unaware. Others simply groaned.

At that point, he proceeded to read three or four scriptures from chapter 1 of the book of Romans, which, at least on their face, appeared to denounce homosexuality.

Reverend Glenn then walked to the edge of the platform and vociferously preached:

"Judgment is coming to a nation that has turned its back on God!" he said to a quiet roar from the crowd. "So we need to stand up in the face of growing sin and call it what it is. This is not the time to let public opinion or Hollywood intimidate us. God doesn't care anything about being politically correct. He is the same yesterday, today, and tomorrow. This country must turn from its wicked ways and flee all immorality now, sexual or otherwise! Time is running out. Can't you feel it? How much longer until we face the entire wrath of God? God will not be mocked, I tell you. He will not tolerate sin in the camp. Pastor Moses was not afraid of the truth, and neither are we. Because our God is holy and righteous. He alone is worthy of our worship and praise! Somebody in this place needs to stand to their feet and give God some praise!"

At that point, most of the congregation stood up and began shouting praises and thanksgivings to God. Sandy, who was already sitting at the piano, started playing softly as the worship team took their places on the platform and began to sing. Reverend Glenn then made his usual appeal for people to give their lives to Christ or repent from the sin in their lives that held them in bondage. About five or six people came forward and were met by some deacons, who spoke to each one individually. Reverend Glenn walked off the platform as one of the deacons came forward to give the final appeal and benediction.

Sandy was not overly bothered by the sermon. He had obviously heard it all before. With respect to the condemnation of every gay and lesbian person in America, Sandy just thought that either Reverend Glenn didn't really know what he was talking about or he knew a lot more than he was willing to admit. Regardless, in Sandy's humble opinion, the solution to most of the problems in this country lie more with being honest and showing compassion toward others than with how hard one thumps his or her Bible.

Indeed, about police brutality, for instance, no matter how suspicious the shooting, Sandy had never heard of a single instance where any police officer, black or white, who at the time of the occurrence, denounced a shooting that resulted in the death of an unarmed black man. Similarly, he had never heard of anybody who had once openly embraced the gay lifestyle and who now speaks convincingly about how they were delivered from it by God. It appeared that those in the best position to affect the kind of change most of us would want to see were content to remain silent, for some reason.

Usually on Sunday afternoons after work, Sandy just liked to be alone. Sometimes he would go to his mother's house for dinner or something, but he was completely content to do nothing at all. This day was no different. Having fully recovered now from whatever virus he had, he just needed to catch up on things around his apartment, and maybe do his laundry.

Tanya called again, and he spoke much too long to her again about the stresses she was facing as a single parent of her two young daughters, Sophia and Gabrielle, who were five and three. Three years ago her husband up and left her after two years of marriage, and now she was basically miserable. He couldn't remember the last time that she had called him twice in one week, so he speculated that this was an exceptionally tough time for her. Although it bothered him that neither one of his sisters had never fully rebounded from their rebellious teen years, he was relieved to finally get off the phone with Tanya.

For the rest of the evening, Sandy did his laundry, ate some leftover Chinese food, and watched TV with Mel on his lap. Around ten o'clock he received a text from Tony that just said, "Goodnight." He then read his Bible in bed for about an hour. His father had always told him that it was impossible to love God without loving his Word because they were the same thing. Typically, Sandy would read the Bible two or three nights a week, but never when Tony was over, but he seemed to sleep better on those nights when he did read.

Chapter 5

Having missed almost an entire week of work, Sandy was anxious to return to the office. Mondays were always busy, but today he needed to catch up with last week's work before he could focus on the upcoming week. Rachel Glenn was seated at the reception desk when he walked in. Rachel was one of Reverend Glenn's twin daughters who had worked at the church just a little more than a year. She was very overweight and not suited to be a receptionist because she was not very personable. People complained all the time that she had been rude to them, but she always had a reason why she was justified for whatever brash thing she had said.

"Good morning," he said as he hurried on his way.

"My dad needs to talk you," she blurted out.

"Me?" Sandy asked. "When?"

"He said as soon as you came in," was her snappish response. "He's in the conference room."

Sandy wondered what this was all about as he walked toward the conference room. The door was opened and he walked in. Both Reverend Glenn and Reverend Grimes were seated at the table side by side.

"You wanted to see me?" Sandy asked.

"Yes, Sandy, come on in," Reverend Glenn said, "and close the door, please."

Sandy shut the door and sat down across from the two men. Reverend Grimes seemed nervous and didn't look Sandy in the eye. He was about the same age as Sandy and had only been at Mount Moriah for three years. He was originally from Raleigh, North Carolina, and he was married with two little children. He worked well with the teens in the church, and they seemed to like him. Sandy didn't know him well, but always thought he was a good guy.

"I'm not going to beat around the bush here," Reverend Glenn began. "There is a problem. It has come to our attention that you are openly living in sin and moral compromise."

Startled, Sandy responded, "Excuse me, but I don't know what you're talking about."

"Are you really going to sit here and deny that you are a homosexual and living with another man?" Glenn offered. He seemed angry. "Please don't try to lie."

"I don't live with anyone," Sandy calmly said.

Glenn countered, "We have been on to you for some time, but now we have proof. You must think everybody here is stupid!"

"What kind of proof?" Sandy asked. He was genuinely confused about what he was saying.

"That doesn't matter," Glenn responded. "There is sin in this camp, and I will not tolerate it. I'm the pastor here and I'm responsible to protect this flock. I don't care how talented you are or who your mother or father is. Do you hear me?"

"What are you saying?" Sandy asked as he struggled to remain calm. The fact that Glenn seemed to be on the defensive was motivation for Sandy to press him.

"I'm saying that you cannot work here anymore. We will pay you two weeks' severance, but you are through here. Do you understand? Your stuff is already packed for you. Please don't make a scene, Son."

"Don't call me son!" Sandy could not contain his rage any longer. "I'm not your son! And you certainly are not my father! Why do you get to judge me? Who among us is without sin, right? Why is my supposed "sin" so much worse than everybody else's? I never claimed to be perfect. But I have dedicated my life to this church—"

"Sandy, you need to calm down," Reverend Grimes interjected. "We do appreciate everything you have done here. We really do. But please try to understand our position. You simply cannot just live any kind of way and then stand up in front of people on Sunday morning and lead them in worship."

"Why not?" posed Sandy. "Only God knows my heart. You don't know anything about me or how I'm living." Sandy was almost completely out of breath.

"I think we know all that we need to," was Reverend Glenn's quick retort. "You are making this much worse than it needs to be!"

"I don't think you people know anything about the God you claim to serve. Where's the grace and mercy? Where's the love that you're always talking about?"

Sandy was shouting now.

"We do love you, and sometimes the most loving thing we can do, is to tell you the truth," Reverend Grimes attempted to explain.

"Are you kidding me?" Sandy began to laugh, which was merely a defense mechanism, but came across as mockery. "That whole 'hate the sin and love the sinner' thing is a lie. It feels a lot like straight-up hate!" He proclaimed.

"I know that if you do not repent, you will one day lift up your eyes in hell!" shouted Reverend Glenn. "I can promise you that!"

"Maybe, but I'm guessing that you'll get there before I do! How's that for the truth?" Sandy hollered back.

Standing up and pointing toward the door. Reverend Glenn bellowed, "Get out!"

"The truth hurts, doesn't it, Pastor?" Sandy asked sarcastically.

"You need to go. You are no longer welcome here!"

Sandy sprang to his feet and stormed out of the room. His thoughts were spinning around in his head and he suddenly felt sick to his stomach again. The hallway was vacant, and Rachel was no longer at her desk. In front of the door was a big box containing his personal items. Sandy picked up the box and without looking back, he walked down the stairs, out the door, and to his car as fast as he could. By the time he reached his car he was out of breath and sweating profusely. There was no one else around. And for the second time in less than a week, he vomited everything that was in his stomach.

Sandy texted his boyfriend from the car, only to learn that Tony was on his way to Attica Correctional Facility with a colleague to meet with a client in prison. He could not decide what to do next and considered calling his mother, but dismissed the thought almost immediately. He couldn't just go home either. He felt like he needed to talk to someone before he lost his mind. He suddenly regretted that he didn't have any close friends. There were just the people on the worship team and in the choir, but he really didn't associate with any of them outside of church very much. As he was pulling out of the church parking lot, more thoughts raced in his head. He instinctively started driving in the direction for home, but decided to go to the mall instead. After arriving there, he went to the food court, bought himself a latte, and sat down. He had no energy to walk. He could feel his insides shaking and he kept going over what had just happened repeatedly in his head. He was so angry and he wanted to do something, but he didn't know what. He was also deeply hurt—he felt dirty and rejected.

Sandy had been sitting there for about an hour when Tony called. Sandy gave him a quick rundown of everything that had just happened. Tony was angry too, but he tried to reassure Sandy that everything would be alright. They decided that if Sandy didn't want to go home that he should go to Tony's apartment and just lay low until Tony got there. At first Sandy didn't leave immediately, but he abruptly decided to go when he saw a woman he thought he knew from church walking in his direction out of the corner of his eye. Just the thought of having to make small talk made him feel sick all over again.

Tony lived in a two-bedroom apartment near downtown Syracuse. It was an old house that had been remodeled and converted into a two-family duplex. Sandy only went to Tony's place occasionally because he was much more of a homebody than Tony was. He found the spare key that was hidden behind the mailbox and let himself in. Tony was a bit of a slob. There were dishes in the kitchen sink and papers and mail were spread out everywhere. In one swift motion, Sandy began to clean up. He put the dishes in the dishwasher and placed the papers in neat piles on the table. He also took out the garbage, made the bed, and picked up the clothes that were scattered about the floor, both in the bathroom and in the bedroom. When he looked at his watch, he couldn't believe that it was only 11:50 a.m. It felt good to focus on something menial—and he always liked taking care of Tony.

He tried to sleep, but he couldn't. Daytime TV was a joke, and Tony didn't have anything good to read. He probably could have eaten a little something, but there was nothing edible in the refrigerator. He was sitting on the couch in the living room watching an old movie on cable when Tony walked in.

"How you doing?" he asked as he was taking off his coat.

"Okay," was all Sandy could manage to say, fighting back the tears.

"Tell me what they said."

Sandy tried to tell Tony everything that happened without too much editorializing, but it was hard. He kept thinking of things that he should have said. He felt like his whole world had come crashing down in a moment.

"Sandy, baby, I'm so sorry… After all that you have done for that church. Nobody is as dedicated as you are. The ungrateful hypocrites! You should sue the pants off those bastards!"

"Sue them? For what?" Sandy asked.

"For wrongful termination and discrimination...for slander... for the intentional infliction of emotional distress. And whatever else we can think of," Tony freely declared.

"I can do that?"

"Yes, Sandy, you can do that. You can't let them just treat you like that," Tony insisted.

"I don't know…" Sandy was trying to think, "maybe."

"Look, you don't have to decide today. We can talk about it later. Do you need anything right now?" Tony asked lovingly.

"No. Thanks, Tony," Sandy said.

"You don't have to thank me. I love you."

"I love you too," he said calmly

Just then, Sandy's phone rang. It was his mother. He took a deep breath and then answered.

"Hello."

"Sandy, what is going on?"

He heard an edge of what sounded like panic in her tone.

"What do you mean?" he asked cautiously.

"Did something happen at church?"

"Yes, I was fired." He cringed and sighed as the words rolled off his tongue, waiting for her reaction.

"Fired? Why?" She shouted.

"Because I'm a sinner. Haven't you heard?" Sandy's voice quivered, and he swallowed hard to control his emotions.

"I have heard no such thing. What are you going to do?"

"I don't know," he pinched the top edge of his nose and squeezed his eyes tightly, wishing this day away.

"Do you want me to call Reverend Glenn?"

"No, I do not want my mommy to call my boss!" His voice was a bit more forceful and sarcastic than he meant it to sound, but that was the very last thing he needed from his mom.

"Sandy, I'm just trying to help. Sometimes there is no winning with you. I just need to know that you're okay and how to pray." She was already starting to play the victim.

"I know, Mom. I'm sorry. Look, I'm okay…can I please have a moment to try to digest this first? I'm not suicidal or anything, if that is what you're worrying about. I just need to think. I promise I will call you tomorrow. Is that okay?"

"I guess," she conceded. "Just don't forget."

"I won't forget."

"I love you." She just had to say.

"I love you too," was all he could whisper in a melancholy tone.

Sandy stayed at Tony's apartment that night to take refuge, then he got up early the next morning and went home. Mel, who appeared to be happy to see him, met him at the door. Sandy had slept restlessly and his body felt tired, however, he knew that trying to sleep would be a waste of effort. He had three text messages on his phone from the night before, one from Tanya, one from Whitney, and one from Reverend Grimes. All three were asking if he was okay. Sandy responded back to his sisters that he was "fine." He chose to ignore Reverend Grimes. After taking a shower, he made breakfast and ate most of it. Then he laid down on the couch. He fell asleep within minutes, only to be awakened at 10:00 a.m. by the phone ringing.

Still in a bit of a fog, he picked it up. It was Verna Louise. Apparently, she just needed a little time to digest it all too, because now she was approaching category 3 tornado wind-speed intensity. She was furious at Reverend Glenn and the church. She had thought about it overnight and was now convinced that all of this was an orchestrated plot to get back at her. As the former First Lady of Mount Mariah, Verna didn't much care for her replacement, Mercy Glenn. Verna surmised that Mercy had talked her husband into firing Sandy because she was jealous of Verna's popularity with the other women in the church. Although Sandy thought the idea was crazy, he wisely didn't tell her so. Instead, he just listened. She had been embattled with Sister Glenn from the very beginning, and Sandy had learned long ago that there was no reasoning with his mother about "that woman." When he saw Tony calling while he was still talking with his mom, Sandy politely told his mother that he had an important call and had to go. Tony said that he was just checking in and Sandy reassured him that he was okay.

Both Whitney and Tanya called Sandy separately later in the day. He told them what had happened. This was the first time that he could recall when Tanya didn't complain about some aspect of her own life. Whitney, the older of the two, lived on the south side of Syracuse with her twelve-year-old son, Stevie, and her new husband, and she appeared to be in a better place emotionally than Tanya was. At least she never complained about anything to him. He was on good terms with both of his sisters, but it is fair to say that they were not intimately involved in each other's lives. However, both were obviously concerned about him and he answered all of their questions as best he could. Neither one asked for any details about his lifestyle. However, Whitney did ask about his finances, which, frankly, he hadn't considered. He told her that he had enough money saved to survive and she seemed satisfied. He really did appreciate their concern, although he was more than a little relieved when the calls ended.

Sandy knew that he needed to do something with himself because he was starting to feel anxious again. Although his cat was generally very accommodating, Mel would only tolerate so much grooming, and he was about maxed out with how much Sandy had been petting him already. He decided to go to the gym and work out, which was saying a lot because he hated to exercise. The only reason he had joined this gym in the first place was because it was less than a mile from his apartment and the price of membership was greatly reduced for the residents of his complex. Another added benefit was that no one really knew him there. He decided to do his regular routine, which consisted of walking on the treadmill for twenty minutes, doing a couple of sets on two weight machines for his upper arms and legs, and then sitting in the sauna. He felt a little more relaxed when he left the gym just shy of an hour after getting there.

He checked his phone as he was walking to his car and was surprised to see that he had eight text messages. They were all from different choir members wanting to know what was going on. Sandy's heart dropped. Apparently the word had gotten out in some fashion and he was not prepared to face people this soon. It was only at that moment that he realized that he was officially outed and that his life would never be the same again.

Chapter 6

A week later, Sandy and Tony walked into the law offices of Loretta Smiley, Esq. Tony didn't know her personally, but he had asked around, and she came highly recommended. The word on the street was that although she was not a legal eagle or anything, she was very tough and got good results for her clients. Her office was located near downtown in an old office building on James Street. It used to be a mansion or something in the early 1900s, but now it housed offices for a lawyer and therapist on the first floor and an accountant on the second floor. A receptionist told them to take a seat and that Ms. Smiley would be with them in a minute.

Sandy was nervous. He still wasn't sure if he really wanted to sue Mount Moriah. Tony was more than a little insistent, however, that he at least consult with an attorney to see what his legal options were. On the other hand, his mother didn't much like the idea of him taking legal action. He had only discussed it with her in the first place because she brought it up. However, she had made it clear that the Bible says that you should not take your brother to court and advised him that he should just let God take care of it. Tony, however, felt that God had already done enough.

Ten minutes after arriving, the receptionist escorted them into a big office with two large windows and a large messy desk in the middle of the room. There were diplomas prominently displayed on the walls as well as some personal photos scattered around the room. Sandy thought it odd that there was also a rather large black cat sitting in the corner. Loretta Smiley introduced herself and offered her hand to both. She was a white woman in her mid to late 50s. She had dark brown hair that she wore in a messy bun. Both her skin and her voice revealed that she was a smoker. She was dressed very conservatively in a white, long-sleeve collared blouse, grey slacks, and flat shoes. She wore no makeup and her glasses were too big for her face. She told them to take a seat and they both sat down in front of her desk while she walked around and sat behind it.

"How can I help you gentlemen?" she asked.

Sandy and Tony quickly looked at each other. Tony spoke first and explained why they were there. Sandy felt a little like a child having Tony speak for him, and he didn't much appreciate that Tony made it sound like everybody at the church were closed-minded bigots. She listened intently while looking over at Sandy a couple of times and then writing on a legal pad.

Turning to Sandy, she asked, "What was your job title at the church?"

"Minister of music," Sandy said. He squirmed a little in his seat.

"Are you ordained or licensed or something?"

"No," he said while shaking his head.

"Was there some kind of religious ceremony that took place and made you a minister?"

"No."

"Did you sign an employment contract?" she inquired further.

"No."

"What were your specific job duties?" she asked while taking notes and not looking up.

"I was responsible for the music every week," he explained. "I worked with the choir and worship team. I played the piano or keyboard."

"Who chose the music, selected the songs each week, you or someone else?"

"Mostly me. Sometimes Reverend Glenn or one of the speakers would request a certain song. But I figured out all of the arrangements on my own and led all of the rehearsals."

"Sandy, did you ever give the sermon?"

"No. Never." He laughed to himself. Just the idea of it was absurd.

"Did you ever lead Bible studies, marry people, or speak or pray during a service?"

"Not really. I would lead a song every now and then and maybe exhort the people a little to really embrace the worship, but not that often."

"What was your relationship with the Reverend?"

"He was my boss. We were okay, I thought." Sandy started to wonder if he had been naïve somehow.

"No bad blood at all?"

"Nope, not that I was aware of." Sandy considered for a second telling her about his mother's theory regarding Mercy Glenn, but thought better of it.

"How did he find out about your sexual orientation?"

"I don't know," he said. His mouth was starting to get dry and he was suddenly aware of the faint humming sound coming from the lights in the office.

"Who knew about it in the church?" The change in the tone of her voice signified that her interest was heightened for some reason.

"Nobody except my mother," Sandy said assuredly.

"Do you think that she would have told them or perhaps told someone else who told Pastor Glenn?" She pressed.

"I'm pretty sure that she wouldn't," he said confidently. "You'd have to know my mother to understand."

The questioning went on for almost an hour before Ms. Smiley took a short break to ostensibly take a phone call from a judge. She looked a little bothered when she returned and apologized for the disruption. She sat down and read her notes to herself for a moment.

Then she said, "Here's the deal. Because you didn't have an employment contract with the church, you were what is referred to as an "at will" employee. That means that they could have terminated you at any time for just about any reason, and for absolutely no reason at all. But you do have the right not to be subject to discrimination, and that is where you might have them."

"Do you think we have a case?" Sandy asked as he leaned forward slightly.

"I don't know. It's hard to say at this point," she paused thoughtfully. "It is a church, and the law gives them a free pass on many things based upon the idea of religious freedom. But you certainly have an interesting argument, one that could be quite compelling, actually. I find that oftentimes it comes down to which side can tell the best story, regardless of what the law is. You are a good-looking guy who will make a very sympathetic witness. I must say that you came to the right person. In my opinion, this case would best be brought in federal court under Title VII, which means that in order to get into court you would have to get what is called a 'right to sue' letter."

"How do we get that?" Tony asked.

"It's not that big a deal. We have time, and I can help you with that. Once we get the letter, we can drag their butts into court and have some real fun."

"Fun?" Sandy asked before he knew it. His voice slightly raised.

"I'm sorry. I don't mean to be callous. I'm just saying if we can get past all of the procedural stuff, then we can force them to have to explain why they treated you the way that they did."

"How much will it cost?" Sandy inquired.

"Look, out of professional courtesy to Mr. Moreno here, I will not charge you a retainer. If we win, then they must pay your legal fees. If we lose, you pay me costs. This is the best deal in town. Can I write it up?"

"It sounds pretty good to me," Tony said, looking Sandy in the eye.

"What do you say, Mr. Coleman? We got a deal?" she asked, looking directly into Sandy's eyes. He was feeling a little anxious. He had never heard of anyone suing a church before, and he had considered most of the people at Mount Moriah to be family. It was not just about him. He had to consider his family's reputation in the community and his father's memory.

"Will this all be on the news and in the newspaper?" His eyes suddenly got big.

"If we're lucky, it will," she shot back matter-of-factly. "Press favors us because it puts pressure on them to appear reasonable." What she didn't say was that as a matter of course, she always gave the heads-up to a reporter she knew at the Syracuse Post-Standard when she had a case that was going to trial.

Sandy looked at Tony, swallowed hard, and paused for a second. He couldn't believe that this was his life. A part of him hated Reverend Glenn for having humiliated him before the whole world. He was pompous, arrogant, and decidedly unchristian. Then he heard himself say, "Yes, we have a deal."

"Great," she said as she stood up. "I will have my secretary put together the agreement."

As she was headed toward the door, she stopped, turned around, and exclaimed, "You know, the thing that bothers me the most about so-called Christians is that if they truly believe that the Jesus of the Bible is who he said he was, then they should be preaching love and tolerance, even if they don't believe the same way as someone else. I mean, how lost are we as a society if even churches and religious folk think that it is alright to openly discriminate against people? I just don't get it."

For some reason, Tony was elated when they left Ms. Smiley's office, and Sandy was not sure why. He just felt drained. His life had been turned upside down in just a week's time—and now it was about to deteriorate even more. Sandy didn't want to hurt Mount Mariah in any way. He really didn't. His father built the place and had literally died there. He didn't dare allow himself to even think about what his father would have thought about all this if he was still here. Sandy had so many fond memories of growing up in the church, and he would give just about anything to have everything go back to the way that it was before they knew about him. However, he also knew that that ship had sailed. Moreover, as Tony was quick to point out, the church picked this fight, not him. He honestly didn't know exactly what the right thing was to do, because just accepting the abuse and walking away quietly seemed to show cowardice.

He needed to find a job. Despite what he had told Whitney, the little bit of money he had in the bank was not going to last long. He spent the afternoon following the meeting with the lawyer looking at online job postings. He noticed that there were plenty of retail places that were hiring for the upcoming holiday season. He wasn't opposed to working retail as long as it wasn't at the mall, where he risked running into too many people from the church.

Obviously, Sandy knew that he couldn't hide forever, he was just so embarrassed that he could hardly stand himself. There was simply no way that he was ready to face people, many of whom had looked up to him. In response to all the text messages he had received from music people at the church, he just replied that all was well with him and asked everyone to keep him in prayer. He added the last part because it seemed like what he was expected to say. However, the truth is that his faith level was at an all-time low and he really didn't want anyone to pray for him.

He applied to a couple of department stores that were a little off the beaten path. He was also thinking about possibly going back to school. A part of Sandy really regretted that he didn't have a degree. He always figured that he would go back to college sometime down the road when the time was right. Who knows, maybe getting fired was a blessing in disguise? The question now is what kind of program he should study. Business was out of the question. That was clearly a mistake. Maybe his father had been right all along about music. At least now he was open to the possibility.

Sandy promised himself that he would not get too clingy with Tony. He realized that one of the reasons that their relationship had worked in the past is because they both had separate lives and valued their own privacy. He also knew that he didn't want to be anybody's responsibility, and that he needed to fill up his days and nights with something other than Tony if he wanted to keep Tony's respect. He was aware that he may have already spent too many nights at Tony's place this week as it was, but part of the reason for that was because Tony had insisted that he stay. Regardless, he had to be careful not to wear out his welcome.

Verna Louise called him every day. He knew she was very worried about him, so he tried his best to be nice. At some point, however, he was going to have to tell her about his decision to sue the church. They never actually talked for long when she called because it appeared that she only needed to make regular contact with him and nothing more. Say what you will about his mother, but her faith was genuine. She never doubted God about anything. He knew that her life hadn't been perfect and that there had been many tough times for her. Both of his sisters had been holy terrors as teenagers, and there were all the rumors about his father's infidelity and affairs with women in the church. Clearly, Reverend Coleman was never as attentive to her needs as he should have been. But his mother never showed any signs of wear. She was a strong black woman, and he respected her for that.

Chapter 7

There is simply no denying that winters in Syracuse are truly as bad as advertised. Five months of lake-effect snow, dark clouds, and cold. It had been almost two months since he was fired. Sandy managed to find a job working for UPS loading packages. The pay wasn't bad, and it was somewhat mindless work and he discovered that he liked that part of it. The downside was that he worked the midnight shift and didn't get to spend as much time with Tony as he would have liked, which left him alone a lot with his thoughts.

He hadn't been to Loretta Smiley's office since the first time that they had met, and he hadn't given the lawsuit much thought at all until someone from her office unexpectedly called him. Apparently, they wanted him to come in to sign his complaint that was being sent to the Equal Employment Opportunity Commission (EEOC). He promptly complied with the request just to be done with the whole thing. He just signed the complaint where the assistant told him to and left. He didn't read one word of it. Sandy still was not that comfortable with the idea of a lawsuit, so he mostly just put it out of his mind as best he could.

He spent Thanksgiving Day at his mother's house. He was a little apprehensive about going at first because Whitney and Tanya would be there with their families, but his mother would kill him if he even thought about skipping it. Besides, he loved his mother's cooking, and she insisted upon making everything from scratch. Surprisingly, it ended up being a good day. They laughed, joked, and talked over each other the way that they used to do when they were kids. Sandy also got to play with his nieces and nephew, which he thoroughly enjoyed. This was the first time that he could remember that he felt like himself.

The next day he received a voice message from Shonda Jackson wanting to know if he would be willing to come to a small party at her house next Saturday. Some of the team was expected to be there.

"We all love you and miss you," she said. "Please come."

Sandy called her back and explained that he worked the midnight shift and that he could not attend. She asked about the possibility of him meeting up with just a couple of them over Christmas.

"I promise that it won't hurt," she said, trying to reassure him.

He laughed and then he lied when he said that he would love to meet up some time. She said that she would try to set something up and get back to him. Sandy's heart ached, but he tried to sound upbeat when he thanked her for calling and said goodbye. He choked up a little as he hung up the phone.

Sandy received a letter from an EEOC investigator asking him to call to set up a phone interview. He called his lawyer and she told him to make the appointment.

"What do I say on the call?" He was only slightly panicking.

"Just tell the truth. It'll be okay," she promised.

She was right. The investigator seemed very nice. He asked a lot of questions about the day Sandy was terminated and exactly what was said to him. He also asked Sandy to list all his job duties.

"Before the day that you were let go, did you enjoy your job?"

"Yes, very much." Sandy answered honestly.

"Was this going to be a career for you or was it a stepping stone to some other position?'

"I really don't know how to answer that. In a way, it was the only thing that I ever knew because I started so young."

"Mr. Colman, what is it that you want? Do you want your job back? Is that it?"

"Um, no. I will never work there again. I wouldn't go back even if they begged me!" His response was immediate and emphatic.

"Can you tell me why?"

"The trust is gone. I will never completely trust them again." He could feel the hurt rising up inside once again.

***

Christmas was hard, which is saying a lot because usually it was Sandy's favorite time of year. He always liked the fact that the holiday brought out the best in many people. It was one of the few things that he had in common with his father, who had loved everything about Christmas. However, this year Sandy just wanted it to be over. After Reverend Coleman died, his mother started spending Christmas with her sister in Florida, so there wasn't a big family celebration anymore. He usually just sent gifts to his mother and to his nieces and nephew. Last year, he gave Tony something small, but he doubted if he had the energy to do all that this year. He was thinking maybe just gift cards for everybody.

Marco DeSimone, one of Tony's friends, was having party at his house on Christmas Eve and Tony insisted that Sandy go. Most of Tony's friends were active in the gay community and they all seemed nice. He just didn't feel like being at a party. Marco was one of Tony's oldest friends. They were both from Utica, New York and they had first met in high school. Sandy always thought that Marco had a thing for Tony, even though he was living with his boyfriend. Their house was located near Syracuse University, and there were about twenty people there when Tony and Sandy arrived around 8:00 p.m. They were all mostly men, and all of them were white. The house had two floors, but it was old and the rooms were small. Everyone was standing either in the kitchen or in the adjoining dining room. There was plenty of food on the dining room table and drinks in the kitchen. Music was playing in the background, but it was almost completely drowned out by all the loud talking and laughing.

It seemed that most of the conversation was about politics, both local and national. Unlike Tony, however, Sandy wasn't very interested in either one. He kept discretely looking at his watch, desiring only that the time move faster. He politely listened to everyone and laughed when it was appropriate. Sandy knew that he was the one with the problem, and not them. They couldn't have been any more welcoming of him, but he would have preferred to have been home alone with Tony.

The topic went from the oval office to homophobia on the part of mainstream media and Christian conservatives. At one point in the conversation, Tony said that he couldn't believe how the blacks in this country could so easily forget their own persecution and align themselves with the same kind of people who had discriminated against them.

Before he knew it, Sandy had blurted out, "Excuse me?" It was a habit that he had either learned or inherited from Verna. They both tended to reveal what was on their minds without necessarily thinking it through first. Everyone was a little startled by the mild outburst.

Rarely taken aback, however, Tony coolly responded, "Hey, Babe, I'm just saying that it seems to me that African Americans should be the first to see Christian propaganda for the croc that it is because it was once used to justify slavery. They should be leading the charge for gay rights. Instead, they join in the discrimination."

"Maybe it's not that simple," Sandy defiantly suggested, "it's possible to believe that both slavery and gay marriage are morally wrong, you know."

"I know that. But shouldn't they be very skeptical of the very same belief system that led to their own oppression?"

"Maybe they are." Sandy was fighting with all that was within him to suppress his agitation so as not to make a scene.

"Funny way of showing it," Tony wryly responded.

At that moment, one of the women present interjected that everyone discriminates on some level and that it's not just a black-and-white issue. Sandy walked out of the room just as Tony was responding to her. He went into the living room and looked out the window at a neighbor's house that was covered with Christmas lights. He wanted to go home.

"Sandy, you okay?" Marco asked.

A little startled by the break in his thoughts, Sandy smiled and responded, "Yes, I'm fine. I was just looking at the decorations outside."

"Listen, Honey. We all love Tony, don't get me wrong. But sometimes he can be a bit of a twit," Marco paused thoughtfully and rubbed Sandy's left shoulder with one hand.

Marco continued with his thought, "When you act like you think you're the smartest person in the room, most of the people in the room just really want you to leave after a while. He really didn't mean anything by what he said. He just can't help himself."

Sandy whispered under his breath, "I know."

"Can I tell you something?" Marco asked. "I've known Tony a long time. In high school he was one of the cool kids. Obviously, I was not. He had all the girls when he was pretending to like girls and all the boys after he came clean his junior year. All of it comes easy to him. He's had so many relationships that it's impossible to keep up. When something happens, he just moves on to the next one without ever having to change anything about himself. I doubt that he's ever fully committed to anyone. He breaks up with one guy on Monday and comes home from the mall with a new and improved version on Tuesday."

Sandy couldn't help but laugh.

Looking around, Marco said, "Sandy, please don't ever tell him that I said this, but I think that you're good for him. He is a hard nut to crack, but I have noticed some subtle changes in him. I think that deep down inside, he knows that you're a better person than he is. I really do. But that makes you the prize, Honey, not him."

Sandy made a mental note that he needed to think about that.

Just then, Tony came in the room. "Everything okay in here?" he asked.

"Yes," Marco quickly said, "just telling secrets." He smiled at them both and turned and walked away.

Tony eyed Sandy and asked, "What was that all about?"

"Nothing, we were just looking at the neighbor's decorations."

Tony didn't look too convinced, but finally let his shoulders relax and said, "Okay. You want to come back to the party? He indicated with his head.

"Sure," Sandy shrugged and they rejoined the rest.

***

Sandy and Tony spent Christmas day together, just the two of them. They slept in and stayed in bed most of the day. They also exchanged gifts. Sandy gave Tony cologne and two tickets to see Billy Joel at Madison Square Garden in New York City. Tony gave him a gold bracelet and a gift certificate to the mall. It was a good day. It was as if they were the only two people on earth. Sandy wished that it could just stay like this forever. However, he knew that that was impossible, and very soon they would have to let the world back in. Thus, he made every effort to savor each second of the day.

In the past, Tony always spent Christmas with his family in Utica. His mother typically hosted a Christmas day party at their family home and all his aunts and uncles and hundreds of cousins just sat around, ate, and yelled at each other. Sandy knew that Tony loved Christmas at home and that he only gave it up this year because he was afraid to leave Sandy alone. Although he appreciated the gesture, it just made him feel worse. Tony's pity was the last thing that he wanted. Fortunately, Tony's family always did this big thing the day after Christmas at his Aunt Theresa's house, and Sandy insisted that he go. When Tony hesitated, Sandy practically threw him out of the apartment.

Chapter 8

With the New Year came more snow and more depression. One good thing was that UPS offered him a temporary part-time position. He also made an appointment with an advisor at Onondaga County Community College about possibly enrolling there. For the most part, Sandy just went to work, ran the necessary errands, and waited for Tony to be available. He very much appreciated that his mother had stopped calling him every day. She changed it to a couple of times a week, which was much better. Mostly, he and Mel just hung out in his apartment.

He was on the couch reading a book when he heard a knock on the door.

"Who is it?"

"Sandy, it's me, Shonda."

He was shocked. He jumped to his feet, straightened himself up, and opened the door.

"Hi," she said quietly.

"Hi, what a surprise!" Sandy genuinely meant it.

"Sandy, I'm sorry to just show up like this, but I didn't think you'd answer if I called before."

"Come in," he shamefacedly replied. "I would have called you back."

"You look good. How have you been?" she asked.

"Great," he lied. "Doing pretty good. Have a seat?"

She sat down on the end of the sofa. She seemed nervous but spoke right up,

"Now that I'm here, I'm not sure quite how to say this. So, I guess I will just come out with it. Okay, the thing is that …we all hate what happened to you… I don't know everything, but I know how much you love the Lord and how faithful you have been at Mount Moriah all these years. When I think about how you must feel, it breaks my heart. It really does…I just wanted to tell you that you are not alone. We still love you. You're one of the best people I know. Your private life is between you and God. I don't care anything about it."

"Thank you, I really appreciate it." He reached over and gave her a hug.

"How's the team?" He asked, determined to appear normal.

"Not the same." she whispered under her breath as if she didn't want anyone else to hear. "No one can direct a choir like you. You know that," she offered.

"Who's playing for you guys?"

"Some teenager they found somewhere. I guess he's okay; he's learning. They're still looking for someone to do your job though. I do what I can, but it's not enough. I even overheard the First Lady saying how much she misses you."

Sandy made a mental note to tell Verna Louise.

He said, "I miss you all too."

They chatted for just over an hour. Shonda gave him the run down on everything that was happening at the church. A lot of it was idle gossip and Sandy loved hearing it all just the same. It ended when her phone beeped, and she announced that she had to go. He was very surprised at how much he had enjoyed her visit and he hated to see it end. The people at Mount Moriah were his family, and he had been feeling very much like the prodigal son lately, except it was not his choice to leave his father's house. Nor did he believe that he would ever be welcomed back. He thanked her for coming and tried to sound upbeat.

"Sandy, I heard that you are suing the church and I hope that you win. I really do. I miss you so much!"

"Thank you. This means so much to me. You have no idea."

They held on to each other as they said goodbye at the door. She told him to take care of himself and made him promise to answer her messages. He noticed that she was teary-eyed when she turned and walked away.

Unfortunately, Shonda's visit didn't change his overall mood. He was aware that he was more than a little depressed, but just figured that it would lift at some point. After all, he had just been cut off at the knees, so it made sense that it would take some time before he could stand on his two feet again. In the meantime, he was determined to keep his inner turmoil from Tony—and everyone else—as much as possible. Things were good between them, and Tony was being very caring toward him. However, Sandy knew that Tony didn't completely understand what was going on with him. Tony had made it perfectly clear that he was an atheist and that he believed all religion was "a hoax and a crutch." As a result, Sandy didn't believe that anything good could possibly come from talking to Tony about all his feelings.

Tony's birthday was also on April fool's Day. They celebrated with a weekend excursion to New York City. The first night they had a nice dinner in a restaurant in Brooklyn that Tony had heard about and afterward they went to the Billy Joel concert at Madison Square Garden. The weather was usually better in the Big Apple than it was in Syracuse, and Sandy welcomed the change in scenery. It was seventy-two degrees on Saturday as they walked around the city hand-in-hand for hours. He felt more alive than he had in months and was saddened when they had to leave the next morning,

There was a letter from the EEOC in his mailbox when he returned home. He read it but didn't understand what it meant. As instructed, however, he dropped it off at Ms. Smiley's office the next day. She called him later the same day and said that it was a "Letter of Determination," which meant that the EEOC had concluded that the church had discriminated against him in some fashion. She explained that as is their standard practice, the EEOC wanted the parties to work toward a settlement. However, her recommendation was that they not try to settle the case right now. Instead, she wanted to write back to the EEOC and ask for a "Right to Sue Letter." She thought that this should put the fear of God in Reverend Glenn. Sandy told her that she was open to proceed in whatever manner she thought was best.

"You don't sound happy. This is good for us," she said to reassure him.

"No, I know. I'm happy," he uttered. "I'm just tired."

Whitney called and left a message asking if he was available to pick up her son Stevie after school. Occasionally, she would reach out to him if she needed something and he was usually willing to oblige. Apparently, she had a doctor's appointment and Verna had a meeting and was not available. Sandy noticed that

69

she didn't say anything about why her husband couldn't do it. He texted her back that he could help.

Stevie went to one of the middle schools in the Syracuse School District and was in the sixth grade. He wished that Whitney didn't live in the city so that Stevie could attend one of the suburban schools. Although Reverend Coleman pastored a church in the city, Sandy has almost no recollection of going to school in Syracuse. He and his sisters went to schools in the Liverpool School District, which had less problems than the schools in the city had. He really hoped that Stevie wouldn't end up going to high school in Syracuse.

Sandy arrived at the school at 3:20 p.m. just as the bell was ringing. He went to the main office and Stevie met him there. He was tall for his age at almost six feet, with light skin and light eyes. He was very handsome, just a little awkward and uncomfortable in his body. Whitney had became pregnant with Stevie during her senior year in high school. Sandy had no idea who Stevie's father was, and Whitney had been raising Stevie alone prior to her recent marriage. But he was a good kid. He was all boy—he loved sports, superheroes, and all that stuff. Reverend Coleman, who surprisingly had almost no reaction when Whitney announced that she was pregnant, would have adored his grandson, who also bore his name. Verna mostly called her grandson by his full name of Stephenson.

Stevie announced that he was hungry as soon as they got to the car, so they stopped at McDonald's. The kid ate like a champion. Sandy hated fast food and only ordered coffee for himself. For some reason, Stevie had always gravitated to his uncle, and the two of them were buddies. It seemed that the only thing that Stevie loved to do more than eat was to talk. He jumped from topic to topic without clearly stated transition sentences, and Sandy struggled to keep up. He talked about everything from his friends and school to professional basketball players and video games. Sandy was more than a little amused until Stevie mentioned that his mother and stepfather Julio argued a lot and that he didn't like Julio very much.

"Are you afraid when they argue?" Sandy asked in a normal tone.

"No, not really." Stevie seemed proud of himself.

"What do you do?"

"I just go to my room. Sometimes I turn the TV up so that I can't hear them. One time I went to my friend's house, but I got in trouble even though I didn't really do anything wrong. I wasn't gone that long, and we just played video games. It wasn't a big deal. At least, I didn't think so. Do you?"

Sandy didn't really know that much about Whitney's husband. She had many boyfriends over the years, and no one could possibly keep up. Julio Moya was just the latest. He was quiet, and Sandy never gave him much thought, partly because he could count on one hand the number of times he had laid eyes on the guy. Whitney just announced one day that she was getting married. They didn't have a wedding and eloped instead, which was consistent with the whimsical way that Whitney lived her life. At least she had a good job as a secretary for an insurance company and took good care of her son. She deserved some credit for that.

Stevie had long finished eating when Whitney texted Sandy that she was home. He didn't go inside when they arrived there, rather he got out of the car just to give Stevie a big hug and kiss goodbye. Whitney waved from the door and shouted her thank you. Sandy had been telling himself for years that he needed to spend more time with Stevie, and there really wasn't a good excuse now that he had so much time on his hands. He promised himself that he would do better with Stevie.

Sandy's job at UPS ended in May. One of the supervisors there told him about a job at a private warehouse out by the airport and said that he would put in a good word for Sandy. He ended up being hired full time there, which was a blessing in disguise because the job came with health benefits. Sandy worked hard and kept to himself. Most of the other people working the floor were younger than he was, and hearing them talk about their lives was interesting. Sandy couldn't believe how messed up some people are. The world is a lot crazier than he ever imagined, which made him realize that things could be a lot worse for him.

Even so, he continued to struggle with his depression. Something was missing in his life, and he wasn't sure what it was. While he missed directing the choir and worship team, he had to believe that it was much more than that. Losing his job at Mount Moriah was embarrassing, but it wasn't the end of the world. He just kept trying to encourage himself to keep it all in proper perspective. He wasn't so weak that he couldn't take a punch, but this thing had dragged on for much too long now, and something had to give. However, every time he thought he was making real progress, something would happen, or a thought would come into his head, and that empty feeling was there again.

Chapter 9

Sandy never liked going to his lawyer's office. For him, it was worse than going to the dentist. He couldn't decide if he liked Ms. Smiley or not. She was more than a little weird. She was polite, but came across as insincere because she was always in attack mode. She seemed to have agenda, and he suspected that she was an angry person in her private life. The bottom line was that he was not completely comfortable around her. Tony came with him today and they brought with them the "Right to Sue" letter that just came in the mail.

She explained that the next step was for them to file a complaint in federal court. They would have to detail in it all the ways that the church had violated his civil rights and all the harm that had been caused to him as a result. She said that it wasn't a "slam-dunk" case because the church has rights too, including the right to hold its ministers to certain moral standards. Hopefully, the final decision would have to be made by a jury.

"How long will it all take?" Tony asked.

"At least a year, probably much longer."

"Will I have to testify in court?" Sandy asked.

"Yes. You will also probably have to give a deposition before trial too. That is basically where the church's lawyer can ask you questions about your lawsuit before the trial so that they can get

73

an idea of what you will say to the jury. This gives them a chance to decide if they want to settle with you without a trial. We get to depose them too."

"Do you think that they will want to settle?" Tony asked.

"It's hard to say. Maybe."

"Will this definitely be in the news?" Sandy asked.

"I cannot say for certain. However, once we file the complaint, it all becomes public record. The media will have access to all the papers and most of the proceedings. They can report on whatever they want. Trust me, Sandy, the church doesn't want this in the public any more than you do, which actually works to our advantage."

When they left an hour later, Sandy felt sick to his stomach. He wished that there was some way to settle this without having to go to court. However, there was no way that he could drop the case now without feeling like a weakling or disappointing Tony. He felt trapped. At this point, only a very small part of him wanted anything akin to revenge or vindication. The thought that everyone in Syracuse was judging him was simply too much to bear. Other than what Shonda had said to him the day of her visit, no one had asked him anything about the lawsuit. Sandy wondered how much longer that would last, and what his mother would say when she found out. He decided not to worry about it until he had to. Perhaps no one would care after all or everything would just miraculously go away.

A week later Sandy was back at Ms. Smiley's office, this time to sign the twelve-page federal complaint, which alleged several causes of action, including unlawful discrimination in violation of Title VII of the Civil Rights Act of 1964 and the New York State Human Rights Law. Again, he didn't ask any questions and he just signed his name in the places on the document where the assistant told him. The whole thing took about fifteen minutes. Once he was back in his car in the parking lot, he called his mother and told her that he had spoken to a lawyer who advised that he should sue Mount Moriah for discrimination.

"Did you hear me," he asked as he bit down on his lower lip.

"Yeah, I heard what you said. I'm just thinking…Sandy, are you sure there's no other way?" She sounded nervous.

"Yes, I am," he quickly responded.

"Why can't you just go back and talk to Glenn? Have you thought about doing that? I know for a fact that everybody misses you. I hear it all the time," she pleaded.

Sandy interjected, "Have you heard it from Reverend Glenn?

"Well no, but that doesn't mean anything. He doesn't talk to me."

"Sure it does," he insisted. "Look, I don't really want to sue anybody, but I'm not sure I will ever be able to look at myself in the mirror again if I just turn and walk away. Something inside of me just won't let me do that. You always taught us to stand up for ourselves. You taught us to fight."

"I know that I did," Verna said softly.

"Mom, I just can't sit here and do nothing."

Verna was quiet, which was unlike her. Then he just listened as she gradually made her case that he ought to be still and wait upon the Lord. He didn't say much in response to her—which was unlike him.

His phone started ringing just as he concluded his conversation with his mother and was pulling out of the parking lot. Because he didn't recognize the number, he decided not to pick it up. When he checked the message later, he learned that the call was from Reverend Bobby Jones, who just said he needed to talk to Sandy and that it was important. Sandy's first thought was that it was going to be some kind of bad news, but when he listened to the message again, there was nothing there that sounded tragic. Reverend Jones was the Pastor of United Love Baptist Church in Syracuse. Sandy didn't know him at all, but he had heard the name and knew some people who were members there. He decided that he had to call Reverend Jones back.

"Hello," a voice said.

"Reverend Jones, this is Sandy Coleman returning your call."

"Oh, thank you so much for calling me back. I really need to talk to you. I have a problem and I was really hoping that you could help us out."

"What kind of problem?" Sandy asked suspiciously.

"We have our summer revival coming up in a few weeks and we are in desperate need of a musician. We have people coming from out of town and we want it to be nice, you know. It is only for a few nights. I know that it is a lot to ask, but I would consider it a personal favor if you could find a way to play for us."

"Well...I don't know." Sandy was caught completely off guard.

"Before you say anything, can we just meet to talk about it?" Reverend Jones pressed. "I'm just asking that you hear me out. What do you say?"

"I have a job, so I can't promise anything," Sandy quickly responded.

"Understood. All I'm asking is for a few minutes of your time. I just want to talk face to face."

"Okay," Sandy said reluctantly.

"God bless you, Sir. I cannot thank you enough."

The meeting took place the next day at the Starbucks on South Salina Street. When Sandy arrived, Reverend Jones was already there. He greeted Sandy with a handshake and a man hug. Sandy ordered a latte and sat down. Reverend Jones was about five feet ten inches tall, with a slight built, brown-skinned and appeared to be in his fifties. He began by thanking Sandy for agreeing to meet and talk about the upcoming revival. He said that it was a three-day event and that the guest speaker was someone that Sandy had never heard of before, a minister from Detroit, Michigan. Their musician just recently left the church and now they had no one to play at any of the services. Sandy's intention when he agreed to meet with Reverend Jones was to hear him out and then graciously decline. He hadn't played a note since his firing and his heart had soured toward it. However, he could see now that it was going to be harder to say no than he had anticipated.

"Is there any chance that you could see your way to help us out?" Reverend Jones asked and looked Sandy squarely in his eyes.

"I would really like to. But…I don't know if you heard about what happened…" Sandy was starting to perspire, and his hands were wet.

"Yes, I heard. Can I tell you something about me? The Lord called me into the ministry when I was a very young man. I was in my early twenties, probably around your age. I heard the call clear-like, but I was not interested. At least, I wasn't ready. I just wanted to party and do all the things that all the other guys my age was doing. I liked my drink, and I really liked women. All women. Still do. I have twelve children that I know of by six different women. I'm sure that there are probably more out there too. They are all pretty much grown now and most of them are serving the Lord. Praise God! But the thing is…God waited for me. And when I stopped running, he forgave me. I haven't had a drink or been unfaithful to my wife since then, and that has been almost twenty years now."

"That's a great story, but I don't think that you understand—"

Reverend Jones interrupted, "I know what it feels like to feel unworthy and rejected."

"Do you think that I'm eternally damned?" Sandy spoke without forethought.

"No, I don't, Reverend Jones replied. "The underlying message of the Bible is that Jesus died for the sins of the whole world. Fortunately for you and me, that would include us too."

"Do you think God loves gays?" Sandy asked.

"I know he does. Here's the thing, God has many dimensions to him. For one thing, he is both love and judgment. But there is not one single person who is alive and breathing today who has ever experienced the judgment side of God. The Bible teaches that those who die in sin will one day be lost. But fortunately, that day is not today...not today...So I focus on loving people the way that Jesus loves me, and other than that, I just let God be God."

Sandy's heart raced within him and he had a lump in his throat. His eyes became blurry and he couldn't see through his tears. Every word that Reverend Jones spoke cut through his heart like a thousand knives. The next thing he knew he was sobbing, and he couldn't stop no matter how hard he tried. It just kept coming and coming. Reverend Jones got up from where he was sitting across the table and sat next to Sandy. He just let Sandy cry it out. He was quiet for several minutes.

"What do you say?" Reverend Jones whispered. "Come play for us. It is just three nights. It will do you good."

Sandy nodded because he could not speak.

He was a little embarrassed when he left Starbucks. He hadn't really cried from his heart since being fired—at least not like that. His father didn't like it when he cried, so he learned pretty early on that he needed to control his emotions at all times. In fact, his sisters really didn't cry either. They yelled and screamed at each other a lot growing up, but Reverend Coleman's children didn't cry. To Sandy's surprise, he felt a little better.

Also, considering Tony's low opinion of the church, Sandy was more than a little surprised when Tony later agreed that it was probably a good idea for him to play at the revival. Tony said that he thought that it might well be time "to get back on the horse." But Sandy was not so sure.

United Love was a very small church. It was in a structure that looked like an old supermarket or something. Everything inside was old and dated and there was an odd smell in the building. The sanctuary held about 120 people. The chairs appeared to be newer, but they didn't match. There was an old piano on the floor in the front next to an elevated choir stand. It was badly out of tune and Sandy hated it immediately. Reverend Jones graciously granted his request to use his own electric keyboard and play that instead. There were only twelve people in the choir—all altos and sopranos—and none of which were strong singers. Sandy worked with them every night for a week leading up to the revival. Considering the talent level, they did well.

Overall, Sandy somewhat enjoyed the experience, except for the fact that the temperature in the church was around ninety degrees and there was no air conditioning. It was nothing like playing an actual piano with the team at Mount Moriah, but it wasn't as bad as he feared it would be. Sandy didn't much care for the guest speaker, who seemed unprepared and old school. He preached hard and loud and it seemed like he was trying to force a response. However, the congregation clearly enjoyed it and the crowd grew in numbers each night. On the last night, the choir members gave Sandy a small gift, which he didn't expect but appreciated. In addition, Reverend Jones thanked him profusely from the pulpit and everyone clapped for Sandy. He was certain that Reverend Jones was hoping that he would consider playing for them on a regular basis, but that simply was not something that he was either emotionally or physically capable of doing.

***

Summers do not generally last very long in Syracuse. Some say that it goes from spring directly to fall in central New York. However, that is more than an exaggeration. Upstate New York is one of the best-kept secrets in the United States. The truth is that both the summers and fall can be quite remarkable. Neither too hot nor too cold. Tony introduced Sandy to hiking and camping the first summer after they began dating and they spent quite a bit of time in the Adirondack mountains, which are located just a couple of hours north and east of Syracuse. The Adirondack Park and Forest Preserve is one of the largest parks in the United States. Sandy loved the peacefulness and spectacular views. Usually they met up with others, but sometimes they went alone. Sleeping under the stars with Tony made him feel safe.

In September, Sandy enrolled in a class at the community college. The advisor he spoke to thought that it would be a good idea if he took one of the introductory music courses designed for non-music majors in order to get his feet wet. It didn't take long for Sandy to realize that Music Theory I was going to be a problem for him. Most of the other people in the class didn't look old enough to be out of high school, and Sandy felt ancient compared to them. More to the point, however, he had a hard time staying focused. It was not that the class was too easy or difficult, but—like what he experienced when he studied business—the subject matter failed to prick his natural curiosity, in spite of his love for music. However, at this point it didn't really matter. He just needed something that would take up some of his idle time so that he didn't have so much of it to dwell on the past and to feel sorry for himself.

***

Sandy asked Whitney if he could take Stevie camping one weekend. She didn't care, and Stevie was excited to go. Sandy took him out to buy some hiking boots beforehand and he could not believe that Stevie wore a men's size eleven already. Sandy only wore size ten himself. Being October, the trees were still turning, and the colors were magnificent. They took a hike up Bald Mountain on what was almost a perfect fall day with temperatures in the mid 70s. Sandy worried that Stevie was going to slip and fall because the kid showed absolutely no restraint, and the trail was full of roots and rocks. It was a little cold at night and the three of them slept in one tent at a camp site.

"I need to ask a question," Stevie announced at one point.

"What?" Sandy asked playfully.

"How come you two get to cozy all up together and I have to freeze to death by myself."

"Well you can move closer to us if you want."

"Good. I just didn't know the rules."

Tony and Stevie became fast friends. They laughed and joked around as if they had known each other for years. Sandy had introduced Tony to Stevie just as "his friend." He wasn't sure of exactly what Whitney had told her son about his sexual orientation, but Stevie was very bright, and Sandy and Tony didn't try to hide their affection for each other. It was obvious that Tony was enjoying having a kid with them. Stevie was also the first and only member of Sandy's family that Tony had gotten to meet, and Tony clearly wanted to make a good impression. Other than the fact that it rained a little on the second day, the trip could not have gone any better.

Sandy was driving Stevie home and he became keenly aware that Stevie's mood had changed. He seemed somber somehow.

"Hot Shot, is something wrong?" Sandy asked.

"Uncle Sandy, there's a boy on my team who has two moms."

"Really?" was all that Sandy could manage to say.

"Yeah. Some kids think it's weird. But not me. Mom says that all love comes from God. What do you think?"

"Well, the Bible does say that God is love," Sandy replied.

"I know that. But I think that love can be bad too, even though God is never bad."

"Well, you know that Tony and I love each other, and some people think that men should only love women and not other men. Is that what you mean?" Sandy asked and braced himself for Stevie's reaction.

"No, Tony is cool."

"Then what?" Sandy was thoroughly confused.

"I don't know," was all Stevie said.

"When is love bad?" Sandy inquired further.

"When someone hurts the other person for no reason and they're mean," Stevie offered.

"Have you ever seen anyone do that?"

"Yeah, everyone has seen it. It happens every day, and I don't get it."

Sandy was not sure exactly what Stevie was trying to say or how to respond. However, they arrived at their destination and Sandy was left wondering. He helped Stevie carry his stuff into his room and listened while Stevie told his mother about his "awesome" weekend. Sandy promised him that they would go hiking again soon and Stevie gave him a big hug goodbye. Whitney was very appreciative and kissed her brother on the cheek as he was leaving.

The relationship between Sandy and Tony was probably better during this period than it was before Sandy was fired. They were able to spend more time together, which meant that they were more involved in each other's lives. Although Sandy was painfully aware of just how much Tony meant to him, something inside him kept telling him to be careful. Tony remained too much of an enigma to take the chance of losing him by crowding him.

However, Tony was truly wonderful. He was so giving and caring. Sandy simply refused to believe that a loving God would deny anyone something this good. Homosexuals are the same as everyone else. He just wanted to connect with another person in a meaningful way, to love and to be loved.

One difference between Sandy and Tony was that Tony was much more secure in his sexuality than Sandy, which also meant that Tony was much less concerned about other people's opinions. Indeed, Tony had no problem with the public show of affection, whereas Sandy was very aware of the reactions of other people around them. No one had ever actually said anything out of line to them, but the looks on their faces, their leers, and whispers said it all. This was hard for Sandy and he knew that he was going to have to get stronger if he was going to survive.

One night after dinner at Sandy's apartment, Tony mentioned that he thought that he might be getting a migraine headache. Because Sandy didn't have the right kind of pain reliever in his medicine cabinet, he promptly jumped in his car and headed to the supermarket. It was only a few miles from his apartment. As he was walking across the parking lot, he noticed Deacon Eddie Williams pull his van into one of the handicap parking spots in front. Deacon Williams was one of the longest-serving deacons at Mount Moriah. Sandy hurried because he didn't want to have to stop and talk—the man could talk for hours about absolutely nothing.

For some reason, Sandy was having problems finding the medicine and walked up and down the aisle marked for pain relievers several times. Just when he was zeroing in, he heard a big voice from behind.

"You should be ashamed of yourself!"

"Excuse me?" Sandy said as he turned around to see the angry face of Deacon Williams. He had to be in his seventies, with a mostly bald head that showed the hint of grey. He was only slightly overweight, but he had a protruding gut and wore big black orthopedic shoes with Velcro straps.

"You heard me. You should be ashamed of yourself taking the man of God to an ungodly court!" Deacon Williams barked.

"Look, can you just leave me alone?" Sandy pleaded.

"No I'm not gonna leave you alone! You are gonna hear me out whether you want to or not!"

"I really don't want to talk to you about this!" Sandy shouted back.

"God will not be mocked by you and your kind, you hear me? You will surely reap what you sow!"

Deacon Williams was shaking his finger in Sandy's face now and his voice was reverberating. Sandy tried to walk away, but Deacon Williams blocked his path and continued his rant.

"You disgust me! You really do. I loved your daddy. He was a good man. But I bet if he was still alive, he would shoot you dead himself for what you're doing. The blood of Jesus is against you!"

Sandy turned and walked as fast as he could in the other direction. He left the store without buying anything; he was very angry and upset. It was not only what Deacon Williams had said, but also the way that he said it, and by whose authority he claimed to speak.

Sandy was shocked that any Christian could possibly be so out of touch with the tenets of his own faith. Even if homosexuality is a sin—and Sandy was not completely convinced that it was—how is it that any true believer could think that he or she has the right to lord their righteous indignation in the face of others? This is one of the reasons that no one wants to be a Christian anymore and why Christians are so ridiculed today. There is a complete lack of self-awareness specifically related to any of the other things that followers of Jesus have been clearly instructed in the New Testament to add to their faith, things such as brotherly kindness and love. Sandy decided to go to the drug store across the street to get Tony's medicine in order to further escape the wrath of God and holy persecution from one of his saints. He also chose not to tell Tony what happened.

Chapter 10

According to Ms. Smiley, there is something called "full and free pretrial disclosure" in federal courts, which means that Sandy has no choice but to sit for a deposition. The very thought of it terrified him. However, what frightened him even more was the prospect of having to tell Verna Louise that the church wanted to depose her too. Ms. Smiley had no idea why they asked for his mother, but she said that she was not worried about it and that she would prep them both so that they knew what to expect.

After that night in the supermarket with Deacon Williams, however, Sandy became more than a little preoccupied with the thought of running into other people from the church. Obviously, word of the lawsuit had gotten out and he could not handle another confrontation. He was always looking over his shoulders now or trying to figure out the best time to go to some place when his chances of seeing someone he knew was greatly reduced. When he mentioned it to Ms. Smiley, she just said that she could not do anything about the rumor mill and that he should just live his life as normal as possible.

Surprisingly, Verna didn't overreact when he told her about the deposition. She just wanted to know why they asked for her to testify. Sandy tried to explain as best as he could that they were probably just fishing for information to use against him at trial. After that, she didn't say much else, which Sandy thought was odd, but he was not about to look a gift horse in the mouth. The last thing he needed was a fight with Verna.

The day before the depositions, Sandy brought his mother to Ms. Smiley's law office. Ms. Smiley decided to prep them both together. She told them that the examinations would take place at her office and that the entire proceeding was informal in that the only people that would be there would be the parties. She said that a stenographer would also be present to take down the testimony. Other than that, the only other people there would be the lawyers. They were instructed that because there would not be a judge present at the proceeding to act as a referee, the best approach to answering questions was not to offer any additional information and to just answer the specific question that was being asked. She also warned them to be sure that they understand the question before answering. Neither Sandy nor Verna had any questions about the process.

The depositions were supposed to start at 10:00 a.m. They arrived on time and they spoke briefly with Ms. Smiley in her office. That was the first time Sandy realized that Reverend Glenn would be there too. Ms. Smiley said that Reverend Glenn had a right to be there and that Sandy could be present when she took Reverend Glenn's deposition next week. The thought of being face to face with his former pastor was more than a little unnerving for him, although he knew that he could not show it. However, he wished that he was in a better place emotionally.

Sandy went first while Verna sat in the waiting room. He was led to a small conference room and was told to sit in the chair next to the stenographer. Ms. Smiley sat on his other side. A tall, thin, balding white man in his mid-fifties offered his hand to Sandy and said that his name was David Smith and explained that he was the attorney for the church. Reverend Glenn said good morning to Sandy, and Sandy repeated the same words back. Their eyes only met for a split second. Mr. Smith sat directly across from Sandy and next to Reverend Glenn, who was seated to the left. The stenographer asked Sandy to raise his right hand and take the oath to tell the truth, which he did.

Mr. Smith began the questioning by asking Sandy personal questions. He asked about Sandy's age, education, work history and income. He also asked about his job duties at Mount Moriah and about performance evaluations, of which there was only one from several years ago. Sandy was also asked about his employment since leaving the church. That kind of questioning went on for about an hour before Mr. Smith finally got around to asking him about his sexuality.

Q. How long have you been a practicing homosexual?

A. I don't understand the question.

Q. You are a homosexual, correct? Or would you prefer that I use another word? I'm not trying to offend you.

A. I'm not sure what I am. I'm attracted to men, if that's what you mean.

Q. And by attracted, you mean that you have sex with other men?

Ms. Smiley started objecting to the question, and a heated exchange took place between the two lawyers. Sandy didn't really understand any of it. After several minutes, the examination continued.

Q. Mr. Coleman, were you involved in a romantic relationship with another man at any time while you were employed by Mount Moriah Baptist Church?

A. Yes.

Q. And whom would that have been with?

A. I'm sorry. Do you want his name?

Q. Yes, please.

A. Anthony Moreno.

Q. How long have you and Mr. Moreno been romantically involved?

A. Two years.

Q. Is it serious? Are you hoping to marry him one day?

A. I have no plans to marry anyone right now.

Q. Mr. Coleman, why did you keep your relationship with Mr. Moreno a secret?

A. Because I didn't think it was anyone's business.

Q. Were you at all concerned that you would lose your job if anyone found out?

A. No. I never thought about that.

Q. Did you enjoy your job at the church?

A. Yes, very much.

Q. But you never thought that your job would be in jeopardy if it was discovered that you were homosexual?

A. Again, I never thought about it. I didn't want to hurt my family. That was my primary concern. Plus, I really did think that my personal life was just that—personal.

Q. Are you proud of your sexuality?

A. Proud? I don't know. Probably not.

Q. Why not?

A. Because I'm still trying to come to terms with it.

Q. With what exactly?

A. I was brought up in that church. My father was the pastor there for a long time. It has always been a very important part of my life. I never thought that I could do anything that would make the church denounce me or make God turn his back on me. But I was wrong. He did reject me, and I'm struggling now to figure out if I deserved it and how to go on with my life.

Q. How are you struggling?

A. I'm depressed, and I have problems sleeping and eating. I have almost completely shut myself off from the world because I'm afraid of running into people from the church.

Q. Have you sought medical treatment for depression?

A. No.

Q. What about the other things, the eating and sleeping problems? Have you sought treatment from a medical provider?

A. No.

Q. Why not?

A. I'm trying to deal with it all myself. I'm not crazy, and I don't want to take any medications. So I don't see what a doctor can do for me. I'm just going through a very difficult time now, but I'm determined to not let what happened to me ruin my life forever.

Q. I'm trying to understand if the source of your problems is that you are struggling with your own identity, or with something that you think that the church did to you.

A. Honestly, it's probably both. I was not living openly as a gay man when I was let go, which was my decision to make. It should also have been my decision as to how and when I wanted to disclose this very personal information about myself to the world. They not only fired me, but they disclosed this information to the whole world.

Q. So you blame the church because now people know the truth about you?

    A. The truth? I'm not sure I know what you mean. But to be clear, I blame the church mostly for ripping out my heart and crushing my spirit for absolutely no reason other than they could and without any regard for me as a fellow believer. No matter what anyone thinks about me personally or my life choices, I should still matter to people who claim to represent God and who are supposed to love me unconditionally. In all the years that I was there at Mount Moriah, I never saw anyone get treated the way that they treated me.

Sandy was deposed for a total of three torturous hours altogether, during which time he was forced to discuss the timeline of his relationship with Tony. This was extremely difficult to do with Reverend Glenn sitting right there. A couple of times he really struggled to hold it together. He understood now why he didn't particularly care for his own attorney. She was strident, aggressive, and borderline unprofessional; however, he was also very glad that she was on his side. She clearly had gotten the best of Mr. Smith, and he looked more worn than Sandy did by the end. They agreed to take a forty-five minute break and start with Verna at 3:00 p.m. Afterward, Ms. Smiley told Sandy that he had done well. She suggested that he take his mother to the sandwich shop across the street for a quick lunch during the break.

Verna was nervous. Having to sit for three hours had put her on edge. Sandy was a little concerned because he had rarely seen her like this before. She prided herself on her innate ability to keep up with appearances. He felt guilty that he had put her in this position and tried to convince her that it wouldn't be that bad. She already knew that Reverend Glenn was there because they had spoken briefly in the waiting room. Verna still attended Mount Moriah every Sunday without fail, but she was not surprised that no one there had mentioned the lawsuit to her. It took every ounce of restraint that she possessed not to have given Reverend Glenn a piece of her mind already about the way that he had treated Sandy. Regardless, she felt more than a little torn between her absolute devotion to her son and her loyalty to God and the church.

When they reconvened, she was asked to sit in the same seat where Sandy had sat earlier. Ms. Smiley sat next to her and Sandy was now seated at the far end of the table. After Verna swore the oath, Mr. Smith began his questioning of her in similar fashion as he had done with Sandy. He asked her personal questions about herself and her family and about her involvement in the church. She looked only at Mr. Smith and answered all his questions as succinctly as possible. She looked uncomfortable and didn't really sound like herself. Then he started asking her questions specifically related to Sandy:

Q. When did you first learn that your son was a homosexual?

A. Um…when he told me.

Q. And how long ago was that?

A. I don't remember.

Q. Was it before or after he left the church?

A. It was before he was fired.

Q. Did you tell anyone what he had told you?

A. Yes.

Q. Who did you tell?

A. My sister and my daughters.

Q. What is your sister's name?

A. Florence Jenkins

Q. And your daughters?

A. Whitney Coleman… I mean Moya. Whitney Moya and Tanya Arnold.

Q. Did you tell anyone else about your son's sexuality?

A. No.

Q. Did you tell anyone at the church that your son had a roommate?

A. No.

Q. Did you ever tell anyone at the church that your son was living with his boyfriend?

A. No.

Q. Do you remember having a conversation with Rachel Glenn about your son being sick at home and unable to go to work?

A. Yes. Once.

Q. Could you tell me about that conversation?

A. She called me and said that Sandy hadn't come to work and that they were worried about him because he never ever missed work.

Q.And what did you tell her.

A. I told her that I didn't know anything about it and that I would check in on him.

Q. Did you tell her that he had a live-in boyfriend?

A. I never said that exactly. She must have assumed.

Q. What did you say?

A. She said that she was worried, worried that it was someone from the emergency room who had called her… and I told her that it was probably his friend who called.

Q. What friend were you talking about?

A. I don't know his name.

Q. Was your son living with this friend at the time?

A. I don't know.

Just then, a big argument ensued between the lawyers. Ms. Smiley objected to the line of questioning and said that it was entirely improper. Mr. Smith refused to back down and they sparred for what seemed like forever. The air in the room was thick. They threatened each other and talked about calling a judge. At last, the questioning continued:

Q. Have you ever met Anthony Moreno?

A. Who? Oh…no.

Q. Do you know who he is?

A. No.

Q. Do you know if he is dating your son?

A. No… I mean … I already told you that I don't know his name.

Q. Do you believe that homosexuality is a sin?

A. Yes.

Q. Do you think that it is appropriate for a homosexual to be a minister of the gospel?

A. I don't know.

Q. So, you don't have an opinion one-way or the other?

A. Are you asking generally or if I think that he should have fired my son?

Q. Generally.

A. I would not go to a church where the Pastor was gay, if that is what you mean.

Q. Why is that?

A. Because I would be concerned that the full gospel was not being preached, especially if he was trying to say that there is nothing wrong with being gay.

Q. Did you ever tell your son that you believe that homosexuality is a sin?

A. He knows what I think.

Q. Did you ever tell Sandy that he should probably quit his job or not work as a minister or something to that effect?

A. No.

Q. So that I understand, you are saying that you would be completely comfortable with a homosexual like your son being hired as a minister to lead your church's congregation in prayer and worship?

A. Let me put it this way. I took Sandy with me one day to visit one of the mothers from the church who was in a nursing home. He must have been around four years old. I didn't want to bring him with me because there are a lot of germs in hospitals and nursing homes you know, and she was dying, but I had no choice because I could not find anyone to watch him. I made him sit in a chair outside her door and I told him not to move. Well, I was only in her room a few minutes and when I came out, he was missing. I was a little concerned because it wasn't like Sandy to wander off like that and I started looking for him. I finally found him down the hall in the room of another woman. She was sitting in a chair and he had his little hand on her shoulder and he was praying for her... in another language! I mean that the boy was speaking in sentences too! Of course, I had seen people speak in tongues before, but it was mostly some of the older saints in the church. I had never seen him do that before and I had no idea that he even knew what tongues were... The woman was awake, and she was praying along in English. There were tears running down her cheeks... I just watched from the doorway until Sandy finished praying. I knew then that my boy was truly anointed by God and that he was special... So, to answer your question, I don't know if homosexuals should be ministers. But I do know that no one should be cursing anyone who is made in the image of God, not to mention someone who professes to love the Lord and who is trying to serve him as best he can. I don't know much Sir, but I know that.

There was complete silence in the room for what seemed like an eternity and Sandy could hear his heart beating. Both his lips and hands were trembling. It took every ounce of strength that he had to maintain his composure. Mr. Smith fumbled around and asked a few more questions before announcing that he had nothing further.

Ms. Smiley met with Sandy and Verna in her office for a few minutes after and said that she thought that they had both been awesome. She called Verna a "superstar." It was clear, however, that his mother did not feel much like a superstar. She looked like she had just run a marathon and she asked to go to the restroom. When she came out, Sandy helped her put on her coat and they walked to the car without saying a word. Verna began to sob as soon as she sat down.

"Honey, I am so sorry. I did not know what that girl was asking me that day. I would never have said anything to her."

"I know that mom. You did not do anything wrong," he said forcefully.

"But I feel so stupid!" She blew her nose with a tissue.

"Mom, you are not stupid."

Shaking her head in disagreement, Verna asserted, "Sandy, I owe you an apology. I have been praying all this time for what I want. I never asked you what it is that you want. Do you love this man?"

"Yes, I do," he answered somberly while looking straight ahead and purposely avoiding her intense stare.

"Does he love you the same way?"

"I don't know." His heart nearly stopped beating after he spoke the words.

"Well, you better know for sure before you sacrifice your life for him!" Verna decried.

After dropping her off, Sandy cried all the way home.

Chapter 11

Tony knew that he had screwed up. Nevertheless, he was not overly concerned because he told himself that it was only one time and that there was no way that Sandy would ever find out. Besides, it really did not mean anything. Marquise Walker was a law intern in his office. Tony knew that he was in trouble the first time that he met him. Marquise was tall, dark and handsome. He looked like an all-American athlete, albeit a gay one. Late one night after work, a group of them went out to a local bar for drinks. One thing led to another and Tony ended up hooking up with Marquise in the backseat of his car. The truth is that he had not been with anyone other than Sandy since the day they met, which was a record for him. However, this was exciting. He had always had a bit of a wandering eye and he knew that he was not always the best at relationships. But it was different with Sandy, and he did not want to do anything to mess things up. They were good for each other because they made each other better. He was not lying when he said that he loved Sandy, but he was not sure if he even believed in monogamy.

When he first met Sandy, he had just gotten out of a yearlong relationship and he was not necessarily looking to start a new one any time soon. However, he was immediately attracted to the tall, handsome, straight-acting guy that he saw walking into Macy's at the mall. He always went for black guys, so he followed Sandy throughout the store at a distance and waited for an opportune moment to strike up a conversation with him. It was easy, and Sandy laughed a lot. He remembers thinking that Sandy was like a breath of fresh air.

Tony's family was Catholic, although he had not been to mass in years. Suffice it to say, he did not understand Sandy's obsession with his church, or why he was so willing to accept the status quo with his family. All his friends told him that he just needed to be patient and to remember what it was like for him at first. Tony was trying to do just that, but sometimes it honestly felt like he was dating a teenager. He really did enjoy being with Sandy, but he needed more, and he told Sandy as much. His contention is that secret love does not even work out in the movies anymore because there is always an underlying element of dishonesty that ends up wearing on one or both people in the relationship.

Despite his own misgivings about organized religion, he really did understand what Sandy was going through trying to reconcile his faith with his true passions. That had to be tough and he respected the way that Sandy took it on the chin and got back up. However, he knew that if Sandy ever found out about Marquise that it would probably kill him. Tony saw things in degrees, whereas Sandy was more black and white. If his intentions were good, Tony did not think that his actions should matter all that much. Viewed through this lens, he has never intentionally hurt anyone, and he had no intention of ever hurting Sandy.

Tony's own belief is that life is a personal journey to enlightenment. He was not really an atheist, as Sandy believed him to be. Rather, he was more in the agnostic camp. To his way of thinking, no one can definitively say that there is no God, but the reverse is also true in that no one can know for sure that God exists. With all the evil in the world, his leaning was that the notion that the perfect love God of the bible was the master and creator of the universe and that he is active today in the affairs of men is highly unlikely.

Nevertheless, Tony does not personally have any problem with Christians, or any other religious person for that matter, if they do not force their beliefs upon other people. He does not understand how any fair-minded person could think that only their opinions and beliefs should matter. Nothing angered him more than the politics of the religious right and their stated agenda to legislate their own morality at all cost. The fact is that most Christians are arrogant and unloving toward others.

Sandy did not say much about what happened at the depositions. He only mentioned to Tony that his name had come up a few times and that Ms. Smiley thought that it went well. Tony was starting to question whether suing the church was a good idea after all. It had become abundantly clear that Sandy would never be able to move on as long as the lawsuit was hanging over his head. Thus, he was not too surprised that Sandy came home from the depositions even more down than usual.

Tony knew Sandy was really struggling. He could easily see behind Sandy's thin façade. He recognized that coming out was very traumatic under the best of circumstances and what happened to Sandy was particularly mean-spirited. Most nights, Sandy just tossed and turned in his sleep. In addition, his breathing was weird. There were several instances when it appeared that Sandy had stopped breathing completely. Tony wondered if Sandy suffered from sleep apnea or something. He had never noticed him doing that before everything happened. Usually, Tony just rubbed his back until his breathing became noticeable again. Sandy also had a hard time staying asleep and he often woke up several times during the night.

"You know, I'm a little concerned about your sleeping," Tony said one morning.

"I'm okay. I'm just a little restless at night. I'm having trouble getting comfortable. That's all."

"Sandy, I think that it might be a little more than that. You rarely sleep, and when you do, your breathing is all messed up."

"Messed up how?" Sandy asked.

"I don't know. It's like you stop breathing or something. You probably should see someone," Tony urged.

"Well, I didn't know. You never said anything before."

There were a couple more slip-ups with Marquise, but the internship had ended, and Tony didn't anticipate that he would ever set eyes on him again. Marquise was only in it for the fun of it and he fully understood the game. Moreover, Tony was honest with Marquise from the beginning and he told him that he had a boyfriend. He never brought Marquise to his house because he didn't want Sandy to walk in on them. For the most part, Sandy rarely, if ever, just showed up at Tony's place without prior notice, but Tony still refused to take any chances. It was important that he continue to protect Sandy at all cost.

The end of the year was good. Tony spent both Thanksgiving and part of Christmas with his family. Sandy did Thanksgiving again with his own family at his mother's house. However, they brought in the New Year together at a nearby casino with several of Tony's friends. They saw a show and afterward went to a dance party. Tony loved to dance, and Sandy was very smooth on the dance floor. Tony always thought Sandy was very sexy when he danced, and he looked forward to their time alone in their hotel room later. Sandy had no interest in gambling, but he was content watching Tony and his friends throw their money away. It was 4:30 a.m. when they finally got to bed.

Tony's mother had a cancer scare in late January and she had to have a hysterectomy. She also had radiation treatment. She was in a lot of pain and was a very sick woman. Tony was overcome with fear at the prospect of losing his mother, and it was tough going there for a while. But she seemed to be far along on the road to recovery now, and he was no longer that worried about her. He probably would have prayed about it at the time if he believed that there was someone out there to pray to and that it would have helped his mom. Sandy came with him to visit her in the hospital twice and that meant a lot to him. She always liked Sandy. She said that he was "a keeper and a cutie." Tony agreed.

Late in the season, he had gone with Sandy to one of Stevie's basketball games. He was a little surprised to be invited, but apparently Stevie's mother or grandmother didn't often go to watch him play. The game was held at one of the junior high schools on the north side of the city. The gym was huge, but run down. There was plenty of room to watch from the bleachers because there weren't many spectators. Tony couldn't believe that parents wouldn't take the opportunity to come out on a Saturday morning and watch their kids play. His own parents never missed any of his baseball games, even the ones in the rain and cold.

They arrived just in time to see Stevie's team take the floor for warm-ups. Tony could not help but notice that he was the only white person there, except for one of the referees. All the kids appeared to be either black or Hispanic or some combination of the two. He and Sandy sat close to the court and had to wave several times before they were able to get Stevie's attention. Within minutes of the game starting, it was readily apparent that Stevie was the best player on either team. He had very quick hands and amazing leaping ability. The kid was simply unstoppable. If it were not for some rule that required every player on both teams to have some playing time in the game, Stevie probably would have scored around thirty points. As it was, he ended up with eighteen points and a ton of rebounds, and his team won quite handily. Tony could see him having a real future in the game.

They took Stevie out for lunch after the game. He was in a good mood.

"I thought that you had a great game there, Bud," Tony said as he touched Stevie playfully on the shoulder.

"Thanks. I missed that shot at the end though. Did you see? The ball slipped out of my hands. I think my hands might be growing or something. That's what mom says, anyway. I'm the second tallest kid in my school, besides Trevor. But he can't shoot at all from the outside. Coach really gets mad at him."

"Are you tired?" Sandy interrupted.

"No, I'm not tired. Me and my friend Kevin are supposed to hang out today at his house. We'll probably just be in his basement the whole time. Do you think we can stop and get something to eat?"

Tony didn't have any nieces or nephews himself, so he was not used to being around someone with so much energy. However, he enjoyed Stevie, even if he was little exhausting. Sandy was good with him too, and Tony liked seeing this side of him. Sandy's family was so different from his own. Tony always felt supported by his parents and his sister and by his extended family, who, it seemed, were always in each other's business.

In comparison, Sandy's family seemed to have so many boundaries that were never ever crossed. It was an isolated existence to which Tony just could not relate. Sandy had put up walls a mile high just to hide from the judgement of the people he loved. But he was always fully engaged when he was with Stevie and never showed any signs of depression. The three of them had a good time, and Sandy seemed to be much more relaxed when they dropped Stevie off at home.

After lunch they decided to catch a matinee and dinner. Tony spent the night at Sandy's apartment and left early the next morning to go home to change and shower because he needed to go into the office to catch up on some work.

Tony loved everything about his job, except the low pay and constant stress. He hadn't always wanted to be a lawyer. At first he thought he wanted to be a teacher. He attended State University of New York at Oswego and earned a teaching degree in secondary education. But after graduating, he realized that he really didn't want to be a teacher after all. He decided to take the LSAT as an afterthought, but was only a little surprised at how well he did on the test. For some reason he always performed well on standardized tests, no doubt partly because he was always a veracious reader.

Self-confidence was one thing he never lacked. Although he was aware that some people found him to be a little arrogant, he really didn't care much what others thought about him. He didn't believe that he was arrogant at all; he just wasn't afraid to have an opinion. Most people, he reasoned, were too concerned about what other people think to be honest about their true beliefs and opinions, unless they can hide behind their laptops and social media. Tony always said that most people are fake and cannot be trusted.

Syracuse Law School was very good for Tony. He loved his time there. He also rather enjoyed the unlimited supply of undergraduate boys and he managed to go through quite a few of them. However, he didn't consider himself promiscuous. It was just that he was young and in the prime of his life. He didn't want to wake up one day as an old man and regret not having taken advantage of the opportunities that were once available to him. He also had high standards when it came to men. Even his few one-night stands were all with the best and the beautiful.

There was simply no way he could ever work in some stuffy law firm, and it was always his intention to end up somewhere in the public sector. He really wanted to do something that made a real difference in people's lives. Writing appellate briefs and then arguing in court for someone's freedom from prison because their conviction was somehow unlawful or unjust was a humbling responsibility. Most of his clients had no one else in their corner—he was it. No one came to the prison to visit them or even bothered to send a birthday or Christmas card. These are the people in our society who we have simply thrown away.

Tony believed that the notion of justice under the law was a myth. The problem was that there can be no justice without compassion and understanding. To that point, justice can never be truly blind. Tony saw his job mostly as trying to get people to look at some despicable soul who most of us would just rather not see. Unfortunately, he was rarely successful in these efforts, which meant that he had to get used to a lot of failure. Burnout was a distinct possibility in this profession, and perhaps teaching high school kids how to write just might be in his future after all.

He believed all along that the people at Sandy's church were just using Sandy; they were barely paying him minimum wage and yet their demands were ever-increasing. There was always some special service or a wedding or funeral where he was expected to play the piano. Tony knew that eventually Sandy would see it for what it was, and that is pretty much what happened. When they found out he was gay, they never even asked to hear his side of it. They just tossed him aside without any thought at all. Although it was inevitable, Sandy's fall from grace took an even greater toll on him than Tony had anticipated. Now Sandy spent his days being angry with God, when he really should have focused his rage on those hyper-spiritual Jesus freaks who only ever cared about feeling superior to everyone else and lining their own pockets. The level of their hypocrisy in the world is astonishing.

Chapter 12

After her deposition, Verna was so angry with herself that she wanted to scream. She could not believe she had let Rachel Glenn outsmart her like that. Truthfully, she could not even remember exactly what she had said to that girl on the phone that day. After she heard that Sandy was sick, all she remembered thinking was that she needed to get to him because he was never sick and she was worried that it might be something serious. She vaguely recalled Rachel asking questions about who the guy on the phone was and why she thought Sandy hadn't called himself, but at that point Verna just wanted to get off the phone. Now, if whatever she had said to Rachel ultimately became the reason why Sandy was fired from the church, she would never forgive herself. It turned out that Rachel was far worse than her mother ever was.

It was very hard now for Verna to sit in church and listen to Reverend Glenn preach every Sunday. The only reason she continued to attend Mount Moriah in the first place was that she didn't want anyone thinking that they had ran her off. It wasn't a secret that Verna was never a fan of Reverend Glenn. When the board of trustees voted him to be the new pastor after Stephenson died, she was very upset. Reverend Glenn seemed arrogant, and she was not at all impressed with the fact that he had graduated from some Bible college in Indiana or wherever. Verna wanted someone more like her Stephenson, someone with charisma. Reverend Glenn was a bit of a boob. She feared that people would leave the church in droves if he became the pastor, and all the work that they had put into building up the ministry would have been for nothing. There was a young man from New Jersey who they had interviewed, and she had liked him much better, but Deacon Sykes managed to convince a majority to go with Glenn. She came close to leaving Mount Moriah a couple of times after Reverend Glenn came, but she feared that it would have caused too much of a stir if the grieving, former-first-lady left and went to another church in Syracuse. So she was stuck. However, she did resign from the trustee's board three months after Glenn was hired.

Although Reverend Glenn was never her cup of tea, Verna had to admit that he had done a better job with the church than she thought he would. Unlike his wife, he always treated her with respect, so she was content to be a regular member. Besides, she absolutely loved watching Sandy direct the choir and worship team. She was so proud of her son. He had clearly been anointed by God to be a minstrel in the courts of the Lord, and nothing touched her heart more than watching him serve God that way. Everyone always said that Sandy was her favorite—and maybe that was true—but that was only because he was the only one of her children who seemed to have any heart for God. Whitney and Tanya were always too distracted by the things of the world to have much time for God. They reminded Verna of the women in her husband's family.

Verna had known her husband for just about her whole life. They had grown up only a couple of blocks from each other in Brooklyn, New York. He was five years older than she was, so they were never in school together. He was very popular with all the girls, not just because he was so handsome, but also because he could sing. He was friends with her older brother Russell, so it seemed like he was always around. Although they rarely spoke, Verna had a hard time taking her eyes off him. He was very engaging and was always singing. He would break out into spontaneous song at every opportunity. Everybody was convinced that he was going to be a big star one day.

Verna and her two siblings were raised by her grandparents. Their mother had died of sickle cell anemia when Verna was just three years old and her sister was only a baby. She had no recollection of her mother other than from some old photos. Her father felt that he couldn't take care of three children by himself and he just disappeared one day.

Verna was fifteen years old when Stephenson began flirting with her. When her grandmother got wind of it, she threatened to send Verna away somewhere if she went anywhere near that "grown man." In hindsight, her grandmother was right that she was out of her league with him. Nevertheless, he was just so much bigger than life and she could not help herself. She had a huge crush on him—and he knew it. He would laugh and joke with her whenever he had the chance when her grandmother wasn't around. One Sunday he showed up at their church, which she thought was very odd at the time because he had never been there before. However, he seemed to enjoy it and started coming on a regular basis. He eventually became a member and started singing in the choir. It wasn't long after that when their pastor started working with Stephenson and he announced that God had called him to the ministry.

They were married a week after she graduated from high school. Her grandmother wasn't very happy about it either, but her grandfather gave them his blessing. The early years were quite lovely. Stephenson was both very protective of his young wife and very attentive. They didn't have a whole lot of money, but they didn't need much. He took a job working for the New York City Transit Authority and they had a nice apartment right there in Brooklyn. He was very much against her working outside of the home, and Verna spent most of her days taking care of the apartment and preparing meals. Stephenson loved her cooking from the very beginning and he gained ten pounds that first year. Verna became pregnant almost immediately, but she had a miscarriage early on. Other than that, their life together was nearly perfect.

Stephenson was also working hard at the church. In addition to singing in the choir, he was being groomed to be in the ministry. God's people were very needy and there was always some meeting that he had to go to or someone who was in some manner of crisis that Stephenson needed to address. Even her grandmother was impressed by how hard he worked. Verna resented it a little, but she also understood that God's work was important and she needed to be supportive.

Besides, she could hardly wait to become a pastor's wife. It turned out that Stephenson was very ambitious and his goal was to have his own church one day. There were many nights when she fell asleep in his arms listening to him talk about it. He was contagious, and soon his dreams became her dreams too. In fact, she was already living a dream—and loving every minute of it.

It took nearly five years for Stephenson to become the assistant pastor. By that time, they had two children. Whitney was almost four years old and Tanya was just an infant. Verna was still recovering from having the baby and she was moody and tired most of the time. Had it not been for her grandmother, who came to the apartment almost every day and was always taking the girls for the night, Verna probably wouldn't have made it. Believing parenthood to be mostly woman's work, Stephenson didn't think

110

to help with rearing their children. He never changed a diaper or got up during the night to comfort either one of his screaming daughters. But Verna never resented it because he was a good provider and she understood that he really didn't know any better. The real problem was that he also seemed to not have any respect or appreciation for anything that she did, and that really weighed on her after a while. However, she never said anything to him about that either.

The promotion just meant that Stephenson was more focused on the church than ever before. He was teaching Sunday school and Bible study, in addition to all his other duties. When he was home, he was tired and distracted. Verna found it hard to even get up each mornings, not to mention to go to church on Sundays. However, she went; appearances were always important to her and she had absolutely no intention of letting anyone know that she was in any kind of distress. Right when she thought that she had turned the corner and was starting to feel a little better, however, she discovered that she was pregnant again.

Fortunately, everything about this pregnancy was different. Not only did she not get sick, but she also didn't gain as much weight as before. She knew all along that she was carrying a boy this time. She knew it in her heart and was very excited at the prospect of presenting her husband with a male heir. Stephenson had said all along that it didn't matter to him, but she still noticed a little extra pep in his step the day they brought the baby home from the hospital. Verna wanted to name him after his father until Stephenson said that the Lord told him that the child's name was Isaac. But for some reason, Whitney took one look at her baby brother and started calling him Sandy. To Verna's dismay, the nickname stuck.

Sandy was a good baby. If he was dry and fed, he never cried. She could put him down for long periods and he always slept through the night. That was really a blessing because the girls were a handful. Even with Whitney being in school, it just seemed that she could never catch up. As much as she loved her children, Verna often felt like she was in prison. Other than her grandmother and her sister, she rarely had a meaningful conversation with anyone. As attentive as Stephenson had been to her in the beginning, he barely spoke to her now. It was obvious that his career was his first love—and she feared that she would never be able to lean on him again.

The move to Syracuse was a real shocker, and it almost killed her. She and Stephenson had never discussed even the possibility of ever leaving Brooklyn and they were not looking to relocate. He heard through a friend that there was a good-sized church in Syracuse that was looking for a pastor and, although he was intrigued at the possibility, he knew that he was still young. He only decided to interview for the position to get the experience of going through the process. Verna didn't even go up to Syracuse with him that day. She was planning to go, but Sandy suddenly came down with a fever and she was not comfortable leaving him overnight. The interview was on a Saturday, and, as part of it, he had to preach to the congregation on Sunday. When he returned home, all he said was that it had gone well and that he liked the church. A week later, he was offered the job.

Leaving Brooklyn and her family was the hardest thing that Verna had ever done. She knew Syracuse was only four hours away, but it seemed more like a million miles. She thought that upstate New York was too cold and too country. The people at Mount Moriah were very nice, but it didn't matter. She just felt so alone. On the other hand, Stephenson was so excited that he could hardly contain himself. She was proud of him for fulfilling

112

his dream to become a full-time pastor, but she never realized that for it to happen, she would have to move to a city where she didn't know anyone—away from everyone and everything she'd ever loved. He knew that she was not at all happy about the move, but he still didn't go out of his way to try to reassure her. Simply put, for him, there was never any question about whether he was accepting the position so there was really nothing to talk about. Verna cried every day that first month in Syracuse.

In contrast, Stephenson had hit the ground running and was at the church every chance he got. She tried to focus on getting the house together. It was close to the church and she did like it. Someone from the church had recommended the house, and it was much nicer than their apartment in Brooklyn. It had a fenced-in backyard and an attached garage. They needed new furniture because most of the furniture they owned had been given to them and was not worth bringing to Syracuse. Stephenson had said that she could buy whatever she wanted. The only thing that had been left in the house when they moved in was an old piano. It appeared to be in good condition but was badly in need of tuning. It must have been too much trouble for the previous tenants to take with them, but Verna didn't mind because she had always wanted to learn to play. The thought entered her mind that maybe this was a sign from God that she really was home after all.

It took about a year for Verna to fully settle into her new life. Her grandparents and her sister came to Syracuse to visit twice, which helped. In addition, there was a group of four women at the church who befriended her and made her transition complete. Sophia Sykes, Carmen Johnson, Lisa Terrell, and Rosa Perez were all about the same age as Verna. Lisa was a little older than the rest of them at age forty. Only Sophia was originally from Syracuse. These women were all bold and brash and they liked to have fun. Their company gave Verna something that she never had before, a healthy outlet for stress relief. It took a while for her to warm up completely, but eventually they became her life support.

In addition to seeing them at church every week, they would go out to eat together at least once a month. She so looked forward to their outings, which were always filled with laughter. For the benefit of their husbands, they referred to their outings as prayer meetings, but the truth was that they rarely prayed about anything when they came together. It was just a safe forum where they could share what they were going through and be themselves.

Verna had no official duties as the pastor's wife. However, she insisted upon being on the trustee's board because she wanted to be respected in her own right. More importantly, the only women in the church who she trusted around her husband were the women in her prayer group. One of the things that one of the older women in her church back home had told her, was that it was her responsibility to keep the women at the church off her husband. Truthfully, Verna didn't trust Stephenson with women because she believed all men were weak. Besides, he loved attention too much, and she feared he would most certainly fall when the right opportunity presented itself. So she was determined to limit his opportunities. That is why she did things such as bring him dinner unannounced when he said that he had to work late or show up at the office just to drop off a cake she made.

Furthermore, she absolutely forbade him from counseling any women in the church alone. She knew his schedule better than he did. She was not naiive enough to think Stephenson had never stepped out on her, but if he did, it was all about the physical and didn't have anything to do with the emotional; that type of connection required the kind of investment of time that he simply didn't have to give.

114

In addition to watching over her husband like a hawk, Verna had to hold down the fort at home while Stephenson followed God. This, it turned out, was no easy task. Both Whitney and Tanya were very rebellious teenagers. They were disrespectful and disobedient. Moreover, they were not afraid of either one of their parents. Other than insisting that they attend church every Sunday, Stephenson was absolutely no help at all. He never had a father when he was growing up, or any other positive male role model, for that matter. He was raised by a bunch of women whose sole purpose in life, it seems, was to get drunk and fight—when they were not fooling around with somebody else's husband. Although it was not entirely his fault, Stephenson was mostly clueless about how to be a good father.

That left Verna to do it. She decided that the best route to go was to pick her battles very carefully and when she did, she had to show no mercy. She discovered that the girls were less inclined to misbehave if they thought that their mother was going to completely overreact or somehow embarrass them. Also, while Verna was not in love with the idea of physical punishment, she did have to spank them a couple of times. When she got that certain look in her eyes, they generally backed down. She prayed with them every night and prayed over them every morning before they went to school. Her plan worked for the most part, until they got to middle school.

Verna never actually understood why Stephenson was so hard on Sandy when he let the girls get away with murder. Because he loved his sports so much, she thought that he would really embrace this opportunity to do these things with his son. However, she was wrong. When Sandy was a toddler, Stephenson was completely focused on trying to establish himself at the church and didn't have much time for anything else. Verna believed that he would eventually come around, but he never did. As Sandy got older, Stephenson just grew more indifferent to him.

The thing was that Sandy was a lot like his father. They looked alike and had many of the same mannerisms. Maybe Stephenson was jealous or something, it was hard to tell. All he ever said to her was that she was spoiling Sandy too much. But she didn't care what he thought, and there was no way that she could ever just stand there and watch while someone mistreated her child—she didn't care who it was. The worse arguments that they ever had during their marriage were about something he had said or done to Sandy. Verna was careful not to criticize her husband in front of the children, which was very hard not to do. But she would let him have it with both barrels later when they were alone. If nothing else, Stephenson knew not to go too afoul of her, at least not in her presence.

Sandy never complained to Verna about his father. He also never confronted his father or disrespected him. It was just so upsetting to her because Sandy really was an exceptional child. She knew he was badly hurt by Stephenson's rejection, but there was only so much she could do about it. Stephenson was wrong about her coddling Sandy too, because, if for no other reason, Sandy would have no part of it. He absolutely hated to be fussed over. If nothing else, all three of her children were very resilient and very much wanted their independence from her. As a result, she had to learn when to pull back, lest she risk driving them further away.

One afternoon when she was in the kitchen preparing dinner she heard someone playing what sounded like a song on the piano. Although she didn't recognize the tune, it was clearly music, as opposed to the banging noise that she had long grown accustomed to hearing from the kids. At first she thought one of them must have let someone in the house, but was shocked, however, to walk in and see four-year-old Sandy sitting there at the piano. She stood at the door and listened for a minute.

"Who taught you how to play that song?" she asked.

"Nobody."

"Then how do you know how to play it?"

"I don't know. It's easy." Sandy didn't look in her direction.

"Can you play anything else?"

"Yeah." And he did.

"What song is that?" she asked.

"I just made it up," was his response.

After that, she made it a point to pay closer attention. Apparently, Whitney and Tanya had decided that the TV room belonged to them alone, and Sandy had been banished to the living room where the piano was. Rather than complain to Verna, he decided to occupy his time by tinkering with it. She never could figure out how long this had been going on or how it was that she never heard him play before. When Stephenson came home, she made Sandy play for him, and even he was impressed. The next Sunday, he had Sandy play for Juliette Jones, the church pianist. Sister Jones, who had been playing for the church choir for several years, was also a music teacher at one of the elementary schools in Syracuse After hearing Sandy play, she offered to work with him a little for free. She said that she had never seen any child quite this gifted before. Unfortunately, she became seriously ill the next day and was unable to provide him with even one lesson. They never sought out another teacher for him after that, mostly because Sandy didn't seem much interested in a teacher.

Nevertheless, within a year he could play just about anything the choir sang and he started accompanying his father a little during the service. Had she not known better, Verna would have thought that Stephenson was proud of his son, the way that he always made a big production out of having Sandy play for him. He would pretend that the idea to have Sandy play just popped into his head and he would call his son from the pews up to the piano. The truth is that they had rehearsed the song sometime during the week. The people, of course, loved it, and Stephenson would sing the song's refrain repeatedly as the Spirit of God moved among the people.

To his credit, Sandy was not at all impressed with himself. He obviously enjoyed playing the piano, but he would have been content to keep it all to himself. The thing about Sandy was that he was always a little embarrassed by the extra attention and acted as if he just could not figure out what all the fuss was about. For him, it was only about the music. He was born with the heart of a worshiper and he never much cared about who was listening or what people thought of him.

In contrast, both of his parents loved to show him off, especially Stephenson, who had figured out quickly that Sandy was a big asset to him on his out-of-town speaking engagements. Stephenson was typically invited to speak at other churches outside of Syracuse about five or six times during the year. Verna rarely went with them and she worried a little about Sandy being alone with his father. However, Sandy always wanted to go and he never reported to her that anything bad had happened. Verna knew that deep down that Stephenson really did love his son, he just had a hard time showing it, for some reason. Still, she was always a little on edge when they left.

It was when Whitney turned thirteen that the Coleman household was first turned upside down. By then, they had moved out of Syracuse and had bought their own house in suburban Liverpool. Verna was afraid of the junior high schools in Syracuse, and Whitney was going into the seventh grade. Stephenson didn't put up any resistance when she told him that they needed to move, but Whitney was beside herself. She didn't want to leave her friends or go to a new school. She was very angry about it and made sure that everyone knew it. Verna thought that it had been bad before, but this was an entirely different thing altogether. Whitney simply refused to do anything around the house and she would pick on Tanya mercilessly, which meant that the two girls were constantly fighting. Verna tried to fight back, but she was outnumbered and there was just was no way that she could outlast them. No one could. To make matters worse, Tanya was showing the potential to be worse than her sister was. She was just a different verse of the same song. Verna loved it when they were in school because she could finally hear herself think. However, the reprieve was never long enough because the sparks would start to fly again as soon as they got home.

Stephenson was oblivious to most of it. When one of the girls misbehaved in his presence, the most they got from him was a mild rebuke as he left the room as fast as he could. As a result, they didn't have a healthy fear of their father. Unfortunately, his wrath was reserved for Sandy's minor offenses, such as not closing the door when he came into the house or not taking the garbage out to the curb on trash collection days. Verna was left to fight the real battles alone, and the truth was that she almost didn't make it. One Sunday when Whitney pretended to be too sick to go to church, Verna returned home early to check on her, only to find her in a compromising position with a boy in the TV room. Verna was so angry that she physically beat her daughter with her hands. However, it didn't matter because Whitney was not deterred in the least.

Neither was Tanya, who had been suspended from school twice for fighting and was caught shoplifting from one of the stores at the mall. At one point she was failing every subject in school, including gym. If there was trouble to be had, Tanya was always in the middle of it. Verna knew that she had more than met her match in her daughters. The entire situation had left her feeling defeated. This went on for several years until they both graduated from high school and left home as fast as they could.

Verna didn't know what hit her when Stephenson suddenly died. Her grandfather had passed away just a year prior, but he had been sick for a while and it was a relief when he finally died. However, this was different. Stephenson was never sick. He was strong and larger than life. One day he was there, and the next day he was gone. It didn't seem real at first. When the pastor of a church dies, however, the whole church grieves together. The feeling of loss was substantial—but at least everyone was in it together. Stephenson was loved greatly by the people, so it wasn't as bad as it could have been for Verna. At least she didn't feel alone.

The funeral was a beautiful celebration of life. There were people from across the country in attendance, including state and local officials and other pastors who knew her husband. Altogether, there were some fifty clergy in attendance. Reverend Tyus Winston, Moderator of the Northeast Baptist Association, officiated. And to her utter surprise, Sandy decided to sing a solo. True to character, he had told no one beforehand. However, it was one of the most amazing things that she had ever experienced. The choir sang two songs and then took their seats. Sandy remained at the piano and began to play a soft melody that she didn't recognize. He allowed the music to saturate the air for about a minute or two. Methodically the volume inched upward. The tension in the room was palpable and started to rise slowly with the striking of every chord. Then he began to sing. His voice was angelic, and the music resonated throughout as it began to pierce the hearts of the people like arrows from heaven. Note by note, it seemed to penetrate to the depths of the soul. At first, there was complete silence from the people sitting and standing in the church that was filled to overflow. Suddenly, a quiet roar could be heard that gradually grew louder and louder as people began to wail and tremble. At the same time, there was the faint sound of something like wind that filled the room. Whitney and Tanya, who were seated next to Verna and her grandmother, were sobbing uncontrollably, as was everyone else in the church. That is, everyone except Verna and her son. She never took her eyes off Sandy and he never took his eyes off his beautiful Savior.

***

Verna's adjustment to life without Stephenson was familiar. In many ways, it reminded her of how it was when they first moved to Syracuse because there was so much to do, yet there was an ever-present sense of dread and apprehension. She had to tell herself repeatedly that she could do this because she knew that her children needed her now more than ever. It helped that Sandy was still living at home at the time, so she was not all alone in the house. Deep down, she knew that God had prepared her for this. Fortunately, she didn't have to be too concerned about finances since Stephenson had two life insurance policies. She also still had her friends to lean on and to help pull her through. The hardest part came every time she walked into Mount Moriah, and she was reminded that something was different in her life. She missed her husband, but oddly, she missed being the pastor's wife more. However, life goes on, and one day slowly turned into the next. The next thing she knew, she had survived again.

Chapter 13

Pastor Glenn was pulling into the church parking lot when he saw two deer grazing on the open lot across the street. Surprisingly, the City of Syracuse had a huge deer problem. Apparently, the deer had learned how to cross the highways in search of food without incident and had grown very comfortable around people. But this was the first time that he had observed any this close to the church. It was 6:00 a.m. on a Sunday morning and there was no one around. He had been an early riser ever since his days in the army and he liked to arrive at the church early so that he could make any final changes to his message. Usually he just read it to himself repeatedly until he had it almost memorized. His strength was always his preparation and his biggest fear was being unprepared or not having enough material to fill up the allotted time.

As he pulled into his parking spot right next to the church, he had to admit that he was very proud of how far he had come. Dennis Glenn was born and raised in Rochester, New York. His parents never married, and his father left them when he was just a baby. His mother raised him and his sister Ruby by herself. Dennis never really knew his father, who apparently relocated to Buffalo shortly after the breakup. He would call his children only occasionally, usually on holidays. However, he never remembered their birthdays, never sent money or gifts, and never came to see them. His mother had several jobs over the years, but she worked the longest as a maid in one of the big hotels downtown. She did the best she could, but it was always a struggle. She also had several boyfriends over the years and eventually had two more children by two different men.

The day after Dennis graduated from high school, he went downtown to the army recruiting center and enlisted. He became a medic and spent time overseas in both Korea and Germany. While he was in Germany he struck up a friendship with a guy who talked him into going to church. Dennis had little experience with religion. His grandmother and aunt would take him to church from time to time, but his mother never went. She said that it was just too boring for her, but he suspected that the truth was that she felt guilty about the way she was living. Being on his own, he managed to regularly attend the chapel services with his army buddy, at least whenever he was not too hungover from Saturday night.

His sister Ruby died unexpectedly while he was in Germany. The Rochester police said that she had jumped off a bridge to her death. Apparently, she was high on cocaine at the time. Dennis was out in the field with his unit the day that she died, and he received word of her passing from the Red Cross upon his return. He missed the funeral, but he was not sure that he would have gone anyway. He loved his sister, but she was running wild for so long that he barely knew her. At first he tried to pretend that it was no big deal, but he completely lost it the first time that he went to church shortly after she died. It surprised him a little because he didn't shed a tear when he first heard the news. Everyone he knew back home was either in crisis or coming out of one. Because despair was all that he ever saw, he felt empty inside and believed his life had no meaning.

A man in the service apparently noticed him crying and walked up to him, put his hand on Dennis' shoulder, and began praying for him. Dennis was embarrassed because he could not remember the last time he had cried about anything, much less cried in front of someone. However, he was unable to stop, so he just closed his eyes and waited for it to pass. Apparently, someone else came over to pray for him too because he could hear him praying in what sounded like a foreign language. Suddenly, the hairs on the back of his neck stood up and a strange sense came over him. That is when he heard the Spirit of God say in his heart, "Dennis, I have called you this day to minister my word and to tell my people of my great love." The command was repeated three times. It was clear and unmistakable. He was shaking uncontrollably because he knew it was real. He never thought to respond to the voice in any way. But it really frightened him, and he didn't know what he was supposed to do next. It was months before he told anyone about what had happened.

Initially, nothing about his life changed very much after he heard the call to ministry. He continued to drink too much and to attend church every so often. He fully recognized that army life was good for him because he needed the structure. Many of the other black soldiers he met had a hard time with authority and discipline because they never really had it at home. Growing up, he never felt settled himself, but he secretly craved it. His mother was a good woman in many ways, but she knew very little about raising children because she was just a child herself. The army was a blessing for him because it gave him the additional time that he needed to grow up. When the time came, Dennis considered reenlisting. He didn't want to go back home to Rochester, but he wasn't sure if he wanted to be in the army for another two or three years. In the end, at twenty-two years of age, he figured that he was probably ready to face the real world again.

After being home one week, he decided to keep a promise that he had made to visit an army buddy in Cleveland, Ohio. While there, he met his friend's younger sister, who had the most beautiful smile that he had ever seen. Her name was Merciree Evans, but everyone called her "Mercy." There was something very special about her and he was smitten immediately. She was kind-hearted and warm. He had never met anyone like her before. She liked him too, and their courtship progressed rapidly. To the dismay of his mother, the two were married three months after first meeting.

Dennis moved to Cleveland and quickly found a job as an orderly at Fairview Hospital. He loved being married. Mercy had a job working as a waitress in a diner and they enjoyed spending whatever free time they had together. She had a big family right there in Cleveland and they were all very close. There was a small Baptist church that they all attended together and there were these big family dinners on Sunday afternoons at her parents' house where they all gathered and just loved on each other.

The Evans family seemed to fully accept him into the fold, and he began to feel like maybe he could be happy after all. Suddenly his life had real direction. Much of it was because there was a lot less dysfunction in Mercy's family than in his own, and he began to see for the first time that it was possible to live a peaceful existence without having to worry about money or the drug dealers on the corner all the time. Meeting Mercy changed the course of his life. He liked to joke that it took him longer to fall in love with Jesus than it took him to fall in love with his wife.

Although he was extremely apprehensive, he also began taking classes at a small Bible institute. His classes were much more difficult than he had ever imagined. First, he had no background in Christianity so almost everything was new to him. He hadn't been baptized, nor had he ever taken communion before. Moreover, he knew absolutely nothing about the Bible and most of it didn't make much sense when he did try to read it. His understanding was limited to things he had picked up here and there, which was mostly Christmas and Easter stories. Mercy knew much more than he did, and she was helpful. He asked many questions. His development was slow, but he worked hard because he really wanted to learn as much as he could about the God who had called him by name.

At the heart of his problems in school was his secretly-held belief that he could not learn because something was wrong with his brain. This notion was reinforced by his poor grades, and he knew that the army would not continue to pay his tuition if he failed his classes. He was starting to panic. At one point he realized that he simply didn't know how to study. He managed to get through high school and four years in the army without having to study anything. Whenever he had any kind of test, he just answered the questions as best he could by relying on what he remembered from what had heard in class. He never read anything, or even took notes. However, that was not working now, and he was becoming more and more discouraged. Apparently, Mercy must have had a conversation with her pastor about Dennis because Reverend Sykes called him one day and asked if they could get together for coffee or something. This ended up being one of the most important meetings of his life.

They met at one of the donut places near the hospital where he worked. Reverend Sykes was tall and handsome. He was about fifty years old, with a little grey starting to appear in his temples. He also was very soft-spoken and had a way of drawing people in when he talked. Dennis noticed how he was very thoughtful and chose his words carefully. At first he thought that Reverend Sykes probably just wanted him to volunteer to do something at the church. He had officiated at Dennis' wedding and seemed nice, but the two men had never really spoken. Their meeting began with Reverend Sykes asking him questions about his background. Dennis slowly began the open up and ended up telling him about the voice he heard that day.

"What do you think it meant?" Reverend Sykes asked matter-of-factly.

"I don't know," Dennis responded.

"Have you tried to find out?"

"I don't know what you mean," Dennis admitted, feeling foolish.

"Have you prayed to God to reveal his plans for your life to you?"

"No, not really." Now Dennis was embarrassed.

"Do you ever pray to God yourself? Do you know how to pray?" Reverend Sykes asked.

"No." Dennis lowered his head.

"You need to develop a prayer life. Prayer is just talking to God the same way we are talking now. You don't have to use any special words, just speak to him from your heart and be yourself. Tell him about your secret thoughts and your needs. He knows all about them anyway. Ask him to help you with your problems."

"I hear people pray in class all the time. I just never did it," Dennis confessed. "It looks hard, and sometimes I have problems putting my words together. I'm so afraid they'll call on me to pray and I'll make a fool out of myself."

"Nonsense. Even a small child can pray. Listen to me, Son. When God calls people, he also prepares them. The Holy Spirit will equip you and cover you. As powerful as that experience was that day when you heard his voice, it will never sustain you, because you need more. You have to pursue God. It sounds like you have already started to do that, which is good. I'm proud of you. But ministry is about more than learning about Scriptures and the sacraments. There are so many who are lost in this world without hope. You may be the only part of Jesus that they ever see. Ministry is about learning how to love God's people and how to serve them. In order to do that, you need to be developing relationships with them."

"I know I need more, but I really don't know anything. All I know is that God is real because he came to me," Dennis lamented.

"Then let me ask you this. Do you believe that you are a sinner who is lost in this world without Jesus?" Reverend Sykes asked.

"Yes, I do."

"Have you accepted Jesus as your personal Savior?"

"Yes, I have."

"Are you willing to give him your life, the good, the bad, and the ugly? All of it? Are you willing to serve him for the rest of your life?" Reverend Sykes recited.

"Yes," Dennis managed to say through his tears and the lump in his throat.

"Then you're ready. Not necessarily for ministry, but you're ready to be used by him, and that is how it starts. Remember everything we do is for his glory and not for our own."

They talked for almost three hours. Dennis had so many questions. Reverend Sykes told him that he needed to be discipled and offered to work with him. Dennis readily accepted and was relieved that finally someone was going to help him. He realized then that he probably should have spoken to Reverend Sykes earlier, but he could never bring himself to do it. He knew that this was all Mercy's doing, and once again he was so grateful for the wife that God had given him.

Being discipled by Reverend Sykes turned out to be much harder than Dennis thought it would be. Reverend Sykes required him to be in service every Sunday and they met for at least an hour each week. Sometimes they just prayed together, sometimes Reverend Sykes just asked him questions. On more than one occasion, they worked together on one of Dennis' homework assignments. Slowly he grew in confidence and his grades got better. More importantly, however, he was also growing in his walk with the Lord.

Near the end of one of their meetings one afternoon, Reverend Sykes introduced Dennis to a young boy named Andre, who apparently had been waiting out in the hall for them. Dennis thought that he recognized the boy from the church, although he couldn't be certain. Apparently, Andre, who was fifteen years old, had been arrested for assault stemming from a fight at school and had been suspended. He had gone to court and was required to do community service at the church as part of his sentence. Reverend Sykes decided to put Dennis in charge of Andre, which meant—as he explained it—that Dennis had to meet with Andre regularly. While he didn't say anything, Dennis was not exactly excited about this assignment.

Turns out, neither was Andre. Dennis quickly discovered that talking to him was pretty much like talking to a rock. Matter of fact, a rock was likely to be more communicative. Andre spoke without expression and without making eye contact. Most of the time it was impossible to tell if he even heard you because it took him so long to even attempt to respond. He was buried so deep inside himself that it would take a creative miracle just to have a conversation with him, let alone to reach him. Dennis understood why Reverend Sykes wanted him to mentor a teen, but this simply was not a good match.

Mercy had a good idea. She suggested that he keep digging until he found something that Andre was really interested in and then force him to talk about that. It made sense, so he began there.

"What do you like to do for fun?" Dennis asked.

"Nothing," Andre muttered.

"What is your favorite sport?"

"I don't know?" Andre's voice was barely audible.

"Do you like football?"

"No," Andre mumbled as he rolled his eyes.

"Basketball?"

"No."

Annoyed, Dennis inquired further, "Do you like music? Who is your favorite group?"

Andre just shrugged and looked away.

Dennis tried several times, but nothing worked. He was always glad when their time together was over. The kid was dead weight. There were times when they barely spoke during their meeting. Dennis would just make him clean the bathrooms or something. The community service part of Andre's sentence was just eight weeks, but before that could end, a representative of the church was required to attend a meeting at the school and discuss Andre's progress. If all went well, Andre would be permitted to return to school. Reverend Sykes said that Dennis had to go to the meeting.

The school meeting took place in the counselor's office. Andre's grandmother was there. He had no mother or father. Apparently, his mother was an addict, and he never knew his father. The dean of students was present too. He was a black man named Leon Turner. He looked like he should be playing linebacker for the Cleveland Browns. The counselor, Ms. Siegel, was a white woman with salt-and-pepper hair and appeared to be in her fifties. She started the meeting by skimming through about twenty pages of prior offenses, which included numerous fights, abuse of staff, and incidents of insubordination.

"Andre, can you tell me why we should let you come back to school?" she asked gently.

"No," was his terse response.

"Do you want to be a student here?" She wondered.

He just shrugged.

She tried again. "Do you have any plans for what you would like to do or be after you get out of high school?"

He just looked straight ahead without a word. There was no light in his eyes.

At that point, Dennis interrupted the questioning and asked if he could speak to Andre alone. The two got up and walked out into the hall. Dennis noticed that there was an empty office right next to Ms. Siegel's and he pushed Andre through the doorway and up against the wall. Andre tried to push back, but he was no match for Dennis.

"Listen to me, you little thug wannabe. I have had enough of this crap! I didn't come all the way up here to watch you act stupid. You must be out of your mind. I used to eat kids like you for lunch. So let me tell you how this is going to work. You are going to go back into that office and you are going to tell those people that you are sorry for getting into that fight and that it will not happen again. If you don't, then you and I are going to have a come to Jesus meeting in the parking lot and we are going to see just how big a man you really are. If you think I'm lying, I dare you to try me. I dare you! Do you understand me?"

Andre didn't say anything. He just looked away with a scowl on his face.

Now out of breath, Dennis yelled, "I asked you a question, Boy. Answer me!" At this point, Dennis moved even closer and now they were face to face. Andre flinched first.

"Yes," he whispered.

Dennis let him go, sighed heavily and they calmly walked back into Ms. Spiegel's office. Dennis announced that Andre had something that he would like to say.

Andre mumbled, "I'm sorry. Can I come back?"

Mr. Turner tried to speak some words of encouragement to Andre, which no one in the room believed. He also warned Andre that this was his last chance, and no one believed that he either. He then told Andre to go to homeroom.

After that, their meetings were much more productive. When Andre refused to talk, Dennis would get in his face or yell at him. Eventually, Andre disclosed that he actually loved basketball. Dennis did too, so that first year he ended up taking Andre to two Cavaliers games and to an open practice. Progress was slow, but eventually Andre became a part of the family. He was a funny kid, and the two of them would go after each other. Everyone thought that they were brothers, and strangers would often comment on how much they looked alike. It was not too long before Andre was invited to the Sunday dinners with the Evans family and he started calling Mercy "Mom." He was never suspended from school again and graduated on time with his class. The three of them cried like babies the day he left for army boot camp, exactly one week later.

Andre and Dennis graduated the same month. Mercy was pregnant with the twins at the time. Dennis was now the youth pastor at the church and occasionally ministered the Sunday message to the congregation. He had grown so much in just four years. He simply was not the same man that he was when he first left the army. His life was already much more than he ever dreamed it could be.

As happy and content as he felt, Dennis continued to be insecure in some areas. The problem was that he was so aware of his perceived shortcomings that he was obsessed with trying to make up for them, or at least with trying to cover them up. Without a doubt, it's difficult to break a belief system that one has fed into and carried around for a lifetime. Black men really struggle with this. Apparently, there is an ongoing debate in Christian circles about whether God has predestined the lives of both believers and nonbelievers alike even before we are born. Dennis never could completely grasp the issues. Personally, there was just no denying that God had chosen him, which had absolutely nothing to do with anything in him or about him. If left to his own devices, there was just no way that he would have ever chosen to become a Christian. At least for Dennis, the matter was settled. He was no better than anybody else, probably worse than most. Why God would choose to save him and not his sister Ruby was a question that only God could answer.

Dennis also discovered that God never stops molding us throughout the course of our lives. As soon as we get comfortable in one area or phase, then something changes and we must start over again. In Dennis' case, the birth of his daughters required him to regularly reboot. Specifically, they didn't know beforehand that they were having twins and two babies at one time almost drove them entirely over the edge. Dennis' job at the hospital changed over time. By the time his daughters were in school, he was working in the records department, which meant that he was keeping regular hours and he had every weekend off. He loved being at home with his family. Unfortunately, as Reverend Sykes's confidence in him grew, he found himself spending more and more time at the church. In addition to working with the teens, he taught adult Sunday school and assisted with men's ministry. In effect, Dennis was acting as the assistant pastor, although he was never actually given that title. It was a small church, and he was content to serve God in this capacity for the rest of his life, if that was what he was called to do.

Reverend Sykes had an older brother who lived in Syracuse. He had mentioned his brother a few times to Dennis and their common ties to central New York. One Sunday afternoon, Dennis just happened to be sitting with Reverend Sykes in his office when the brother called. The two spoke for just a couple of minutes. Afterward, Reverend Sykes immediately told Dennis that his brother was just telling him about a church in Syracuse whose pastor had just died suddenly, and they were conducting a search for a new pastor. Reverend Sykes said that he was pretty much locked in where he was in Cleveland and he asked Dennis if he might be interested in the position. Immediately, Dennis shook his head to indicate that he had no desire for the job. Reverend Sykes looked disappointed and told Dennis that he thought he was ready and that opportunities like this didn't come often. He urged Dennis to go home and talk to Mercy about it.

Surprisingly, Mercy was very excited when he told her about the prospect. Frankly, he could hardly fathom the idea of uprooting his family and moving away, but she said that she was willing to go wherever God sent them. Her unfailing support, which allowed him the freedom to pursue God, was worth more than gold to him. It made him feel good too that she thought that he could get a job like that. Part of his own reservation was that deep down inside, he knew that he didn't have a chance in hell of being offered that position.

The first time he saw Mount Moriah he became lightheaded. It was such a big church. His interview was scheduled the weekend of his birthday. For his sermon, he preached from the book of Genesis about how even while Abraham was being obedient unto the Lord when he took his son, Isaac, up to Mount Moriah to be sacrificed, that Abraham never doubted for a moment that God would deliver his boy. The title of his message was, "The Rewards of Obedience." The truth was that Dennis was preaching from his heart to himself because, although it took some time to get there, he had come to fully understand and appreciate the fact that God is always faithful to the end and that he will always love and provide for us. As a result, it was always easy for him to minister these kinds of messages, and his first sermon at Mount Moriah went well. Regardless, he was shocked when he received the job offer approximately one month later.

The actual move to Syracuse went smoothly. Mercy did most of the work. The twins, who were almost ten years old, were excited. They had each other so they were not too bothered by having to leave Chicago. Dennis himself had mixed emotions. His whole family from Rochester came to see him be installed as the senior pastor. Reverend Sykes was there too. It was a wonderful day. Everyone was so accepting of him and his family. That is, everyone except for Verna Coleman, who, along with her little entourage, were noticeably distant. She also seemed to particularly dislike Mercy for some reason. He tried to tell his wife not to let it bother her, but women tend to struggle with those kinds of interactions. Amongst themselves, they often would refer to Sister Coleman as "the Queen Mother."

Reverend Glenn never had a problem with Verna's son, Sandy, who was always respectful and hard working. His musical gifts were obvious, and the congregation just adored him. At first, he didn't know what to do when Rachel told him what she had found out about Sandy's secret lifestyle. He discussed it with a few leaders and with his wife. Mercy, for one, was not convinced that Sandy's private life should matter as long as he was not flaunting it before the congregation. They called Reverend Sykes in Chicago, who unequivocally offered that Sandy should be removed for moral failure. Reverend Glenn also felt that Sandy had deceived him. Moreover, he was concerned that Sandy carried a spirit of lust and rebellion and that there was just no way of knowing how Sandy was using his influence in the church. Pastors have a responsibility to protect the people spiritually. The bottom line was that they would just have to find someone else to play the piano for the choir.

Chapter 14

S andy had absolutely no desire to attend the depositions of the people from the church. However, Ms. Smiley told him that it was important for him to be present. She said that his presence was invaluable because it put added pressure on them to be careful about what they said. In addition, if they tried to lie about something, at least they had to do it to his face. The date of the depositions kept being changed, which was fine with Sandy. At first, Ms. Smiley was only planning to depose Reverend Glenn and Reverend Grimes, but she made an additional request for Rachel Glenn as well.

Sandy could not sleep at all the night before. Tony was out of town and he ended up watching TV all night. He had passed the sleep test that he took at the sleep center, but his doctor still prescribed him an anti-anxiety medication. He didn't believe that he needed it, but Tony strongly disagreed. Reluctantly, he promised to take it, but hadn't filled the prescription yet. Staring at the clock at 3:30 a.m., he conceded that that was probably a mistake. When he left his apartment that morning, he was exhausted and had a terrible headache.

The law firm where Mr. Smith worked was in a small office building near downtown, not that far from Ms. Smiley's office. There was plenty of available parking and Sandy parked his car as far from the building as he could. He immediately recognized Reverend Glenn's black Toyota Camry parked near the entrance. He sat in his car until the very last second. His stomach was in knots and he needed to go to the bathroom so he stepped out of the car. The wind outside was brisk. He went inside and gave his name to the receptionist, who directed him to the conference room and to the bathroom. He went to the bathroom first and sat in one of the stalls for a few minutes. Afterward, he soaked his face with cold water and dried off. Then he exited the bathroom and slowly walked in the direction of the conference room like a man walking to death row.

Ms. Smiley smiled when she saw Sandy walk in the room and gestured for him to come sit next to her. Reverend Glenn and Reverend Grimes were already seated next to the stenographer, who was the same woman from the previous depositions. Sandy sat down and said hello to everyone, but to nobody in particular. He was shaking a little inside but felt a little better. Mr. Smith asked him if he wanted anything to drink and he asked for water. Mr. Smith left the room shortly and returned with a bottle of water, which he handed to Sandy.

"Who do you want first?" asked Mr. Smith.

"Mr. Grimes," replied Ms. Smiley. "Also, I'm going to ask that Reverend Glenn sit outside until his deposition."

"No way," Mr. Smith said, red faced. "He is a party. He has the right to be here."

"He is not a named party. He is not the church."

"But he is an officer of the corporation that is the church, and therefore, he has every right to be here."

"No, he doesn't. He is not named personally in the complaint. He is just an employee of the corporation," Ms. Smiley argued.

"He is the senior pastor and CEO. You are wrong!"

"No, I'm not. The board of directors runs the church. It is up to you; either he leaves, or we do."

"I'm going to call chambers," Mr. Smith threatened.

"Go ahead. I'm good with that."

Mr. Smith left the room and everyone else sat there in awkward silence. He returned five minutes later and asked to speak to Reverend Glenn. When he came back this time, he was alone. He looked angry as he sat down. He turned to the stenographer and said that he wanted to put something on the record, and proceeded to explain what had just transpired, stating that while the defendant objected to the request to exclude Reverend Glenn from the deposition, that they would proceed in that manner in order to save time. He said that he had attempted to call the judge, but was unable to get through.

Ms. Smiley asked that the witness be sworn. Afterward, she explained to Reverend Grimes who she was and asked that he remember to speak all his answers in words and not gestures so that the stenographer could take down his answers. She started out by asking him questions about his background and how it was that he came to be employed at Mount Moriah as the youth pastor. At first, Reverend Grimes appeared nervous, but he seemed to relax after a few minutes. It was apparent that he was concentrating very hard on each question because he was looking down at the floor and not directly at Ms. Smiley. He described Sandy as a friend and a gifted musician. He also said that to the best of his knowledge, Sandy's overall job performance had been very good, and that most of the people at Mount Moriah really liked him. At one point, she directed his attention to the day that Sandy was terminated.

Q. Do you remember that day?

    A. Yes, I do.

Q. Do you remember a confrontation between the Reverend and my client?

    A. I remember the meeting we had with Sandy.

Q. How was it that you happened to be in that meeting?

    A. I was asked to be there.

Q. Asked by whom?

    A. By my pastor, Reverend Glenn.

Q, Why you?

    A. I don't know. You'll have to ask him.

Q. What was your role?

    A. Just to be a witness.

Q. What did you witness?

    A. I witnessed Sandy being told that he was terminated.

Q. Why was he terminated?

    A. Because he was found to be unfit.

Q. Found to be unfit by whom?

    A. By the church.

Q. Could you be more specific? The church is not a natural person.

    A. By Pastor Glenn.

Q. He made that decision by himself?

    A. No, there was a meeting.

Q. Who was at this meeting?

    A. The executive team.

Q. And who was on this executive team?

A. Pastor Glenn, his wife, Sister Glenn, and Reverend Graham.

Q. Who is Reverend Graham?

A. The assistant pastor.

Q. What is Sister Glenn's first name?

A. Mercy

Q. So you were not in that meeting?

A. No.

Q. When was the meeting?

A. I don't know.

Q. What was the purpose of the meeting?

A. To decide what to do about Sandy, I think.

Q. You said that Sandy was found unfit. Unfit how?

A. Because he was living in open sin.

Q. And how was he doing that?

A. Because he is homosexual living with another man.

Q. How do you know that?

A. I'm sorry.

Q. How did you find out that Sandy was a homosexual?

A. Pastor Glenn told me.

Q. When did he tell you that?

A. The same morning that Sandy was terminated.

Q. Who told you that Sandy was living with another man?

A. Pastor Glenn.

Q. When did he tell you that?

A. The same morning.

Q. So before that morning, you didn't know that Sandy was homosexual?

A. No

Q. Did you suspect that he might be?

A. No. Not really. I mean, it was none of my business.

Q. Was Sandy terminated because he was homosexual or because he was living with another man?

A. Both.

Q. How do you know that?

A. Um…Because that is what Pastor said.

Q. What exactly did Reverend Glenn say to Sandy that day?

A. He said that he was being terminated. That's pretty much it.

Q. What did Sandy say?

A. He was very upset and was raising his voice a lot.

Q. Did Reverend Glenn ever raise his voice?

A. Well…Yes.

Q. So both of them were emotional.

A. Yes.

Q. Did Sandy admit that he was homosexual?

A. Not exactly…but it was inferred.

Q. Did Sandy admit that he was living with another man?

A. No, he denied it.

Q. Did you hear Reverend Glenn threaten Sandy in any way?

   A. No, there were no threats. He said that Sandy was terminated. That's all.

Q. Did he tell Sandy that he was going to go to hell?

   A. Um…I don't recall.

Q. Do you believe that the firing was justified?

   A. I don't know.

Q. So you supported it?

   A. I was there because Reverend Glenn said that he wanted me there. I didn't volunteer to be there, and I didn't want to be. I already told you that I was not a part of the decision-making process.

Q. But that is not what I asked you. Do you agree that my client deserved to be fired?

   A. I honestly don't know what I think.

There were several breaks during Reverend Grimes' testimony. One was so Ms. Smiley could take a phone call. Another was because the stenographer said that she needed to change her tape. During one such break, Sandy and Reverend Grimes found themselves in the men's room at the same time. Both were ill at ease and Sandy tried to avoid having to make eye contact. Finally, Reverend Grimes spoke up,

"Look Sandy, I just wanted to say how sorry I am about all of this. Man, it's not personal."

"That's funny because it feels really personal to me," Sandy quickly replied.

"I know, but it wasn't me, I had nothing to do with any of it." Grimes implored.

"You could have warned me. You could have told me what was coming. Instead, you let me walk into an ambush and you said nothing. Not a word," Sandy shot back. Now they were facing each other and looking eye to eye.

"You're right. And I'm sick about how it all went down. I swear I didn't know. But Pastor wanted you gone. It's just that plain and simple."

"Why? What did I ever do to him?" Sandy inquired.

"I don't know. He was just so mad. But you had to know that someone was going to find out about your situation eventually. What did you think was going to happen when they did?"

The question stung Sandy a little before he replied, "I guess I expected more from people who were supposed to love me."

"Are you kidding?" Grimes questioned, now on the offensive. "God's people aren't any different than anybody else. They only do right when God makes them do right."

"What are you saying? Love is a lie?" Sandy wondered.

"No. Just that only God loves us perfectly…nobody else. So… are you okay?"

"Actually, I'm pretty messed up."

"I just wanted to say that I was sorry and if you ever want to talk, I'm here."

Sandy didn't reply, he just nodded to end the conversation.

The two men walked out of the bathroom together and went back to their separate corners. Only the stenographer was in the room. The two lawyers had disappeared. It entered Sandy's mind that maybe they wouldn't come back at all and that the nightmare would be over. He checked his phone, and there was a text from Tony wishing him good luck. He wished that Tony had been permitted to be there; he felt very much alone. Unfortunately, he had fallen into the bad habit of feeling sorry for himself a lot.

Mr. Smith came in first and started talking about a big win for the Syracuse University football team last night. Sandy didn't have a clue what he was talking about, but Reverend Grimes apparently did know and the two of them had a great time reliving some magic moment. Mercifully, Ms. Smiley ventured into the room, took her seat, and resumed her questioning. Most of her questions were about what happened after Sandy was fired. For instance, she wanted to know if anyone was ever hired to replace Sandy, and the answer was that no one had been. She also inquired about the existence of any documentary records or emails relating to Sandy's termination. She was reading her questions and seemed to know the answers to them before asking them, because she never looked up. Reverend Grimes could not hide his relief when she told him an hour later that she didn't have any more questions. They decided to break for lunch and to resume at 2:00 p.m.

It was one of those days when the snow and the cold reigned supreme in Syracuse, so Sandy had no desire to venture anywhere for lunch. He really wasn't hungry anyway. He thought about going out to his car just to get some fresh air, but decided otherwise when he looked out the window at the unfolding wintry mix. In the end, he stayed in the conference room by himself. He had no idea where everyone else had gone, but he was glad for the chance to be alone with his thoughts and not have to make small talk with anyone.

Sandy believed that Reverend Grimes was sincere when he said that he didn't like the way that Reverend Glenn had treated him. Nevertheless, his regret fell noticeably short of supporting Sandy in his right to continued employment at the church. He was not surprised by this, but he was a little disappointed because it meant that someone at the church for whom he did have some measure of respect thought that he had disqualified himself from being lead musician at the church.

For Sandy, the more important issue wasn't how he was treated that day, it was the apparent inability of the people he had worked and worshipped with for several years to look beyond their warped theology to see him as a person God loves to the exact same degree that he loves them. Their image of him changed overnight—and he was now apparently worse than just about anyone else walking on the face of the earth. Other than Shonda and his mother, no one had offered him even one ounce of support. He felt like a spiritual leper and was deeply wounded.

Ms. Smiley was the first to return from the lunch break. Apparently she had left the building because her hair was wet and askew and she was short of breath. Sandy thought it unlikely that she cared that much about how she looked. The stenographer walked in the room a couple of minutes later. She was completely dry and didn't say anything. Mr. Smith and Reverend Glenn walked in together. Clearly, neither one of them had taken on the outside wind either. Reverend Glenn sat down without acknowledging Sandy or his lawyer.

After getting through again what was obviously her standard preliminaries, Ms. Smiley wasted no time in addressing the central issue:

Q. Can you tell me why you terminated Mr. Coleman?

A. We felt that he was no longer qualified to serve in leadership.

Q. Why was he disqualified?

A. Because of his homosexual lifestyle.

Q. How was his lifestyle homosexual?

A. He is a gay man.

Q. How do you know that?

A. He admitted it.

Q. When did he admit that to you?

A. When I confronted him?

Q. What exactly did he say?

A. I don't recall.

Q. You don't recall?

A. No.

Q. How did you know to confront him with being a homosexual in the first instance?

A. I recently learned about it.

Q. And how did you do that?

A. I'm not sure what you mean.

Q. Who was the first person to tell you that Mr. Coleman was homosexual?

A. My daughter told me.

Q. What is your daughter's name?

A. Rachel Glenn.

Q. What did she tell you?

A. She said that Sandy's boyfriend had called and said that he was sick and that he would not be coming in to work that day.

Q. How did she know it was Sandy's boyfriend who called?

A. Sister Coleman told her.

Q. Is that Sandy's mother?

A. Yes.

Q. Did his mother say that Sandy was living with his boyfriend?

A. Yes.

Q. But he lives alone. What if he really wasn't living with anyone?

Mr. Smith objected to the question, for the record, but he said that it was okay for Reverend Glenn to answer if he had an answer.

A Doesn't really make a difference. He is having sex with men.

Q. How do you know that?

A. He admitted it.

Q. He admitted that he sleeps with men?

A. Yes.

Q. He told you that he has sex with men?

A. Yes.

Q. Reverend, need I remind you that you are under oath and that it is a sin to lie?

Mr. Smith vehemently objected to the question. He warned Ms. Smiley that he would end the deposition if she did that again. However, Ms. Smiley appeared to be neither impressed nor deterred.

Q. What did you say after he told you that?

A. I told him that we had to let him go.

Q. Who is we?

A. Mount Moriah Baptist Church.

Q. Come now, Reverend. You made the decision. Didn't you?

A. I'm the senior pastor. So yes, it was my call. I have a responsibility to the congregation.

Q. So you do not want any homosexuals in your church?

    A. Not in leadership.

Q. I'm glad that you brought that up. Was Sandy really in leadership?

    A. Yes, he was. He was over the music.

Q. But he had no staff under him, right?

    A. Yes… I mean, no staff.

Q. And he had no authority to hire or fire, correct?

    A. Yes.

A. He was the only paid musician? Correct?

    A. Yes.

Q. He just played the piano?

    A. He also led the rehearsals and selected the songs that were used in the services.

Q. But didn't other people suggest the songs too? It wasn't just Sandy?

    A. Yes, but it was mostly him.

Q. And he was pretty good at it, wasn't he?

    A. Yes, he was. That wasn't the issue though.

Q. Exactly what was the issue?

    A. His lifestyle was the issue. Like I said—

Q. But you didn't know anything about his lifestyle? Did you ever ask him anything about his lifestyle?

    A. I know he is a homosexual, and that homosexuality is condemned in the Bible.

Q. So this is one of the major tenets of your church?

    A. I didn't say that. But the Bible is very clear about the qualifications for leadership. He was in a position to assert influence over other people. He was a representative of God.

Q. And everyone who represents God must not be doing anything in their private life that is not according to the Bible or they are disqualified from serving in your church?

    A. I don't understand the question.

Q. I think that you do. Are you a perfect man, Reverend? Do you ever do anything that the Bible calls sin?

    A. I never said that I was perfect.

Q. Did you think that Sandy was perfect before you decided to terminate him?

    A. No. But I didn't know that he was gay.

Q. So is there something in the Bible that says that homosexuality disqualifies a person from serving in the church, but other kinds of sinful behavior are okay?

    A. Not specifically.

Q. Can you explain the difference to me?

    A. I see what you are trying to do. But it really doesn't matter to me what you think. I answer only to God. I make mistakes just like everyone else. But to the best of my knowledge, I'm not living in sin. If I do something wrong, I confess it and try to do better next time. I don't embrace the sin or try to pass it off as being right. Homosexuality is a sin, and Sandy knows it. But he still refuses to repent or renounce it. I'm not saying he is a bad person; he's not. But I want the person who is leading my people in worship every Sunday to have a healthy fear of the Lord. I want his life to be an example for others.

Q. Reverend, I know you think I'm trying to pick a fight with you, but I assure you that I'm not. I'm just trying to understand why you did what you did. Did you tell Sandy that he was going to go to hell?

A. The Bible says that the unrighteous will not inherit the kingdom of God. The world is a dark place and it has been corrupted by lust. That is a fact.

Q. But you never asked Sandy anything about his behavior or what was in his heart, right? Maybe he asks God for forgiveness every night and every time he prays; maybe not—but you wouldn't know that because you never asked him about it, did you?

A. You cannot separate belief from behavior.

Q. Says who?

A. Says God himself!

Q. So in your mind, you can do whatever you want to the people who work at the church regardless of the impact on them because you answer only to God?

A. I'm not a monster! I'm just trying to serve God and my people to the best of my ability. Mount Moriah is not the only church in Syracuse. Sandy is free to go to any other church that he wants to. I'm the overseer at Mount Moriah. Nowhere else.

Q. Do you believe in the forgiveness of God?

A. Yes.

Q. And isn't it true that a lot of people struggle in their relationship with God?

  A. Yes. Everyone struggles from time to time. The Bible says that all have sinned and fallen short.

Q. And isn't the church in the business of forgiving sins?

  A. The church is in the business of teaching the gospel of Jesus and changing lives. Only God can forgive sin.

Q. Can anyone beside God condemn a man to hell?

  A. I guess not… I should not have said that. I'm sorry. But I will never forsake my responsibility as the pastor.

Q And you were Sandy's pastor too, correct?

  A. Yes.

Q. Would you say that by firing Sandy you were trying to get him to change his life? Is that what you were doing?

  A. I was trying to protect my congregation.

Q. From what?

  A. From the influence of a poor leader.

Q. Why was he a poor leader?

  A. The Bible is very clear about the qualifications for leadership.

Q. The Bible is clear about who can play the piano in a church service?

  A. He was one of my leaders!

Reverend Glenn asked for a break. He left the room immediately with Mr. Smith trailing after him. Ms. Smiley turned to Sandy and asked him what he thought. He just shrugged, trying to hide his dismay. In actuality, he had hung on every word that Reverend Glenn had spoken. For months, he had relived the day that he was fired repeatedly in his head. Reverend Glenn was right about one thing. Sandy believed that the Bible condemns homosexuality. However, it's also true that he didn't ask to have these feelings, and he would gladly give them back if he could. His love for Tony was special, and people search their whole lives to find something this good. Sandy had always been taught that the primary attribute of God is love. He could not count the number of songs that he sung over the years about our God of love, mercy, and grace. The Jesus that Sandy grew to love had demonstrated his love for humankind long before man repented of his sin. Jesus loved sinners, and specifically said that the reason that he came into the world in the first place was to save people and not to condemn anyone. It was all so confusing. Somewhere along the way, he had completely lost his way and he didn't have a clue what to think or which way to go.

Reverend Glenn didn't look very happy when he returned. Both of his eyes were red, and he was fidgeting. Sandy had to admit that he enjoyed watching him squirm when Ms. Smiley went into attack mode. Everybody at Mount Moriah treated Reverend Glenn as if he was God, so he was not used to being challenged about anything. Sandy had no idea what went on in the Glenn house, but at the church, his word was law. Although he was capable of extreme acts of kindness, he could also be a bit of a diva. He was a lot like Sandy's father in that regard. Perhaps it was a requirement for the job. Ms. Smiley resumed her questioning of Reverend Glenn as soon as he took his seat:

Q. How many people are employed at your church?

    A. Fifteen

Q. Full time?

    A. No, I'm sorry. Twelve are full-time and three are part-time. We also have volunteers.

Q. How many people would you say that you have fired from their job at the church over the years?

A. I don't know. A few.

Q. Other than Sandy, have you ever fired someone because they were disqualified for moral reasons?

A. I don't know how to answer that. We had to let a person go one time because she was stealing stuff.

Q. Stealing is a crime. That is not what I'm asking. Reverend, have you ever fired anyone beside Sandy because you found their personal life to be unacceptable morally?

A. No, I don't think so.

Q. Only Sandy.

A. Yes.

Q. Reverend, is there anyone on your staff who has ever been divorced?

A. I don't know.

Q. Isn't that something that you would want to know? Isn't divorce a sin?

A. I don't know that divorce is a sin. But the Bible does speak against it.

Q. Well, what about having a child out of wedlock? Isn't that a sin?

A. Sex outside of marriage is a sin. Yes.

Q. And that would disqualify someone from working at the church?

A. Maybe...I really don't know.

Q. Living with someone out of wedlock is a sin too, correct?

A. Yes.

Q. And committing adultery is sin, correct?

A. Yes.

Q. So is it fair to say that you are not in the habit of policing the people on your staff to make sure that they do not have any moral sin in their lives?

A. Yes.

Q. Who made the decision to only give Sandy two weeks' notice?

A. I did. If he had resigned or left his job on his own, I would only have expected two weeks' notice from him. I think that is pretty standard. But once I became aware of his issue, I could not in good faith allow him to lead worship ever again.

Q. What did you tell people?

A. I'm sorry. Tell who?

Q. What did you tell the parishioners and the other musicians as to why Sandy was no longer there.

A. We just told them that he was no longer employed at Mount Moriah.

Q. So you didn't tell anyone that you discovered that he was homosexual?

A. No. But people know.

Q. Who knows?

A. It is a small church. Syracuse is a small town. Word gets out.

Q. Did you tell anyone on your staff that the circumstances surrounding the termination was confidential and were not to be disclosed to anyone?

A. No… Like I said, Syracuse is a small town.

Q. Okay, tell me this, was your decision to fire Sandy, personal to you?

A. No, it wasn't. Sandy might think so, but I would have done the same thing if he was my own son. I do not hate homosexuals. God does not hate homosexuals. What he hates is disobedience. We can't say that we love God, and then live like we don't.

Ms. Smiley continued with the questioning for another hour. Reverend Glenn was clearly annoyed several times, but he never lost his composure. He also never looked in Sandy's direction—it was clear that he was very angry with Sandy. One thing Sandy discovered is that as much as he wished otherwise, Reverend Glenn's opinion of him still did matter to him. This was more than a little upsetting because Sandy was sure that Reverend Glenn could not have cared less what Sandy thought about anything. When his deposition ended, Reverend Glenn got up abruptly, sighed heavily, and left the room with Mr. Smith. He never returned.

Instead, in walked Rachel Glenn. She was wearing a matching animal-print top, leggings, and boots. She also had on too much yellow lipstick. Her hair was constructed in such a way that it looked like something had crawled up on top of her head, rolled itself into a blond-and-red ball, and died. She greeted Sandy coldly as she sat down where Mr. Smith directed her to sit and then asked for a glass of water. Like her father, she didn't look at Sandy directly; she didn't show much emotion at all. Mr. Smith asked Ms. Smiley how long she thought she would be with this witness, and she indicated that it would not be long. Sandy looked at his watch and was surprised to learn that it was already 4:30 p.m. when his lawyer began:

Q. Can you state your full name?

A. Um…Rachel Elizabeth Glenn.

Q. Where do you reside?

A. 242 Spring Street, Syracuse, New York.

Q. Do you live alone?

A. No, I live with my twin sister.

Q. And what is her name?

A. Trina…um…Katrina

Q. Where do you work?

A. At the church. Mount Moriah Baptist.

Q. What do you do there?

A. I'm the receptionist.

Q. How long have you worked at the church?

A. About two years.

Q. Could you tell me exactly what your involvement was in the firing of Sandy Coleman?

A. Um…no.

Q Excuse me?

A. No, because I wasn't involved.

Q. Aren't you the one who told Reverend Glenn something about Sandy?

A. I just told my father what happened.

Q. What did happen?

    A. Somebody called and said that Sandy was sick. I called his mother to see if she knew anything about it and she said that she didn't know anything, and that it was probably his boyfriend who called.

Q. His mother told you that?

    A. Yes, she did.

Q. Did you try to call Sandy directly to see why he was out?

    A. No. I only called his mother.

Q. Did you know before then that Sandy had a boyfriend?

    A. No I didn't, but I wasn't surprised.

Q. Why not?

    A. Because of the way he acted.

Q. How did he act?

    A. I don't know.

Q. You don't know?

    A. No.

Q. Are you trying to say that he acted like a homosexual?

    A. Um…He acted stuck-up-like, you know, like he thought he was better than everyone else.

Q. You didn't like Sandy very much, did you?

    A. I didn't have anything against him. I just didn't think that he was all that like everyone else did.

Q. So you wanted to get him fired?

A. See…no you don't. I didn't try to get him fired. He got himself fired. I'm not the one who made him be gay. That's on him. All I did was tell my father what his mother said.

Q. Did your father tell you why he fired Sandy?

A. Yes, because he was a minister living in sin.

Q. Did his mother tell you that Sandy was living with this boyfriend?

A. Yes, she did. She said she knew all about it.

Q. What exactly did she say to you, as best that you can remember?

A. Um…I said that some strange guy had called in for Sandy, but he didn't leave his name or say who he was. She said that it was probably the guy that he was living with. I said that I thought that he lived by himself. Um… she said that they had been together for a while and that she didn't even know his name because Sandy didn't like to talk about it.

Q. Did she say anything else?

A. Nope. Just that she would go check on him.

Q. How long after you hung up with Mrs. Coleman did you tell your father about the conversation?

A. I told him as soon as he came in.

Q. What did your father do after you told him this?

A. We went to Sandy's desk to look for evidence.

Q. Evidence of what?

A. You know like pictures and such.

Q. You mean that you were looking for photos of Sandy with the guy on the phone?

A. Yes.

Q. Whose idea was it to search Sandy's desk?

A. I don't remember.

Q. The two of you searched his desk?

A. Yes, we did.

Q. Did you find anything?

A. No.

Q. Before that day, had you ever searched anyone's desk at the church before?

A. No. That was the first time.

Q. Beside your father, have you ever told anyone else what Mrs. Coleman had said to you?

A. I don't know. Maybe a couple of people.

Q. Who did you tell?

A. I don't know. Just family, you know.

Q. Did you tell anyone at the church?

A. I don't remember.

Q. Isn't that gossiping? Isn't that a sin?

A. I didn't say anything that wasn't the truth. Besides, I ain't no minister.

Q. So your father fired Sandy based on some gossip you told him without any other proof?

A. Um…like I said, I had nothing to do with all that. So let's not go there, please. I was just doing my job. You should have asked my father about that if you really wanted to know that bad. I'm not the one, okay?

Q. Well, maybe you're right. I have no more questions. Thank you.

By the time Sandy left Mr. Smith's office, he was completely exhausted. He felt like he had just been hit by a truck or something. His body ached all over from the stress of it all and he was hungry from not eating anything all day. He decided to stop on his way home and pick up a pizza. He also got his prescription for the anti-anxiety medication filled at the pharmacy. The last thing he needed was to be up all night again with his thoughts. He had yet to figure out how to turn off his brain and he was already anticipating that this could be a bad night. However, he was glad to finally be home and was even happier when a snow-covered Tony walked through the door at ten o'clock.

"Hey, thought you might like some company," Tony said with a smile.

Mel, who was sitting next to Sandy on the couch at the time, took one look at Tony, jumped down, and ran away.

"How did it go?" Tony asked.

"It's over, that's all I care about now."

"What about me? You care about me?" Tony joked.

"Maybe a little," Sandy said and they both laughed.

The day ended for Sandy much better than it had begun. With Tony next to him, he managed to get a couple of hours of sleep. Unfortunately, he found himself wide awake again at 3:00 a.m. and he never could go back to sleep.

Chapter 15

Sandy earned a grade of ninety-eight percent on his midterm exam without even studying. In fact, he got the highest grade in the class. Unfortunately, the grade was meaningless to him. He had stopped taking notes after the first two classes, although he had completed all the required readings. For him, this was high school all over again. He was there, but only physically. His mind was always wandering. He was embarrassed one day when the professor unexpectantly called on him in class and he never even heard the question because he was daydreaming.

Thanksgiving was another masterpiece by Verna. Like the previous year, he ended up enjoying the day immensely, even though he hadn't been looking forward to it. There was just something about being around the three kids that seemed to bring out the best in him. He especially enjoyed Stevie, who insisted on sitting next to his uncle during dinner and entertaining everyone with his quick wit. At one point after dinner, Sandy somehow dosed off on the couch, only to wake to find both of his nieces curled up next to him and sound asleep.

His sister Whitney did seem a little distant, but she had always been moody and hard to read. She was different from Tanya, who always wanted everyone to know how she was feeling in real time. Tanya was more like their mother in that regard. When they were younger, Verna and Tanya did most of the talking, and Whitney just sat back and judged them. Typically, Reverend Coleman would only say something if the discussion started to become too heated, or if he wanted something done for him.

Sandy knew that he had been only a casual observer at Coleman family holiday events over the years. That is, he was never a true participant, not that he ever wanted to be. The point is that he also was never even considered. Christmas was a little different because of all the gifts he usually received, but even then, he was always quickly ignored right after he had opened the last box or bag of Christmas wonder. In Verna's defense, she was always so busy preparing and cooking that she didn't have much time for anything else. While she usually led the dinner conversation, no one ever asked him what he thought about anything or even about what was going on in his life. Truthfully, he never felt that bad about being isolated because a part of him preferred it that way. He never liked too much drama, and the more they talked, the greater the likelihood that someone was going to become upset about something. He thought it better to just remain quiet.

Tony spent Thanksgiving with his family again. He and Sandy were together the night before at Sandy's place and then went their separate ways first thing in the morning. Although this was hardly typical behavior for most couples, they were hardly a typical couple. Tony was planning to stay most of the weekend at his parent's house, so Sandy figured that he probably wouldn't see him again until sometime next week. Unlike Tony, he had to go to work on Friday.

Stevie kept hinting that he wanted Sandy to take him to see some new superhero movie on Saturday. It was intriguing to Sandy just how different he was from his nephew. Even as a teenager, Sandy was never the least bit interested in superheroes or action movies. His preference had always been for a good story with well-developed characters. Still, he readily agreed to take Stevie to a matinee as long as Whitney was okay with it, which he knew that she would be.

What Stevie and his mother conveniently neglected to mention was that he had a basketball game at 10:00 a.m. on Saturday morning, which meant that the 12:10 p.m. matinee that Sandy had planned was out of the question. He was supposed to pick up Stevie after the game and he arrived at the school gym at 9:45 a.m. Two hours later, he was still waiting for it to be over. Again, Stevie dominated the game and Sandy enjoyed watching him play. However, it was a close game this time and Stevie's team ended up winning by just one point in overtime. The problem was that he really needed to take a shower before they could go to the mall, which meant that Sandy had to take him home because the showers at the school weren't working.

Sandy had only been inside Whitney's apartment a few times. It was small, but neat. He was more than a little surprised at that because her room always looked like a tornado had just blown through when they were growing up. She was home alone when they walked in. Stevie promised that he wouldn't be long and ran upstairs to shower and change. Sandy sat at the kitchen table and Whitney made him a cup of coffee without asking him if he wanted one. They chatted about Stevie's game a little before she adeptly changed the subject.

"Um...I have been meaning to ask you something, but I have been afraid to," she said.

"What is it?" he asked.

"How long have you known that you were gay? I mean, did you know when we were kids?" She seemed uncomfortable.

"Actually, I didn't. I kind of just realized it that year when I went to Morrisville."

"So, before that, you didn't have a clue?" Whitney inquired further.

Sandy paused for a moment before verbalizing, "Looking back, there were signs. But I didn't really think about it."

"Are you afraid of getting…um…AIDS…or something?" She managed to ask.

"I'm careful, and I get tested regularly."

"I'm sorry. It just makes me nervous," she admitted and looked away.

"I know. But I don't sleep around."

"Oh, I know," she said immediately. "But I'm not sure that you can ever really trust people to be honest with you. Especially men."

"You sound like Verna Louise," he said with a smile.

She laughed. "I know I do, but I'm not saying anything against you. I'm sure this guy you're seeing is really nice and all, but are you sure you can trust him?"

"Let me put it this way, I refuse to be anybody's fool." Sandy felt defensive.

"I'm glad to hear that, but sometimes it's hard to get out once you're in." She whispered, and her voice trailed off.

"Whit, what about you? You wanna get out?" he asked pointedly.

"I want a lot of things," was all she said before jumping up and pouring him another cup of coffee.

Just then, Stevie rushed in.

"Boy, that was too quick! Did you use soap?" asked his mother.

"I always use soap," He insisted, already heading toward the door.

"Right. Well, you guys have fun," she said.

Sandy stood up. He wished that they could have had a few more minutes alone to finish their conversation. He was purposely trying not to pry too much into her life because she was even more private about some things than he was. Her husband never came to holiday dinners with her, so it was hard to read anything into that. However, she never talked about him either.

They just made the 1:20 p.m. movie. It was sold out and there were about a hundred hyperactive teenagers in the theatre. Stevie pretty much consumed an entire bucket of large buttered popcorn along with a large drink all by himself. Moreover, he loved the movie. He seemed to be transfixed by all the fake drama.

Sandy didn't exactly hate the movie. He thought it was okay, if one could somehow completely suspend all sense of reality for two hours and fifteen minutes. Nevertheless, it was a nice break for him and they ate at the food court afterward. They also ran into some of the choir members from Mount Moriah, who seemed genuinely glad to see him. He noticed that he wasn't quite as fearful of the possibility of running into people as before, which was a very good sign. He also managed to pick up a few things for Christmas before they left the mall, including a gift for Tony.

The forecast for the winter season was record high snowfall and record low temperatures. Sandy hoped that they were wrong, but it wasn't looking too good at the start of it. It was hard enough to maintain one's sanity when the weather was decent. But the combination of the cold and the lack of sunlight was very hard to overcome. Although he was a fighter, he was just barely holding on. He felt like he just needed a break, for one good thing to happen. Hopefully, his breakthrough was right around the corner.

Chapter 16

The knocking at the door startled Sandy. It was 5:15 a.m. Tony was snoring again and obviously didn't hear it. Sandy thought to himself that the outside door must be broken again because it was supposed to be locked, and visitors must be buzzed in—but there was no buzz, just the knocking. Unless, of course, it was someone who lived in the building who was at the door. Sandy got up and put on a pair of jeans. Unlike Tony, who always slept in the nude, Sandy usually slept in a t-shirt and boxers. As he looked through the peephole, he asked,

"Who is it?"

"It's Syracuse P.D., Mr. Coleman. We need to talk to you."

"What is it?" Sandy asked even before he was able to get the door fully opened. Standing there were two uniformed police officers. One was a white male, and the other was an African American female. The male officer was tall with piercing blue eyes. Sandy could not help but notice that he was very handsome.

"Can we come in?" he asked.

"Yes, please. What's wrong? Did something happen?"

"I'm Officer Murray, and this is Officer Thomas. Yes, there has been an incident involving your sister, Whitney Moya, and we need you to get dressed and come with us to the hospital."

"Whitney? Is she okay?" He demanded, and his heart raced.

"We don't have all of the details, Sir, but it is important that we get you to the hospital as soon as possible."

"Okay, give me one minute to get my shoes." Sandy rushed back into the bedroom. He was feeling anxious. Tony was awake now.

"What's wrong?" Tony mumbled.

"I don't know. Something must have happened to my sister. Two cops are here, and they say that I have to go to the hospital right now," Sandy blurted out the words as he sat on the bed and put on his socks.

"Do you want me to go with you?" Tony whispered.

"No, you have to go to work. I'll call you as soon as I know what's going on."

"Okay. Hey, don't forget to take your phone and your wallet." Tony muttered and pointed to the wallet on the nightstand.

"Thanks," Sandy said as he grabbed it and hurried out of the room.

There was a police car parked on the sidewalk right in front of the door. Officer Thomas opened the right rear door and Sandy sat in the back seat. Officer Murray drove the car. They didn't talk at all, and the only sound in the car was the chatter coming from the police radio and the sound of the car's engine. They had the heat cranked up and it was too hot inside the car. It was snowing lightly and there was no traffic on the roads. Christmas lights and decorations shined and sparkled in every direction that he looked. Sandy's heart was racing, and he started to pray in his heart before he realized what he was doing and stopped himself.

There must have been at least ten police cars parked outside the emergency room entrance to the hospital. Officer Murray parked right in front of the main door and the two officers escorted Sandy inside. The lobby was very crowded and there was a lot of commotion. Sandy was led through a set of double doors and down a long hall. They stopped at a closed door where another police officer was standing guard.

"This is the uncle," Officer Murray whispered.

Sandy heard what he said and froze in place. The officer opened the door. Sandy tried to walk but his feet would not move. Then he saw Whitney. She was seated in a chair next to a female police officer. The room was not well lit, but he noticed immediately that the front of Whitney's shirt and slacks appeared to be covered in blood. As soon as she saw Sandy she jumped up and ran into his arms. She became hysterical and was pulling at him.

"What happened?" he heard himself yell. "Somebody tell me now!"

"Stevie is dead! He shot him! My baby! Oh my God! Somebody please help him! I need to take him home now! Sandy, please go help Stevie!"

Her words resonated in his ears and shook him to his core. Sandy's heart was palpitating so hard that it felt like it was going to come out of his chest. Nothing was making sense. His first thought was that there must be some kind of mistake. But there was the blood. It was so dark. It had to be real, right? But why would anyone shoot Stevie? He was just a boy. Suddenly Sandy felt lightheaded, and everything went into slow motion. He could hear his heart beating as the room began to slowly spin. Just then, the female police officer suddenly stepped in.

"Whitney, you need to calm down," the officer directed. "Remember, you said that you would try. Honey, we need your help to find the man who did this. Don't you want to help us? Let your brother go. I promise that he will not leave you."

Whitney released her hold on Sandy and she let the officer lead her back to her chair. She was still crying and her nose was running profusely. Another police officer approached Sandy and introduced himself. Sandy shook his hand mechanically but he didn't catch the name. He sat Sandy down in a chair and gave him a bottle of water. He ordered Sandy to take a drink, to which Sandy complied.

"You okay?" the officer asked.

"No. Please tell me what happened to my nephew."

"Well we do not know everything. Apparently, your sister and her husband got into it really good last night. It seems she was afraid he was going to hurt her and she ran into the bedroom, locked the door, and pushed a dresser or something in front of the door. When he was unable to get in, he went into the other bedroom, shot the minor in the chest, and fled. At this time, we do not know where he is."

"Is Stevie really dead?" Sandy asked.

"Yes, Sir, he is. I'm so very sorry."

"Can I see him please?"

"I'm sorry, but that is not really possible. Do you have any idea where the suspect might be?"

"Me? No. I barely know him!" Sandy didn't intend to yell.

Unfazed, the officer continued, "Okay. Then I need you to start thinking about who else needs to be notified. I'm talking about other family members, possibly some clergy. This is going to be all over the news in a few hours and you don't want people finding out that way."

"Okay…Can you tell me how bad he suffered?"

"It was one shot to the chest. Most likely, he didn't feel anything."

Sandy nodded, dropped his head, and cried a little. He suddenly noticed the dried blood that was on the arm of his jacket and just stared at it. This had to be a nightmare. Who was going to tell Verna? Just then, his phone began to ring. He took it out of his pocket. It was Tony.

"Hello?"

"Sandy, what's going on?" Tony pressed.

"It's Stevie. He was shot and killed tonight." His voice caught in his throat as he spoke the reality of it.

"What? What did you say? Oh my God! Sandy, where are you?"

"At Upstate Hospital. There is blood and everything. I don't know what to do," Sandy confessed through his tears.

"Hold on, I'm coming," Tony asserted.

Sandy hung up. He immediately dialed Tanya's number. When she answered, he told her. His words hung in the air. She was silent and then asked to speak to Whitney. Sandy took his phone over to where Whitney was seated. As she spoke to her sister, Whitney was becoming hysterical again, and Sandy walked away while she and Tanya conversed. When Whitney gestured to Sandy to come get his phone a few minutes later, he spoke briefly to Tanya again, who said that she would be coming home as soon as she found someone to watch the girls. Sandy hung up and started looking frantically through the contacts on his phone until he found his mother's friend, Lisa Terrell. When she answered, he explained the situation and asked if she could go and tell his mother and bring her to the hospital. She kindly agreed.

Just then a different police officer approached and told Sandy that they wanted him and Whitney to go with them to the police station. He said that the hospital needed the space and that there were several more questions they wanted to ask. Additionally, he said the police investigators were still collecting evidence at the apartment, and that it was probably not a good idea for Whitney to return there until they had found the suspect. Sandy texted Tony and Miss Lisa that they were on their way to the police station.

Now he and Whitney were together in the back of a police car. Two different officers drove them. It was just beginning to get light outside. At the suggestion of one of the nurses, Whitney had changed into hospital scrubs before they left. Only her labored breathing gave away that she was still crying. He held her hand. Otherwise, there was no sound emanating from inside of the car. Sandy was calm himself. At least, his emotions were back in check and his anger and confusion were pushed down far enough inside so he could think a little. He still couldn't believe that any of this was happening, and there were about a hundred questions running around in his head.

Once inside the police station, they were taken to a conference room with a big table in the middle surrounded by several chairs. The room itself was not that big and looked like it got a lot of use. It could have used a good cleaning, and the garbage can in the corner was full and needed to be emptied. The woman officer from the hospital was there along with several others. Someone asked them if they wanted coffee, and for some reason Sandy said yes, while his sister declined. He and Whitney sat together at the table without saying a word. No one approached them for several minutes.

It turned out that Whitney had married a criminal. Julio Moya was a dangerous guy. One officer told Sandy that Julio had multiple felony convictions on his record, including some for guns and drugs. He had served time in state prison and was presently on parole. Apparently, Whitney had separated from Julio about two months prior, and had an order of protection against him based upon an incident of domestic assault. The police were looking for him, but they didn't have much to go on. Julio was originally from the New York City area, and they thought that there was a chance that he was on his way back there. They said that because he was in hiding, it could be a while before they found him.

Sandy's head was spinning. He couldn't imagine what Whitney ever saw in a guy like that in the first place. That she would even consider letting someone with that kind of record anywhere near Stevie was unconscionable. He always knew that she was fighting her own demons, but he was completely unaware of the depth of her struggle. She just had always refused to listen to anyone about anything. She was a mess, and now he didn't know how she was going to live with this.

A black man walked into the room. Sandy immediately recognized him to be the police chief. He was on the news almost every night. He walked over to them.

"Hello, I'm Chief Tomkins. I just wanted to let you both know how sorry I'm for your loss."

"Thank you." Sandy said.

"Is there anything that you need? Something we can get for you?"

"No, thank you."

"Well if you think of something, please do not hesitate to ask. I know how hard this is for you," the Chief kindly remarked.

Just then, Verna walked into the room with her friends, Miss Lisa and Miss Sophia. She let out a loud shriek when she saw

Sandy and Whitney and ran to Whitney. The two women sobbed as they embraced. Chief Tomkins graciously stepped aside, and he gestured to Sandy that he was leaving. Sandy just nodded as the Chief walked away, watching as his mother and sister gave in completely to their grief.

Whitney kept saying, "He killed my baby. He killed my baby."

His mother's friends were trying their best to console them. It was too painful to watch. Just then, Tony walked in. Sandy turned and walked toward his boyfriend.

"Oh Sandy, I'm so sorry. I don't know what to say. Are you okay?" Tony said.

Sandy just looked at Tony. A gush of emotion hit him. He simply didn't know what to say. There simply were no words. He tried to think, but nothing came to mind.

Tony whispered, "It's okay, Baby. It's okay."

Sandy fell into his arms and cried for several minutes. Tony led him over to the far corner of the room and sat him down. Sandy fought to recapture his composure, but he just could not get there. Tony, who was also crying, just held him close.

"Sandy," it was Verna.

He looked up and their eyes met. Then he stood up and she put her arms around him.

"Do not despair, my son," she urged with bated breath. "This is not the end, for God is not through with us yet."

She kissed him on the cheek. He hugged her hard for a couple of seconds and then let go. She then turned.

"You must be Tony," she said.

"Yes ma'am. I'm so sorry—"

"I know," she said while reaching out for his hand. "It's nice to finally meet you. I've heard good things."

"Me too," Tony responded.

"Tony, I need you to do something for me, "she began. "I need for you to take care of my boy. See, his heart is so tender, and this is so awful. I'm his mother, and he won't let me. But he trusts you. Will you do that for me? Please?"

"Yes ma'am," was all that he could say through his tears.

"Thank you," she said while looking deeply into his eyes. She seemed relieved. "I can tell that you have a good heart too."

She pulled him to her and gave him a brief hug. Then she turned and walked back to her daughter.

They didn't leave the police station until eleven o'clock that morning. A woman from a victim's advocacy program spoke to them briefly before they left. She said that the medical examiner would not release Stevie's body for at least another twenty-four to forty-eight hours. In the meantime, they needed to select a funeral home and begin making arrangements. She said that Stevie's name had been released to the public, so they should expect that people would start calling. Out-of-town family members needed to be contacted. Stevie's school had been notified, and grief counselors had been sent there already. She gave them a list of other things that needed to be done. At the bottom were the names of several counselors in the area, and she strongly recommended that they each talk to someone.

Whitney went home with Verna. As she got into the car, she looked even more shell-shocked and she could not stop shaking. The coat that she was wearing had just been given to her at the hospital, and it was much too big for her. Apparently, she had left her coat at her apartment. Fortunately, Verna was a bit of a packrat, so Sandy was confident that she still had plenty of old stuff that Whitney could wear. The police had closed off her apartment, which meant that she would have to do without any of her own clothes or personal items. Stevie's room was now a crime scene.

The plan was that Sandy would go home and they would all meet at Verna's house later in the afternoon. It was cold outside when Sandy and Tony left the building and they walked fast without talking. Tony had parked his car on the street several blocks from the police station, and the cold wind went right through them. Sandy barely noticed. The smell of snow was in the air, but it wasn't snowing anymore. The sky was grey and overcast, as usual.

Sandy had forgotten that he was supposed to be at work at 9:00 a.m. He called the warehouse and explained to his supervisor what had happened. He was given the rest of the week off. Apparently, Tony must have called into work as well because he was still there when Sandy came out of the shower. He was watching TV.

"You could have gone to work. I'm okay."

"I'm worried about you," Tony said.

"I'm worried about me too," Sandy laughed. "But there isn't really anything that anyone can do to make it better."

Tony replied, "Babe, I think that you might need to call your doctor. Ask if he can give you something to get you through the next couple of days."

"Something like what?" Sandy asked.

"I don't really know. You already don't sleep."

"Well, I don't want anything," Sandy maintained. "Did you see anything on the news?"

"No," Tony lied.

"Do you think that Julio is still here in Syracuse and that there is a chance that he is going to come after Whitney?" Sandy questioned.

"No, I don't," Tony stated definitively. "He knows that the police are looking for him. Most likely, he is long gone. And he could have shot her too if he really wanted to harm her. Looks like he wanted to hurt her through Stevie."

Sandy thought about that for a minute. It made sense. He wondered how much abuse Stevie had been subjected to over the past year and why he didn't say anything. It occurred to Sandy that maybe Stevie had tried to tell him and that he hadn't been listening. Sandy suspected that there was plenty of guilt to go around here and he just needed to own his. He sat down, pressed into Tony and closed his eyes. He wished that there was a way to go back to the day before Whitney met Julio. Before all this stuff ever happened with the church and he was in control of his life. It was not that long ago that he was happy and in love. Right now he was exhausted. Mercifully, he drifted off to sleep.

He woke up confused. He had no idea where he was. There was a feeling of gloom present inside him, but he could not remember why. It took a couple of seconds before things started to come into focus. He was on the sofa covered in a blanket. The TV was on, but the sound was muted. He sat up and looked around. Tony was not there. Then he remembered. Stevie was dead.

It was 4:10 p.m. He could not believe that he had slept for over four hours. Tony must have gone to work after all. Sandy had a headache. He used the bathroom and took a couple of ibuprofens. Then he slowly got dressed. On his way out the door, he found Tony's note.

> Sandy, I hope that you feel better. I had
> something to take care of at the office. Call me

if you need me. Otherwise, I will see you later
tonight. Love you very much.

T.

There must have been twenty to twenty-five cars parked outside his mother's house, including a police car with someone sitting inside. The thought of facing all those people was overwhelming. He parked down the block and just sat there for a moment. For some reason, he hadn't anticipated this. He tried to think of a way he could avoid having to go inside, but nothing came to mind. He checked his phone. There was a text message from Tony and voice messages from both Verna and Tanya. He decided not to listen to the voicemail and slowly got out of the car.

Tanya met him at the door. They embraced. Considering the number of people who were there, it wasnt that loud. She said that Verna was busy being "the perfect host" and Whitney was upstairs sleeping.

"How is she doing?" he asked.

"Not good, Sandy. I feel so bad for her. Poor thing is up there crying in her sleep."

"What did you do with the girls?" Sandy wondered.

"They are with my girlfriend. But I need to drive back to Buffalo tonight."

"What's with the police car?"

"I don't know," she responded. "The police chief called and said that he was stationing a car outside of the house for a couple of days. I guess that they are just trying to be safe."

"Tanya, did you know all this was going on with Whitney?" Sandy asked. "I can't believe that she married a gangster."

Tanya hesitated before admitting, "Um…I knew some stuff. I knew that she was afraid of Julio and that she had kicked him out of the apartment."

"How come she never said anything to me?" he wondered aloud.

"Don't ask, don't tell. Isn't that how we do it in this family?" she replied dryly.

He let it go.

There was a huge spread of food in the kitchen. People must have started cooking immediately after getting the news. It suddenly occurred to him that he hadn't eaten anything all day and that he was a little hungry. He put a piece of chicken on a paper plate and took a bite. He didn't like it and immediately spit it out and dropped it in the trash. Verna came over and kissed him on the cheek when she saw him but didn't say a word. She was doing what she does best, smiling and keeping up with appearances. He realized, of course, that it was not necessarily a bad thing. His mother was the strongest person he knew.

Most people were just sitting in the living room or standing in the kitchen eating and talking quietly. Sandy knew most of them. Several came over to him to express their condolences, and he was gracious, but he took the first opportunity that he could to go sit in the family room by himself. He texted Tony back. There was an additional message from Reverend Grimes, saying that he had heard the news and was praying for the family. Sandy ignored that one.

His mother's old piano was still there. He tried to ignore it too, but he found that he kept staring at it. He was not tempted to touch it at all. It was as if they were former lovers who hadn't spoken in months and accidentally ran into each other on the street. And since there had been no closure, the feelings were still raw, and the moment was quite awkward. He tried to ignore it—to hate it even. He was suddenly perspiring and experiencing such a rush of unexpected emotions. Much of it felt like anger, but that didn't really make sense. After all, it was just a piano. However, the tension in the room was real and it kept rising. It was a mistake to have gone into that room. He sat there for as long as he could before he got up and made his way up the stairs to check on Whitney.

She was not asleep. Rather, she was sitting up on the bed in the dark. From what he could see, it appeared that both her eyes were red and swollen.

"Hey Whit, you okay?" he tried to sound upbeat.

"Yeah," she said with a quiet sigh.

"Can I get you something to eat? There's plenty of food downstairs."

"No, I'm not hungry."

"Mind if I sit with you? I can't take all the people that are here."

"No, I don't care," she whispered.

"Whitney, I'm so sorry that I let you down," he managed to say through his tears. "You needed me, Stevie needed me, and I wasn't there. I'm so sorry." He felt completely broken.

She shook her head and took his hand. "It is not your fault. It's all mine. I was Stevie's momma, and I didn't do right by him. I killed my baby. Nobody else."

"That's not true," he replied. "You're not responsible for Julio. He did this. Whit, listen to me. It is not your fault. You are an excellent mom and Stevie loves you. For some reason, God allows things to happen that make no sense. We will probably never understand. Sweetie, I know that it hurts. But Stevie is with

Daddy now and he is happy. He will always be happy. No one can hurt him anymore."

Just then, Tanya walked in the room and shut the door behind her.

"Can I hang out with you guys?" she asked in a whisper and sat down on the bed without waiting for a response.

"Yeah, why not?" Sandy replied. "But if Verna Louise comes up here and tries to breastfeed somebody, I'm out. I'm just letting you know now."

The three laughed together. Then they cried together.

Chapter 17

Verna Louise made all the arrangements. Calling hours were at the funeral home from 3:00 to 7:00 p.m. and the funeral was the following day at Mount Moriah, which just happened to be four days before Christmas. She selected the coffin and even purchased the clothes that Stevie would wear. She also had someone from the church make a video out of photographs of Stevie and the family. Whitney was incapable of thinking about any of it so she gave her mother free rein. Accordingly, Verna took full advantage of the opportunity to do it all her way. She didn't ask for anyone's opinion on anything. Sandy wasn't thrilled in the least that the funeral was going to be at Mount Moriah or that Reverend Glenn would be officiating, but he kept his objections to himself. Whitney probably hadn't been to church since Reverend Coleman died, and Stevie had only been to Mount Moriah a couple of times in his whole life. Sandy doubted if most of the people at the church even knew that Verna had grandchildren.

The calling hours were at the Franklin Brothers Funeral home in North Syracuse, the same place that that handled the arrangements for his father. It took place exactly one week from the day of the shooting. The medical examiner's office had some unexplained difficulty with the autopsy and didn't release Stevie's body for three days. Verna was furious about that, for some reason.

Sandy really hoped his mother wasn't going to make everything about her because he didn't have the strength to fight with her.

Other than the day of the shooting, Sandy had managed to sleep only a couple of hours here and there. He kept thinking about the last day he had spent with Stevie and how much fun they had. Tony refused to leave him alone at night, so he had pretty much moved into Sandy's apartment. That was both good and bad. Because Sandy was overtired and moody, he had snapped at Tony a few times. He always felt bad about it afterward, but he couldn't help himself. He was just so tired and angry and hurt.

However, Tony never responded back in like manner. Nor did he ever pull away. One of the big concerns that Sandy had always had about Tony was whether he would stick around if things between them ever became too messy or complicated. For that reason, Sandy always tried hard to keep his own drama to a minimum. The little bit that Tony had said about his past relationships revealed that he was easily spooked. Now, one of the worst things that could ever happen in anybody's life was splattered all over the newspapers and TV and Sandy couldn't help but wonder if Tony was a little embarrassed to be associated with him.

Verna wanted an open casket. Sandy tried to talk her out of that for Whitney's sake, but Verna would not hear of it. She said that it would help everyone to have a proper goodbye. However, she was wrong. Whitney never saw her son's body. As the family was walking into the room for a private viewing before the calling hours were to start, Whitney fainted. She fell hard—no one was able to catch her or break her fall. When she regained consciousness, she was uncontrollable and refused to go near the coffin. As a result, the receiving line had to be relocated to the back of the room and away from the casket.

Hundreds, if not thousands, of people came to pay their respects. Verna stood at the head of the line. Whitney was seated next to her. Tanya and her girls came next with Sandy, followed by Verna's sister and brother. A video displaying family photographs featuring Stevie played in the background. Several classmates came with their parents and their reactions to seeing their friend lying in a coffin was almost too much to bear.

Tony appeared with both of his parents, and he introduced them to Verna. Sandy couldn't hear what was said, but Tony's mother had tears streaming down her face by the time she got to Sandy. She kissed him on the cheek and gave him a warm embrace. Sandy was truly touched by their kindness. After they had gone through the line, Tony took a seat in the far corner and stayed there the rest of the time.

The receiving line moved at a good pace, which helped because each new face was a welcome distraction. Sandy realized that many people came for the sole purpose of supporting him, because they didn't know Stevie or his family. He didn't expect that at all. Even Ms. Smiley came through the line at one point. She had tears in her eyes when she greeted him and gave him a hug. Sandy was particularly touched when three or four people from his job showed up, including his supervisor, who told him that he could take as much time off as he needed.

Some of Tony's friends came too, including Marco. What surprised him the most was how good it was to see all the Mount Moriah church family, especially people from the choir and worship team. To be honest, he had been dreading it, but everyone said how much they missed him and talked about getting together with him at some point. Shondra was the one who was most overcome with emotion herself while talking to Sandy. She could barely speak at all. He could no longer deny that he really did miss all of them very much.

Sandy just happened to notice the four well-dressed white people when they first came into the room. They seemed out of place somehow, but lingered up front near the casket for a considerable amount of time. It appeared to be two couples, one older and one younger. The latter pair appeared to be in their thirties. As they approached the receiving line, the younger man looked somewhat familiar, but Sandy didn't fully recognize him. He must have been about six-foot-five-inches tall and was sobbing pretty good. The woman with him, who was much more composed, was rubbing his back and trying to console him. Sandy guessed that he was one of Stevie's basketball coaches. Eventually, the older man walked over and whispered something to Verna and Whitney, both of whom immediately left their place and walked over to the other side of the room for a private conversation. Sandy was confused and looked at Tanya.

"What's going on?" he asked.

"You don't know who that is?" Tanya responded with a surprised look on her face.

Sandy looked harder. "No, I don't," he confessed, shaking his head.

"That's Andy Kaufman. He's Stevie's father." She whispered and partly covered her mouth with her hand. "You don't remember him from high school? He was some kind of basketball star and played for some big college. He and Whitney were really hot and heavy there for a while, but his parents wouldn't allow it."

All at once, Sandy couldn't take his eyes off the guy. Stevie didn't look like him exactly, but clearly, he was going to be tall like his father, whose hands and feet were huge. It was impossible for Sandy to ascertain any shared mannerisms, but he was certain that there had to be some. Sandy was suddenly painfully aware of the fact that there were many different things going on around him when he was growing up about which he was oblivious. He wasn't quite sure of the reason for that and it made him wonder what else had been kept from him. Obviously, every family has its secrets, but it seemed that all too often he was the one who was purposely left out. He watched closely as a crying Andy Kaufmann walked out of the room. Verna and Whitney returned to their place in line as if nothing had happened. For some unknown reason, Sandy felt even worse at that moment.

Reverend Jones came through the line with his wife and a few of his choir members. Sandy hadn't seen any of them since he played for them at their revival. Reverend Jones gave Sandy a big hug and told him that he had never stopped praying for him. There was something about Reverend Jones that gave Sandy hope. He smiled warmly and handed Sandy a business card. He explained that the card belonged to a Christian counselor that he knew. Sandy thanked him and put it in his pocket.

By the time Reverend Glenn and his wife arrived, most of the people had gone. There were only about twenty or so people in the room at the time, including Tony and the funeral home director. At first, Reverend Glenn hovered around the coffin for a little while and then eventually walked over to Verna and Whitney. The four exchanged pleasantries and Reverend Glenn spoke softly to them. Whitney seemed to be paying attention to him. Reverend Glenn had a Bible and a notepad in his hand and appeared to be taking notes. Then he spoke briefly to Tanya, who was standing alone now without her daughters. Mercy was still talking to Whitney. Turning to Sandy, Reverend Glenn extended his hand and they shook hands. Sandy swallowed hard.

"How are you, Sandy?" Reverend Glenn asked.

"I'm hanging in there, I guess," Sandy said calmly.

"We can't even imagine what you and your family must be going through, but I want you to know that we're here and that we're willing to do whatever we can to help. Please don't hesitate to ask."

Sandy didn't believe that Reverend Glenn was being sincere, and he just wanted his former pastor to move on. Remaining in character, however, Sandy managed to respond, "Thank you. That is very kind."

"When our hearts get broken, they take time to heal. No one is immune to the process. My best advice is to not fight it. Remember that God sees all, and he is a righteous judge. He is not slack in his promises to us or in his curses. We won't stop praying that God will deliver you."

Sandy just nodded, and Reverend Glenn touched him on the shoulder and moved on. Sandy broke out in a sweat and fought through his emotions as best he could. He finally excused himself, found the men's room, and just stood at one of the three sinks and looked at himself in the mirror. He was beginning to feel a little nauseous when he heard the door open. He turned toward it and in walked Tony. Tears welled up in Sandy's eyes.

"I don't know what's wrong with me. But something is wrong," Sandy blurted out. "I never used to get sick to my stomach this much."

"You're just tired and stressed out," Tony responded. "Anyone would be. Give yourself a break. I promise that you will make it through all of this."

"I feel like I'm drowning," Sandy explained.

"I won't let you drown," Tony replied.

Tony reached in his pocket and took out a small plastic medicine container. He opened it and took out one pill.

"Here take this," he ordered.

"What is it?"

"It's for you. Your doctor prescribed it. I called him."

"When? Why? I told you that I wasn't taking any more medication," Sandy protested.

"Actually, you're going to take it even if I have to shove it down your throat." Tony said, red-faced. "I have had it with this act of yours! You don't have to act like a superhero all the time. Okay, we all get it. You don't need anybody. Well, how about this? Everybody needs help sometimes. It doesn't make you weak; it makes you human. So cut the crap. You have exactly five seconds to take this pill."

Sandy slowly took it. He looked at it, then put it in his mouth and swallowed it. He then turned on the water in the sink and drank some of it out of his cupped hand. As they walked out of the bathroom together, they could hear Reverend Glenn leading the family in prayer and they waited in the foyer until he finished. Sandy inhaled a big breath before exhaling slowly, then he sluggishly walked back in to join his family. Tony just took a seat in the foyer.

The funeral home director announced that the casket would not be opened tomorrow at the church and that everyone should take a moment to have a final viewing. He said that they could have as much time as they needed. Everyone except Whitney walked up together. She flatly refused and stayed back with the director and another man from the funeral home. This was Sandy's first time seeing the body. He had gotten a glimpse just before Whitney fainted and never had a chance to make his way up there again once people started to arrive. The whole thing was surreal as he fixed his eyes on Stevie's face. It didn't look like him, rather a caricature of him. His face was swollen on one side and the makeup that they used was darker than his natural skin tone. His lips were also much more pronounced. Verna had him dressed in a dark suit and tie, which made him look much older than he was. Tanya started screaming and Uncle Russell was holding her. Verna was softly crying and praying under her breath.

Sandy recognized Stevie's hands and without thinking, he gently touched them. They were hard and cold. He also noticed that there was a basketball in the coffin that appeared to have writing on it. He picked it up and discovered that apparently all the kids on his team had signed their names. Sandy turned the basketball and read each printed name. They were hard to read because the marker they had used blurred some of the letters. That is when he noticed what was written next to one of the names:

"Sure will miss ya. Have a nice afterlife Stevie!"

Suddenly, the finality in those words struck him hard. His head was spinning out of control as his brain was attempting to process it all. He started coughing and felt himself falling backwards. Just then, Mercy caught him and wrapped him in her strong arms. As hard as she tried, however, he simply refused to be comforted. So she wiped his tears with her hand and never let him fall.

Tony followed Sandy home in his car. Sandy insisted that he was fine to drive the five miles or so from the funeral home to his apartment. Once safely in the parking lot, Tony drove up next to him.

"What do you want for dinner?" he asked.

"I'm not hungry," Sandy mumbled.

"Chinese it is then. I'll be right back."

By the time Tony returned, Sandy had changed into a t-shirt and sweatpants and was sitting on the sofa watching the news. Tony put the food down on the table and took off his coat and shoes.

"You sure you don't want to eat something?" Tony asked.

"I'm sure."

"Then come in here and watch me eat. You know I hate to eat alone."

Sandy came into the kitchen and sat down. He was very tired, but he didn't want another scolding from Tony. Sandy liked the fact that Tony wanted to take care of him, but he also knew that he had to be careful with that because Tony didn't like feeling responsible for others. Still, he clearly was capable of sustaining a loving relationship.

"Do you really think I act like I don't need anyone?" Sandy asked.

"Sorry, babe. I didn't mean it like that. I just want to help you, and seems like you're fighting against me."

"I know. I'm sorry."

"You don't have to be sorry. I understand. What did the good reverend say to you anyway that got you so upset?" Tony asked.

"No, it wasn't that. I just wasn't prepared to deal with everyone from the church. It was a lot all at once. I guess that he tried to be comforting in his own weird way."

"Can I ask you something? Are you…ashamed of us? Are you ashamed of me?"

"No, I don't think so," Sandy offered while searching for the right words to say. "It's a lot more complicated than that. It's hard when everyone you love thinks you are wrong."

"Do you think that you're doing something wrong by being with me?" Tony continued.

"I honestly don't know what I think," Sandy said almost under his breath.

"Because I love you, you know? And I'm very proud of what we have."

Sandy searched his heart and said, "I love you too, and that's not it. I can't even imagine my life without you. I want to be with you."

"Then eat a damn egg roll!" Tony proclaimed.

Sandy's phone was ringing. He took that opportunity to escape from the table. It was Verna. Instinctively, he paused to take a deep breath.

"Hello."

"Sandy, how are you doing, Honey?" Verna asked.

"I'm okay. How are you?"

"I've had better days, as you know," she replied, "anyway, I don't want to keep you. I just wanted you to know that I spoke with Reverend Glenn tonight and he said to tell you that it's okay with him if you wanted to play something tomorrow during the funeral. You know, a special song or something."

"Play? I don't want to play!" Sandy was suddenly enraged.

"I thought, you know, that... you might want to do something nice for Stephenson," Verna tried to explain.

"Stevie is dead. Some thug his mother married shot him in the chest!" Sandy countered through a shaky voice.

Unsteady herself now, she uttered, "I know, Son. I know... Tanya said that she would sing if you didn't want to do it. But I just wanted to let you know."

"Thank you. I appreciate it. But I can't. I'm sorry," he insisted.

"Okay, I understand. But if you change your mind, it's up to you."

"I'm not going to change my mind," he maintained.

"Okay...see you tomorrow. Goodnight." She tried not to sound disappointed.

"Goodnight," he said.

He knew that she was disappointed, but he didn't really care. Sandy told Tony what she wanted, but Tony didn't offer an opinion on the matter one way or the other. He just listened. The rest of the evening was quiet. Tony worked at the kitchen table on his laptop while Sandy watched TV in bed and returned his text messages. The pill that Tony gave him did work because Sandy had dosed off by the time that Tony came to bed. After that, he slept sporadically throughout the night.

The funeral was at 11:00 a.m. Tony said that he had to go into the office to take care of an emergency and that he would be at the church later. Sandy wanted to tell him that it was okay if he couldn't come, but he was not sure how that would sound. Before he left, Tony offered Sandy another pill with some juice. Sandy started to protest, but then he thought better of it. He swallowed it without saying a word. According to Verna, he was supposed to be at the church by 10.00 a.m. He had decided that the less time that he had to spend in that building the better.

A hearse and two limos were parked outside the church when Sandy arrived at 10:05 a.m. Also, a police car was parked out front. Sandy seriously doubted that Julio would try to get to Whitney at the church, but it was probably for the best that there was a police presence. He could hear the choir practicing as he walked in. He immediately thought to himself that he would have used the worship team for this occasion rather than the choir if he were still in charge. Knowing his mother, however, she wanted to have the choir there because they made for a bigger show. The church still smelled the same. It appeared that nothing had changed about the place at all in the year or so since he was fired.

Besides the choir, there were about ten ushers setting up in the sanctuary when Sandy walked through the doors. Two men from the funeral home were fidgeting around the coffin in front. It was completely covered with flowers. Next to it was a big photograph of Stevie. It was a close-up of him playing basketball. Sandy had never seen it before. It was beautiful.

He saw Tanya standing near the piano. She had her back to him so she didn't see him as he approached. She smiled when she turned and saw him. She was dressed all in black and looked nervous. He gave her a quick hug. The twenty-something young man on the piano stopped playing and introduced himself. He said that his name was Trevor Turner. He wore his hair in shoulder-length braids and, while both of his ears appeared to be pierced, he was not wearing any earrings. They shook hands and Sandy deliberately avoided looking at the piano.

Tanya said that she had just finished going over her song and led him to the breakroom where the rest of the family was waiting. Verna was there, along with Uncle Russell and Aunt Florence, and all four of Verna's friends. She wore a black suit and a black hat with a veil attached to it that covered half of her face. She looked good, like a black Jackie Onassis. No one was really talking much, and when someone did speak, it was in a quiet hush.

"Where is Whitney?" Sandy wondered aloud.

"She's in the bathroom," Miss Sophia responded.

"Is she okay?" he asked. "How long has she been gone?"

"I'll go check on her," Tanya said as she turned and walked away.

Tanya was only gone about a minute when she returned with Whitney, who was wearing a black-and-white dress with black boots. Sandy walked over to her and gave her a kiss on the cheek. She half-smiled briefly and then sat down in one of the chairs. She seemed calm, which made Sandy wonder if she had taken medication too—whatever it was that Tony had given to him was working again. It was just enough to take the edge off. He felt as if he was in a bubble looking out.

Reverend Glenn came into the room with his wife. They immediately walked over to Verna, and Sandy couldn't hear what was being said. Someone gave Sandy a program with Stevie's name and picture on the front. That was the second time now that Sandy read his own name on the cover of a funeral bulletin. He didn't open it.

The funeral started on time and was over by 12:30 p.m. It was sad, but bearable. One of Stevie's teachers read a note from his class and his basketball coach cried his way through his remarks. Thankfully, Reverend Glenn was brief. He spoke about the big family reunion that will take place one day in heaven. Through it all, Sandy never reacted. Fortunately, he had recently discovered that there is a place in the corner of his mind where he could go so he didn't have to really think about anything at all. Moreover, he was intent on staying in that place throughout the service. However, he couldn't help but notice the tremendous amount of pain that Whitney was experiencing at the time. He never even looked at his mother. Tanya sang her song. She did a nice job, but again, as far as he was concerned, it was just about getting through this in one piece.

Even though he was not fully engaged, Sandy couldn't help but feel the draw of the Spirit in the piano music during the service. But he would just pull back every time he felt it. He was determined to not yield himself over the way that he had done at his father's funeral. He suddenly realized that this is what he had feared all along. This was the real fight that had been taking place inside of him even before Stevie was killed. His opponent was gentle, but he was also relentless. Sandy promised himself that he would never give in again. As a result, he fought with everything that he had left within him until he had effectively quenched all of the life out of him.

Walking behind Stevie's coffin with his family meant that this part of the nightmare was almost over. At least he could get back to his own private hell where he could suffer alone without everyone watching. The pallbearers were four of the church's ushers and two of Stevie's young friends. They all wore white gloves. The choir was singing again and the video from the calling hours was playing. Tony was seated in the last row and their eyes met for a moment as Sandy passed by. Once outside, he watched as they put the coffin in the back of the hearse and then he followed the rest of his family into a limo.

It was a short drive to Oakwood Cemetery, which is located on a hill that overlooks Syracuse University. It was snowing lightly as they arrived and Sandy wondered how they could do burials in the winter with the ground frozen; he had never thought about that before. His father was buried in Oakwood too, but he died in the summer. Stevie's plot was in a new section of the cemetery. As they got out of the cars, they all huddled together as they walked the forty yards or so to the gravesite in silence. Altogether, there were about thirty people there. Reverend Glenn was all covered up in an overcoat, fur hat, and rubber boots. He looked like a big black bear. He took out his Bible, read a couple of passages from it, and said a quick prayer. Whitney was the only one who was making any kind of sound. She was muttering softly to herself.

Shondra started singing "Amazing Grace" and there were a few more audible cries and sniffles. Sandy looked around and the fallen snow was stunning. Everything was white as far as he could see. It looked like heaven as Reverend Glenn committed Stevie's body to the earth. Indeed, it looked like heaven, but it hurt like hell.

The drive back to the church was quiet. There was a reception planned at the church, but there was just no chance that Sandy was going back in there. When he got out of the limo, he marched over to his mother and told her that he would probably stop by later. He hugged her and Tanya goodbye. It looked like Verna wanted to say something, but she didn't. Every so often, he could sense the depth of her pain. Apparently, someone had already taken Whitney into the church, so he could not say goodbye to her. The pill that he had taken earlier was starting to wear off and he needed another one desperately.

There were still quite a few cars in the parking lot, but the police car was gone. As Sandy reached his car, he saw Tony get out of a small car and walk toward him.

"Hi, Babe," he said.

"What are you doing?" Sandy asked, looking confused.

"Give me the keys, I'm driving," Tony demanded.

"Why? I can drive myself," Sandy protested.

"Just give me the keys, please," Tony insisted.

Sandy complied, opened the door to the front passenger side, and sat down. He was sulking.

"You know, I'm not an invalid, right?" he mockingly inquired.

"I never said you were. You're in no condition to drive. That's all. I never should have let you drive here in the first place. The medication you took is pretty strong."

Sandy decided to mope.

"So, how are you doing?" Tony asked as he adjusted the seat and started the car.

"I'm fine," Sandy sharply replied.

"What does that mean?"

"It means that I'm fine. Where is your car?" Sandy demanded.

"It's at my office. I had someone drop me off." Purposely changing the subject, Tony asked, "Are you hungry?"

"No," was the brisk response from Sandy

"Sandy, are you angry at me?"

"No."

"Did I do something wrong?" Tony harmlessly asked.

"No, you didn't do anything wrong," Sandy said abruptly.

"Then why are you being mean to me?"

"I'm not being mean to you," Sandy argued.

Tony immediately disagreed, "Actually, you are. I'm aware that you have had a bad day. We all have. But please do not take it out on me."

Sandy didn't say anything else. He just looked straight ahead. He knew that he was being a real jerk again, but he could not help himself. In his heart, he wanted to stop—Tony was the last person in the world who he wanted to treat badly. Tony had been so wonderful this past week, and Sandy doubted that he would have gotten through this ordeal in one piece without him. Truthfully, he was very happy to see Tony. If there was one thing he knew for sure now, it was that he could, in fact, depend on Tony to always be there for him. Sandy was more in love with him than ever. After a few minutes of silence, Sandy rubbed his hand against Tony's thigh as he drove them home.

Chapter 18

Suffice it to say, it was not a very good Christmas for Sandy. By mutual consent, the Coleman family decided to skip it this year. Verna didn't go to Florida to visit with her sister as planned and, understandably, none of them had any interest in celebrating anything either alone or together. The only thing Sandy did was give his gifts to Tanya for the girls before she headed back to Buffalo. Tony generously offered to stay with Sandy on Christmas Day, but he flat-out refused to allow that. He wanted to be alone because he wanted to be free to be miserable. He didn't shower or get dressed all day. He did turn on the TV, but he didn't watch it. He just stayed on the couch and stared into space all day. The thing about depression is that it can be a tangible presence that accompanies the person wherever he or she goes. Sandy was more aware of the feeling of despair inside him than he was of its source. He could make his brain forget everything that had happened for a moment, but there was just no escaping the feeling. So he chose to embrace it rather than resist it. The only person he spoke to all day was Tony, who was clearly worried about him and called twice.

He returned to work the day after the funeral, and he would have gone into work on Christmas itself if the business hadn't been closed that day. It helped him to work because it gave him something to do. Warehouse work was mindless, and he didn't have to talk to anyone if he didn't want to. His coworkers were very kind and considerate and no one bothered him. Because so many of them were either on vacation or sick at that time, he took advantage of every opportunity to work overtime. It was the only thing that he could think to do to keep from going completely out of his mind.

There would be no New Year's Eve celebration at the casino for Sandy and Tony this year. Of course, Tony understood, and he was clearly making every effort to be kind and allow Sandy time to heal. They decided on a quiet evening at home with just the two of them. Sandy made dinner and he was pleased with how it came out. It was his first time making lobster. He tried hard to stay in the moment, but he was only going through the motions, and they both knew it. They ended up deciding to just turn in early. Tony was sound asleep at midnight; Sandy, however, was staring at the TV, watching other people celebrate. He had the volume on mute.

Apparently, in order to get the prescription for the anti-depressant medication that he gave him, Tony had to promise Sandy's doctor that Sandy would come in for an office visit after the funeral. Dr. Mark Ingham had been Sandy's doctor since he was eighteen years old. Sandy liked him a lot. Dr. Mark still looked young, being only in his mid-fifties, with slightly greying temples and the beginning of a small pouch in his midsection. He was a partner in a small practice in North Syracuse and was the first person to whom Sandy came out. Sandy was afraid after he lost his virginity in college that he might have acquired a STD or something worse. Dr. Mark explained to him in detail what safe sex was for a gay man. He said that he had several patients who were gay. He somehow managed to make Sandy feel normal again.

Although he called Dr. Mark's office two days after the funeral, because of the holidays, the earliest appointment that he could get was a week later. By then, Sandy was truly desperate. He barely slept at night and his heart was doing a weird racing thing. One night he thought that he was having a heart attack and considered going to the emergency room. Of course, he hadn't mentioned this to Tony. The hardest part about this past week was hiding from Tony how bad he felt. He pretended he was sleeping until he was certain that Tony had fallen asleep and then lied the next day about how much sleep he had actually gotten during the night. He also had what he thought might have been a panic attack at work when his heart started racing for no apparent reason and he broke out in a sweat. It only lasted for a few minutes and he was able to complete his shift with no more problems, nevertheless, he knew that something was very wrong.

Sandy arrived on time for his appointment and only had to sit in the waiting room for a few minutes before his name was called by the nurse. Dr. Mark's nurse's name was Sandy too. She always got a kick out of that and was very chatty with him. Today when he got on the scale, she said that he had lost ten pounds since his last visit four months ago. Sandy was not surprised to hear that since he didn't have much of an appetite and he ate only one small meal a day. He'd noticed that his pants were not fitting properly, but no one had mentioned any apparent change in his appearance. His blood pressure was normal and he wasn't feverish. Before she left the examining room, Nurse Sandy kindly offered him her condolences on the loss of his nephew.

After performing a thorough examination, Dr. Mark sat down next to Sandy and typed on his laptop as Sandy recited all the things that were going on with him. Then Dr. Mark explained to Sandy that our bodies respond to emotional trauma in several different ways. He said that the worst thing that Sandy could do was to ignore what his body was trying to tell him. He also said that he was sending Sandy to the lab for bloodwork and that he was prescribing him a different anti-depressant. Further, he told Sandy that he wanted him to keep a diary of everything he ate and to email or fax it to the office every week. Lastly, he wanted Sandy to see a counselor. He said that the receptionist would give him a list of recommended providers. At the conclusion of the office visit, Sandy was instructed to come back in for another appointment in six weeks.

The list that he was given had the names, office locations, and telephone numbers of five counselors, only three of which were located anywhere close to Sandy's apartment or to his job. The first two were not taking new patients and no one answered at the office of the third one. Sandy was just about to call the remaining two counselors when he remembered that Reverend Jones had also given him the name of a counselor that day at the funeral home. Initially, he could not remember where he put that card. On a hunch, however, he checked the inside pocket of his suit jacket and found it. When he called the number, he was surprised that the counselor answered the phone himself. Furthermore, he indicated that he did, in fact, have a few early morning openings. Additionally, the office also accepted Sandy's medical insurance provider. So he made an appointment.

He mistakenly thought that Tony would be excited that he was going to see a therapist, however, Tony was annoyed that he had chosen a "Christian" counselor. Apparently, he knew of a therapist who specialized in LGBTQ issues and had wanted Sandy to call that person. But Tony had never mentioned this counselor to Sandy before and now he just went on and on about how Sandy needed someone who truly understood what he was going through and how it would be big waste of time to talk to a "so-called Christian therapist who is immersed in religious dogma." Sandy took it for as long as he could. The conversation ended abruptly with him standing up and shouting,

"How about this? You pick your own damn therapist, and I'll pick mine!"

In the past, Sandy had mostly deferred to Tony to avoid getting him too upset. Most recently, he was less inclined to do that. He would say things before he even knew that he had said them. The strangest part was that he typically had no regrets later. He also noticed that Tony wasn't staying the night nearly as much as he had been. Regardless, Sandy was not as bothered by that as he would have been before Stevie died. He simply didn't have it in him to worry about what Tony was thinking.

Shockingly, Verna had started calling him every day again. At least the calls never lasted that long because his mother was never a phone person. She called solely to touch base and then she was gone. He just accepted the fact that this was something that she obviously needed to do. Whitney was in Buffalo with Tanya and the girls. Verna confirmed Sandy's suspicion that Whitney was taking medication before the funeral. For obvious reasons, he chose not to disclose to her any information about himself in that regard.

As it was explained to him, the plan was that Whitney would move to another apartment when she returned to Syracuse, but it was unclear exactly when that would be. She was on medical leave from her job and Verna and her friends had already packed up all her possessions and put most of them in storage. Whitney hadn't been back to her apartment since the night of the shooting. Sandy thought that it was probably for the best that she got away from Verna too. The two of them always had been like oil and water, and Whitney didn't need any additional stress in her life at this time. He was very worried about her.

There was no word on Julio—he just vanished. The police said that he could be anywhere, but they were confident that they would eventually arrest him. Sandy still was having a hard time understanding exactly what Whitney saw in Julio in the first place. She was a beautiful woman, which was most likely part of the problem. She was always popular with the boys, but Julio was as far from Stevie's white middle-class suburban raised father as you could get. It was futile for Sandy to try to figure it out because he was ultimately forced to admit that he never really knew his sister, at least not as well as he should have.

Sandy dropped out of community college. He had concluded that this was the wrong time for him to be in school. Besides, any interest in music that he ever possessed had waned substantially. At some point, he needed to do some serious soul-searching and figure out exactly what it is that he wanted for his life. Obviously, he knew that he wasn't going to work in a warehouse forever, other than that, however, he lacked any vision for the future. The truth is that he was never strong on ambition, which was one of the things about him that his father had always hated.

Ms. Smiley called him, but he was at work and could not talk. He had to wait until his break to call her back. Surprisingly, she picked up the phone herself.

"Sandy, it's me. Thanks for calling me back. How are you doing, Kid?" She asked.

He responded with his overused response, "I'm good. You know…one day at a time."

"Well you hang in there. You're one of the good guys," she reassured. "Anyway, I'm calling to let you know that I received a motion today in your case from the lawyer for the church. The technical name is "summary judgment." What it is in plain English is a motion to have the case dismissed. The church is arguing that you do not state a sufficient claim and that your case should be thrown out. Now I have to respond to the motion and a magistrate judge will decide. It will be several months before we get a decision."

"Does this mean that there won't be a trial?" Sandy asked.

"If they win the motion, there will not be a trial and the case will be over. If we win, then there will be a trial."

"What are our chances?" he inquired.

"We have a shot, but you never really know with these things."

"Will I have to go to court for the motion?"

"No, probably not. Typically, these motions are heard on submission, meaning that the magistrate judge will read the papers and make a decision. However, the judge can require the attorneys to appear in court to answer his or her questions. If that happens, you are free to come along if you like," Ms. Smiley explained in a voice that sounded more hoarse than usual.

"No thanks."

"Do you have any other questions?" she asked.

"No, I don't think so."

"Please feel free to call me if you have any other questions," she urged.

Sandy was not sure what this all meant or if he should be worried. He mentioned it to Tony, who explained that this was just a normal part of the process. Tony seemed much more confident that the judge would not dismiss the case than Ms. Smiley had sounded. Apparently, in order to throw the case out of court based on the motion, the judge would have to find that—even if they accepted Sandy's version of the facts of the case as being true— that no jury could find that the church had done anything wrong in firing him. Sandy wondered how anyone could ever predict what a judge might do. Regardless, at this point, the only thing that mattered to him was that this meant that he would not have to go to court or face Reverend Glenn again any time soon.

Chapter 19

G ary Nelson's business card said that he was a "Clinical Social Worker/Therapist LCSW." It turned out that his office was only about two miles from where Sandy worked. It was in a small plaza that Sandy had never noticed before. It looked like a storefront with the name "Gary Nelson" printed in bold print on the window. His appointment was for 7:00 a.m. By 6:30 a.m. Sandy was already sitting in his car in the parking lot outside of the office. He couldn't sleep so he got dressed and went out to get a latte before his appointment. Tony had stayed at his own place that night. Although Sandy was not nervous, he wasn't quite sure what to expect. He certainly hoped that Tony was wrong and that he was not wasting his time.

He waited until 6:45 a.m. before going in. The front door opened to a very small waiting room. There was no receptionist, only four chairs and a coffee table in the middle with several magazines on it. There were several nice prints on the walls. They seemed to all be ocean views. On the wall adjacent to another door was a sign that read, "Please Have a Seat." The chairs were comfortable. He didn't like any of the magazines, so he checked his phone messages while he waited.

At exactly 6:59 a.m. the door opened and out walked a middle-aged white man and a younger African-American woman. He told her he would see her next week, and she nodded her head in agreement and walked out of the door.

"Hello, I'm Gary Nelson," he said while extending his hand.

"Hi, I'm Sandy Coleman."

"Nice to meet you, Sandy. You can call me Gary. Please come in."

Gary was about six feet tall, medium built with salt-and-pepper hair. He wore round glasses, a buttoned-down blue shirt, khaki pants, and loafers. Inside was a small room with three chairs that were identical to the ones in the waiting room. There was no desk, only a small table. There were some more pictures of the ocean on the walls along with a couple of framed diplomas and certificates.

"Sandy, please have a seat. Do you have your insurance card?"

"Yes, I do."

"Just let me write down the number. I think your insurance copayment is twenty-five dollars," he said as he took the card. Sandy reached in his wallet and handed him the money.

"So how can I help you?" Gary asked and smiled.

Sandy proceeded to give him a rundown of what he had been experiencing. He told him about Stevie's death, his insomnia, and possible panic attack. He also explained that Dr. Mark wanted him to see a counselor.

"Did he prescribe any medication for you?"

"Yes, he did. It's an anti-depressant, but I can't remember the name of it." Sandy recited.

"Are you taking it?"

"Yes, I am."

"Does it help?"

Sandy thought for a moment before responding, "I think so. It's hard to say. I still am having a hard time sleeping at night and I don't really have much of an appetite."

"Did all your symptoms begin when your nephew died?" Gary questioned.

"No. Before."

"How long before."

"Almost two years. It started when I was fired from my job."

"Why were you let go?"

"I worked for a church and I was fired when they found out that I'm gay."

"You never told them that you were gay?"

"No, I didn't."

"Why not?" Gary pondered.

"Because it's nobody's business what I do," Sandy said and waited cautiously for the response.

"So, no one knew that you were gay? You were keeping it a secret?" Gary inquired further.

"I only told my mother."

"No one else?"

"No."

"Are you very close to your mother?"

Sandy laughed to himself and blurted out, "It's a long story."

"Okay, we can talk about it. Tell me how it is that your employer found out about you."

Sandy told Gary everything that happened on the day that he was fired, including Reverend Glenn telling him that he was going to hell. He spoke about how no one came to his aid. He also mentioned the pending litigation and how his entire life was going to be on trial. Once he started talking, he got on a roll and it was easy. Gary just listened as Sandy spoke, occasionally nodding his head. Before Sandy knew it, his hour was almost up.

Gary interrupted him, "Looks like we're running out of time. I have another appointment. But I want to explain to you how this works. I think you know that you have a problem. Depression is real and can be very serious. Instead of your body being sick, your emotions kind of get stuck or scrambled and we get out of balance and need healing. It's nothing to be ashamed of. Some studies show that a large percentage of people in this country will experience a period of depression at some point in their lives. It can happen to anyone. I think I might be able to help you, but that depends on you. I can help you face the issues in your life, but you have to do the work. The process is not pain free. It's about being willing to honestly look at your problems in their true light and to learn new coping skills. If you are willing to try, then so am I. What do you think?"

"What makes you a Christian counselor?" Sandy asked.

"Good question. Well, I'm a Christian, but I'm not a minister. Nor am I affiliated with any particular church. But I have worked with hundreds of Christians. I understand that the way that we see the world is not the same way that other people see it because of the different belief systems. Now, most of the people that I see just happen to be Christians, but not everyone. If someone isn't open to hearing the biblical perspective, then I don't offer it. It all depends on the person. How did you hear about me?"

"Reverend Jones, Bobby Jones gave me your card."

"Ah yes, Reverend Jones has sent a couple of people my way. He's a good man."

"Yes, he is," Sandy concurred.

"Do you have any more questions?"

"No, I'm good…I think that I'm willing to give it a try," Sandy offered, trying to convince himself.

"Good then. I think that once a week is good for you to start. We can always change that if we need to. Is this time good for you?"

"Yes, it is," Sandy said.

"Alright, I will see you next Tuesday at 7:00 a.m. Try to bring with you the name of the medication that you are taking."

"Okay. Thank you."

There was an older woman sitting in the waiting room when Sandy walked out. She seemed happy to see Gary. Sandy couldn't help but wonder what it was like for him to have to sit and listen to people talk about their problems all day. But, then again, it's not exactly hard labor. That is, it's not as if he was digging ditches or something. Regardless, he wasn't quite sure just what he had gotten himself into and he was having "buyer's remorse" already. Talking about anything of substance was not a strength of his, and he was honestly not sure if he could do it. It wasn't that bad today because he didn't have to answer any probing questions. However, Gary was correct, Sandy knew he was in trouble.

***

Sandy's days seemed to run together and he couldn't remember the last time that he looked forward to something. When it was time to go to work, he went to work. When it was time to go home, he went home. When it was time to eat, he at least tried to eat something, the same way that he tried to sleep at night. Whenever Tony called and wanted to do something, he did it. He tried to sound normal. He kept telling himself to fake it until he was over the hurdle. He felt imprisoned in the jail cell that was his life—and it was just about survival now.

Sandy was also becoming more and more aware of the fact that his body had a mind of its own. One change that really surprised him is that his sexual appetite seemed to have gone the opposite direction of his other desires. He noticed that suddenly he was very easily aroused. In the past, he had always enjoyed sex, but this was different. He had never been interested in pornography before, but now he was regularly visiting some gay web sites. In addition, he was fantasizing and masturbating more too. Tony was the beneficiary of the new Sandy, and he didn't seem to mind too much. However, Sandy didn't like it at all because it was more evidence that he was losing control and it scared him.

It was Groundhog Day and the news announced that the little critter had seen his shadow, meaning that there was just six more weeks of winter remaining. Stevie's funeral was just six weeks past, however, it seemed like an eternity ago. Tony wanted to go away for a couple days, but he was swamped at work and Sandy didn't have any leave time left at his job. They agreed to do something as soon as their schedules permitted. Tony suggested that a couple of days in the Caribbean at one of those all-inclusive places might be nice. They had never done anything like that before. However, Sandy was not exactly a beach person. He almost drowned once when he fell in the shallow end of the pool at the YMCA and hit his head on the bottom. He was eight years old when that happened, and hadn't spent that much time in or near the water since. Nevertheless, if Tony wanted to go to Jamaica, then Jamaica it would be.

The second appointment with Gary had to be cancelled due to the weather. A huge snowstorm hit the entire east coast of the United States and Syracuse was buried. Over thirty inches of snow fell in less than a twenty-four-hour period. The airport was closed, as was just about everything else in and around the city. Blowing and drifting snow reduced visibility to almost nothing. The governor declared a state of emergency throughout most of upstate New York counties, and there was a travel advisory in place for Syracuse.

Even after having lived in Syracuse for over twenty years, Verna had never quite grown accustomed to the central New York winters. On a whim, Sandy decided to call her to make sure she was okay. She was not. She had the flu, so he decided that he needed to go check on her. Even though his mother only lived fifteen minutes away, it took him almost an hour to get to her house. For one thing, the snowplows had only gotten to the main roads and, even though it was almost noon, none of the side streets had been plowed. As a result, he could not get to Verna's house by car and he had to leave his car partly on the street and walk from the main road. The snow in her driveway was thigh-deep.

He started to get a little concerned when she didn't answer the doorbell. He had a key, but he couldn't remember the last time that he had to use it. After opening the door, he stepped inside. The house was silent. He turned on the light in the entryway and called to her. There was no answer. After taking off his snow-covered boots and coat, and brushing off the snow from his pants, he approached the bottom of the stairs and called out to her again.

"Up here," she said.

He walked up the stairs and went into her bedroom. She was lying in bed. There was a smell—a bad one. He turned on the lamp on the nightstand and saw her curled up in a fetal position. She also had a barking cough. He touched her forehead.

"Oh my God, Mom, you're burning up. Why didn't you tell me that you were this sick?"

"I thought I was getting better," she said feebly while coughing.

"Did you call the doctor?" he asked.

"The office is closed. They said to go to the emergency room if it was something that couldn't wait. I'm not going to the hospital."

"What hurts?"

"Everything," she whispered through shallow breath.

"Then you need to go to the ER," he insisted.

"No," she replied emphatically.

Then Sandy remembered how bad the roads were. There was just no way he could even get her to his car, parked all the way out on the main street. He thought about calling the 911 dispatch, but it would probably take hours for an ambulance to get to them. He went into the bathroom to get a cold compress. Apparently, Verna had vomited on the floor and that was the source of the sour odor in the room. He walked downstairs and got a small plastic tub that was in the laundry room. He filled it with soap and cold water. Then he got a couple of towels and a washcloth out of the hall closet. He then gave his mother a bath. Afterward, he put a cold compress on her forehead. He then proceeded to clean the bathroom.

"Sandy, you leave that. I can do it later," she implored.

"Mom, I got it."

"I don't want you to have to take care of me."

He didn't mean to raise his voice, but ended up barking, "Why not? Tell me, please, because I would love to know. Your love includes only you. It is all about you and satisfying your fears about us. You know, it's as important to learn to receive as it is to give."

"But it's my job to take care of you kids."

"Actually, it is not. Not anymore," he replied while fighting to hold back his growing anger.

"Sandy, you don't understand, I—"

He interrupted her boldly, "What I understand is that you would rather suffer here alone than to call me for help. I'm sorry, but I have a problem with that."

She said nothing.

He wasn't sure what to do next and he could feel himself getting anxious. It occurred to him to call Tony. Instead, he called Miss Lisa and explained the situation. She told him to find a thermometer and take his mother's temperature. Sandy found an oral thermometer in the medicine cabinet. He took Verna's temperature and reported that the thermometer read 102 degrees. She advised him to give Verna some Tylenol to try to get the fever down. She also instructed him to keep taking her temperature every couple of hours or so. She offered to come there, but Sandy told her not to try. Verna was sleeping now, and he would call 911 if she showed any signs of getting worse.

Sandy went downstairs and turned on the TV. He watched mostly the coverage of the storm. It was on all the channels. Every hour or so he would go and check on Verna. He texted Tony to let him know what was going on, but was careful not to sound too worried. Tony responded back that he hoped she felt better soon. Sandy even managed to doze off once or twice, but he never fell into a hard sleep. There was a time when he would have prayed for his mother and asked God to heal her body. It would have been one of the first things that he would have done after arriving there. However, that was then, and this was now, because the thought never even entered his mind.

Around midnight, he heard Verna get up and go to the bathroom. Shortly after, he made her drink some water and gave her two more Tylenol. When he took her temperature again, it read 100 degrees. He put another cold compress on her head. Although he was not sure that he believed her, she said that she felt better. Regardless, at least she wasn't getting worse. He texted an update to Miss Lisa and to his surprise, she responded immediately. He heard the snow plows outside and hoped that his car was okay.

Apparently, the travel advisory was being lifted at noon. He was told when he called into work that he had to come in at 1:00 p.m. to finish out his shift. He made Verna breakfast consisting of broth and orange juice. He made her sit up, and she managed to take only a couple swallows of each.

"Thank you," she said.

"You're welcome."

"Sandy, there's something I want talk to you about," she forced herself to say through her stuffy nose and congestion.

"What is it?" he asked, using a defensive tone.

"I've been thinking a lot lately. I think that I might be open to moving to Florida with my sister. She is there all by herself, and it might be good for me too."

"You mean sell the house?" he asked.

"Maybe, I'm not sure."

"When?"

"I'm not sure."

"If that's what you want," he said. He tried to sound unruffled.

"I might not be able to do it anyway," she continued. "A lot depends on your sister. I'm very worried about her. I'm worried about you too."

Sandy quickly countered, "You don't have to worry about me. I will be fine."

"I know that. But it is impossible for me not to worry…Sandy, do you remember what I said that day when I had to testify? About you being special?"

"Yes, I remember."

"It's true. I wasn't lying or exaggerating anything," she desperately pled.

"I know that, Mom," he faintly replied.

"What I'm trying to say is that you *are* special. But you don't believe that you are, and that breaks my heart. By trying to hold you close, I think that I somehow managed to push you away. And now you have run so far that you can't see the truth, even about yourself." she cried softly and stopped to cough. "My girls are special too, but not in the same way that you are. People who know their true worth do not settle. If Whitney knew just how special she is, then her life would be different, and maybe our little Stephenson would still be here. I don't know."

"Mom, Whitney made her own choices. None of it is your fault."

"That is kind of you to say, but when you become a parent, you might see it differently. Everybody wants the best for their children, but that's not enough. They have to want the best for themselves," Verna instructed.

"Everybody has to live their own life, and everyone struggles from time to time." He thought about what Gary had said about depression.

The doorbell rang. He went down to answer it. It was Miss Lisa. She was carrying a bag of stuff. He let her in and stayed downstairs while she tended to Verna. Eventually, she came down and said that Verna only had a low-grade fever. She also volunteered to stay while Sandy went to work. He gladly took her up on her offer and went up to say goodbye to his mother. She had changed her gown and she looked better. He told her that he would be back later.

His car had been completely snowed in by the snowplows so he had to walk back to the house to get a shovel to dig himself out. It took him about an hour, which left him just enough time to get back to his apartment, take a shower, and drive to work. The roads were clearer by then, and it was only snowing lightly. All afternoon he thought about what Verna had said to him. She was right that he never felt that he was special. He couldn't help but wonder if anyone other than his mother, and perhaps Tony, ever thought that about him.

Chapter 20

Sandy made his way into Gary's office and sat down. His previous visit was two weeks ago. In addition to the ocean prints on the wall, there was also a framed Bible verse. It was 1 John 4:4, "He who is in you is greater than he who is in the world." Sandy didn't remember seeing that the first time that he was there. He gave Gary the twenty-five dollar insurance copayment and a piece of paper with the name of the anti-depressant that he was taking.

"How are you?" Gary asked.

"I'm good," Sandy answered without thinking.

"I'm sorry that we had to cancel our session last week. That was quite a storm we got."

"Yes, it was."

"How have you been sleeping?" Gary asked.

"Not good."

"Still? How many hours of sleep a night would you guess that you average?"

"Three to four," Sandy estimated.

Gary shook his head and inquired, "What do you do the rest of the night?"

"Nothing. I read or watch TV or get up and clean or something."

"Do you get tired during the day?" Gary questioned.

"No. Maybe a little. But I never nap during the day, if that's what you're asking."

"Are you thinking about anything in particular when you wake up?"

Sandy responded, "No."

"Have you had any more panic attacks?"

"No. My mother was sick with the flu this week and I had to take care of her. I have two sisters, but they are in Buffalo. It was a little nerve-wracking at first, with the storm and all, but we got through it."

"Your mother lives alone?"

"Yes, but she is only fifty-seven years old. She's in good health. She just told me that she is thinking about moving to Jacksonville, Florida with her sister."

"How do you feel about that?"

"I don't know, but it will be weird not having her here. Plus, I'm not sure I want her to sell the house."

"Weird how?"

Sandy explained, "My mother is like the typical helicopter mom, but only on steroids. She means well though, and I love her; I do. But she drives me crazy because at times it's too much. My father was never home, so she really just had us kids, you know. She has always put all of her energy in us."

"Have you told her how you feel?"

"She knows," Sandy stated definitively.

"Do you think she's happy in her own life?"

"I don't know for sure," Sandy admitted. "She's a tough cookie. My father cared more about his job as a pastor than he did about his wife and children. I could tell that she was sad a lot. I'm not sure if my sisters could tell, but I knew."

"Do you think you have a strong bond with your mother?"

"I don't know. Probably. She talked to me about stuff because I was the only one who would listen. I felt responsible for her in a way because of it. I didn't want to do anything or say anything that would make her upset."

"Like what? I don't know what you mean," Gary inquired.

Sandy wasn't sure how best to explain it and took a couple of deep breaths before recounting, "When I was a teenager, my father would take me with him when he went to other churches to preach. We would go everywhere, even out of state. Just me and him. He wanted me to play the piano for him. I never really wanted to go, but I felt like I didn't have a choice, you know? What Reverend Coleman wanted, Reverend Coleman got. Nothing was more important to my father than his reputation as a minister. It wasn't like we shared special moments when we were on the road together. He barely spoke to me. He basically just ordered me around like a dog. There was this one time when we were out of town somewhere and I walked in on him with this other woman in bed."

"Did he know you saw him?" Gary asked and sat up in his seat.

"Yes, he knew. I was stunned and ran away. He told me later that it wasn't what it looked like and that he would beat the hell out of me if I told my mother."

"Did you believe him?"

"I knew what I saw," Sandy stated without flinching.

"No, that's not what I meant. Did you believe him when he said that he would beat you?"

"I don't know. But that isn't why I never told my mother."

"Why not then?"

"I didn't tell her because I knew it would hurt her," Sandy explained

"That is a pretty big secret to have to keep."

Sandy muttered, "Come to find out that our family is pretty good at keeping secrets."

"Well, how was it with your father after that?"

"I'm not sure what you mean. He pretty much ignored me before that, and he ignored me after. Except when he wanted to show me off at church."

Gary didn't respond immediately, and Sandy's words just lingered in the air for an awkward moment.

"You must have been really good on the piano," Gary finally said.

"It's a piano. I was a kid. I taught myself how to play it. Not really a big deal. People just thought it was cute."

"I don't think that's true," Gary protested. "It sounds to me like you are something really special. You don't think so?"

"I don't know," Sandy responded and started thinking about what Verna had just said to him the other morning. He started to tear up but was able to suppress it.

"Do you think that you loved your father?" Gary pressed.

Sandy hesitated before answering. "Yes, I loved him. But he didn't love me back."

"You say that so easily," Gary continued, "maybe he just didn't know how to show his love for you."

"Or maybe he was just a selfish asshole who only cared about himself!" Sandy exclaimed. "Sorry…Maybe, he didn't even love God, just used him."

"Sounds a little harsh," Gary rebuked.

"He was a little harsh," Sandy countered dismissively. He was embarrassed, however, by the unexpected rush of emotion.

"You sound angry when you talk about your father. Are you aware of that?"

"I'm not angry."

"Bitter then," Gary suggested.

"I guess I always resented him," Sandy reluctantly admitted.

Gary asked, "How did he die?"

"He had a heart attack. He wasn't sick or anything. Just came out of nowhere."

"How did you feel when he died?"

Sandy promptly replied, "I don't know."

"Sandy, I'm not sure if you are aware, but you like to say 'I don't know' whenever I ask you about your feelings. I would like for you to stop and think about it before you answer and then try to articulate your feelings for me. Okay?" Gary directed.

"Yes. I'm sorry," Sandy replied.

"Were you sad when your father passed away?"

Sandy took a couple of seconds to consider because he had never thought about it like that before.

"I was mostly scared," he finally uttered.

"About what?"

"About how my mother would handle it, and what was going to happen to our family," Sandy explained.

"Have you ever wished that you had a chance to settle things with your father before he died? Many people desire closure of some kind so they can move on. When someone we are in a relationship with leaves suddenly, there are usually a lot of loose ends that need to be tied up. Do you think about that concerning your relationship with him?"

"No, never," Sandy said without hesitation.

"Sandy, tell me what it was like growing up in your family home for you."

He spent the final twenty-five minutes or so talking about Whitney and Tanya and their misspent youth. He also spoke in some detail about high school and the absence of friends. Gary listened intently. He was taking notes, which is something else that Sandy didn't remember observing at the first session.

"Well, our time is up," Gary said, looking at his watch. "Before I let you go, can you tell me how you feel about our conversation today?"

"I don't understand. I feel okay. Why?" Sandy asked.

"No reason. I just want to make sure that you are not feeling bad about anything that I asked you or about something that you said," Gary stated matter-of-factly.

"No. I understand that you have to ask me tough questions."

"Good. See you next week."

Sandy was glad to be leaving. He sat in his car for a few minutes to digest what he just experienced before heading to work. That was harder than he thought it was going to be. He didn't particularly like talking about Reverend Coleman. It seemed disloyal somehow. He didn't blame his father for the way that his life turned out. He made all his own choices. Nevertheless, that stuff about his father having done the best he could was total nonsense and made him mad. Still, while it wasn't easy being Reverend Coleman's son, he fully recognized that other people had it much worse than he ever did. The point is that he made it through. The past was literally dead and buried. He might not be a good candidate for counseling after all. He wondered what Gary thought about him.

The rest of the week went by slowly. On Saturday night he and Tony attended a panel discussion up at the university and then they went out to dinner with some of Tony's friends. Sandy was mostly bored but tried hard not to let it show. Tony was in a good mood because he had just learned that he had won a case and that his client was granted a new trial and was scheduled to be released from prison any day. He talked a lot about it. Sandy was happy for him and was determined not to ruin the evening for them. It was a little after midnight when they finally left the restaurant. It was freezing rain. They decided to go to Tony's place because it was closer, and the roads were slippery. By the time that Tony awoke the next morning, Sandy had cleaned his entire apartment.

"Good morning," Tony said while sitting up in bed.

"Good morning."

"Hey, how is it going with the therapy? Do you think it's helping you?" Tony asked.

"I honestly don't know. I have had only two sessions."

"Is he a pastor or something?"

"No," Sandy replied. "He is not affiliated with any church. I think that he is just a certified therapist."

"Well do you like it? Do you think it will help?" Tony wondered.

"I don't hate it, if that is what you mean, but it is harder than I thought it would be." Sandy paused to find the TV remote before continuing, "Last time we talked about my family...my father. I don't really like to go there because I don't see the point. No one will ever be able to explain my father to me."

"Did he tell you that it's your issues with your father that made you gay?" Tony inquired in a sarcastic tone.

"No, he never said that, and I don't think he will. He's just trying to get me to talk about my feelings," Sandy explained defensively.

Tony persisted, "Did he ask you any questions about me? About us?"

"No, not yet. Like I said, I have only been there twice, and the sessions are only for one hour. Besides, it is impossible to talk about you in just an hour. That topic alone could take several months."

Tony smirked and said, "Make sure that you tell him that you can't get enough of me."

"Who told you that?" Sandy asked straight-faced.

"Come on, who could resist all of this man?" Tony proclaimed as he got out of bed and was standing there in all of his glory."

"So it's all about you. You really think that you got it like that, huh?" Sandy provoked.

"You know it, Babe."

It was Sunday. For most of his life, Sunday had been the most important day of the week. This was the case long before he ever started working at the church. Reverend Coleman not only insisted that his family attend church every Sunday, but he didn't let them do too many other activities after church either. Because he considered Sunday to be the Sabbath, he didn't permit any kind of cooking, cleaning, or unnecessary work. He always said that it was a command of God that his people rest that day. This meant that Verna usually prepared Sunday dinner the night before, or they went out to dinner. Occasionally, someone from Mount Moriah would prepare dinner for them. When you were raised that way, it becomes a part of who you are. Tony said that Sandy had been brainwashed, but Sandy wondered if the reverse was not actually the case, meaning that the people who take the Sabbath for granted have been brainwashed into thinking that it is alright to completely disregard what the Bible teaches. Whatever the case may be, Sandy now felt that there was something odd about the fact that Sunday was now just another day for him.

He read his messages while Tony was in the shower. There was a reminder from Dr. Mark's office that he had an appointment this week. Sandy didn't want to go, and he just remembered that he had never sent them his eating diary. There was also a text from a number that he didn't recognize. It read:

> Sandy, you might want to check your man Tony
> before I take him from you. I have to admit
> that he sure is tasty. From one black queen to
> another...lol.

He read it again. It was as if time stopped. He was angry because he knew what this meant. He tried to think. The question was what to do about it. If he confronted Tony, he would just deny any wrongdoing or having any knowledge of the author of the text. He knew it because that is what men who cheat normally do in this situation. He considered calling the number, but for what purpose? What would he say? Even if the guy answered the phone, what exactly was there to talk about? Maybe they could compare notes. Sandy was trying to stay calm, but he was losing that battle. He needed to go somewhere and think this through. He jumped up and started putting on his coat. Just as he was opening the door to leave, Tony walked into the room.

"Hey, where are you going?" he asked.

"I have to get out of here," Sandy said. He was shaking uncontrollably.

"What's wrong? Did something happen to your mother?" Tony inquired, his voice evincing his concern.

"No. I just heard from your special friend," Sandy mocked.

"What friend?"

"The one you've been sleeping with!" Sandy shot back.

"I don't know what you're talking about," Tony looked like he was about to have a panic attack.

Sandy read him the text. The words had even greater impact when spoken aloud.

"Let me see that," Tony demanded. He took Sandy's phone and read to himself.

"I swear, Sandy, I don't know what this is. It's not what you think. Please just calm down so we can talk."

"I don't want to talk!" Sandy shouted.

"We have to talk. I don't understand why you're so upset."

"Maybe because you're a liar!" Sandy exploded.

"Excuse me? I have never lied to you," Tony pled.

"I trusted you. You must think I'm so stupid. Whoever this is, you better call him and tell him not to text me ever again or I will find him. Do you understand me? Never again!"

"Okay. Okay...Just don't go," Tony begged and reached for Sandy.

Sandy jumped back. "I have to go before I say something I won't be able to take back. You disgust me!" Sandy shouted just before he slammed the door.

Just when he thought that he could not take any more, then this. His whole world was crumbling down. He just started driving. He was so embarrassed. He wondered how long Tony had been cheating on him, probably from the very beginning. Who else knew? Were people laughing at him? He just kept driving to nowhere in particular. His phone kept ringing. He knew it was Tony. There was no way that he was going to answer. All he wanted to do was drive off a cliff somewhere and put an end to all this pain and despair. Instead, he drove around for nearly an hour before he parked the car, got out, walked up to the front door and rang the doorbell. The door opened slowly.

"Sandy? Oh, Honey, what happened?" Marco asked. His eyes were as big as saucers.

Sandy began to cry. He tried to talk, but he could not.

"Come in. Sit down here. Let me get you something to drink," Marco said.

He left Sandy sitting on the sofa and returned with a bottle of water and handed it to Sandy.

"What is it? Tell me," Marco urged.

Sandy handed him his phone, and Marco read the text to himself.

"Oh Sandy, I'm so sorry...Did you show this to Tony?"

"Yes."

"And what did he say?"

"What do you think he said? He said that it is not what I think."

"Well maybe it isn't. Maybe there is a logical explanation," Marco suggested.

Sandy just stared at him.

"Well what are you going to do?" Marco asked.

"I don't know. I feel like such a fool."

"If you love him, then you have to talk to him. I really don't know what he has or has not done, but I know that he loves you. That's something, right?"

"I can't handle this right now, Sandy vented. "I really can't."

"I know. How about this? How about we spend the afternoon together. Do you like old black-and-white movies? Jonathan is working so I would love the company. We can just enjoy the rest of the day. Just you and me. What do you say?"

"Are you sure? I probably shouldn't have come here," Sandy offered.

"Nonsense. You came to the right place. We've all been there. We don't even have to talk if you would rather not. How about it?"

It was 9:00 p.m. when Sandy left for home. He felt a little better. Marco was funny and easy to talk to. But it was yet another reminder that he didn't have any friends of his own outside of Tony—just one more thing that he needed to work on. Tony called several times. Marco just looked at him each time the phone rang, so Sandy eventually turned it off altogether. He was not really trying to punish Tony. He simply could not bring himself to talk to him. If he broke it off with Tony over this, then he would literally have no one. The truth is that he simply wasn't strong enough right now to just walk away from the only man that he had ever loved.

He saw Tony's car outside his apartment as he pulled into the parking lot. Initially, he considered not going in. However, he had nowhere else to go. He certainly couldn't go to his mother's house. Talk about making matters worse. Besides, he knew all along that Tony would be here. No, he had to face him at some point.

As he opened the door, he could hear the TV in the bedroom. He took off his coat and shoes and walked into the kitchen. Tony appeared.

"Sandy, you okay?"

"What do you think?"

"I don't understand why you won't talk to me."

"Because I don't want to hear your lies. Oh, but I actually do know someone who would love to talk to you. I can give you his number if you like," Sandy said, looking abased before he looked away.

"I know you're angry, but it's not like you to not be fair."

Sandy interrupted, "You do not know what I'm like. You don't know me at all. Because if you think that I'm going to just sit here and let you treat me like this, you are out of your mind, Babe!"

"So, what are you saying? You're not even going to give me a chance to explain?"

"Why should I?"

"Because I love you. And because maybe you don't know everything just based upon an anonymous text message that you received on your phone. All I'm asking you to do is to listen to me for a minute."

"You slept with him," Sandy declared soberly.

"I didn't. I swear that I didn't. Sandy, you gotta believe me. He's just a guy I met at work. We were just talking, and he got the wrong idea. I told him I was in a relationship, but he wouldn't give it up. I would never do anything to hurt you. Don't you believe that?"

"No. I mean…no," Sandy stammered.

"If we were going all hot and heavy, then why would he contact you? Don't you see that he is just trying to break us up?"

Sandy didn't know how to answer that, but he was shaking so much inside that it was hard to think.

"What's his name?" Sandy demanded.

"Sandy, it doesn't matter—"

"What's his name?" Sandy persisted. "He knows mine. It is only fair."

"Marquise. His name is Marquise Walker," Tony acknowledged.

"Did you call him?"

"What?" Tony asked.

"I told you to call him. Did you do it?"

"Yes," Tony affirmed.

"Did you tell him what I said?"

Tony was not exactly sure what Sandy was referring to but rather than asking Sandy to clarify he said, "Yes,"

"If I find out that you are not telling the truth—" Sandy contended.

"I'm not lying. I swear," Tony maintained.

Sandy abruptly turned and went into the bathroom. He turned on the water and let the full force of it mask the sound of him crying. He was confused and sad. He felt hopeless. If Tony was lying and he did sleep with Marquise, then he most likely would do it again. More importantly, this meant that he was all alone in the world. It took a couple of minutes before he was able to compose himself. Finally, he took a deep breath, swallowed what was left of his pride, and walked back into the arms of the man he could never fully trust again.

Chapter 21

Tony wasn't lying about everything. He called Marquise as soon as Sandy stormed out. It was a call he regretted having to make, but he really had no choice. Maybe he could talk some sense into him before this went any further.

"Hello, Lover, imagine hearing from you," Marquise said wryly.

"What the hell is wrong with you Marquise?" Tony erupted. "What are you trying to accomplish?"

"I warned you, but you didn't want to listen," Marquise reminded. "Did you really think that you could get rid of me that easily?"

"I never lied to you. I told you from the very start that I had a boyfriend!" Tony shouted in disbelief.

"Yes, you did tell me that. But that didn't stop you from getting with me. What was I supposed to think? We both know that you don't care nothing about this little boyfriend of yours or you never would have pursued me. You need to just be honest."

"What? I didn't make you do anything that you didn't want to do. I most certainly didn't pursue you. You sound crazy!" Tony argued.

"I'm just crazy for you, Lover. Why can't we get together? I know what you like. He doesn't have to know. It will be our little secret. You just say when."

"You're insane!" Tony shouted into the phone. "You need psychiatric help! Let me be as clear to you as possible. Stay away from me! I do not want anything to do with you and I'm sorry that I ever met you. Don't forget that, unlike you, I'm a lawyer and I know how to deal with psychopaths. I recorded this call too and I will have you arrested if you try to contact my boyfriend or me again. Got it?"

Tony hung up. He was incensed and partially in shock. He was mostly angry with himself. It was clear now that he had seriously misjudged Marquise. He used to be good at spotting the looneys. However, he clearly had missed the signs with Marquise, who started calling and texting again about two months ago to say that he missed Tony and that he wanted to try to make it work. At first, Tony told him that he was too busy to meet, but the calls and text messages increased in frequency and Marquise also started calling on the main line at the office and going through the receptionist. Tony finally met with him the morning of Stevie's funeral at a small coffee shop downtown. He tried to explain delicately that it was over between them, but Marquise threatened to call both Sandy and his boss and tell them about the affair. Tony's response was that he would destroy him if he did either one of those things. Apparently, Marquise had just called his bluff.

Tony was optimistic that Marquise was gone for good until Sandy received the text from him. He felt guilty that Sandy had to deal with this on top of everything else going on in his life. He feared that this would be the last straw to push him over the edge for good, especially if Marquise contacted him again and provided more details. He had never seen that look in Sandy's eyes before and it broke his heart. He was very worried after Sandy ran out of his apartment that he would do something crazy. Tony hoped that Sandy had just gone back to his apartment to cool off, but the place was dark when he arrived there an hour later. Rather than running away as he usually did, Sandy's cat glared at Tony when he first walked in, as if he knew what had happened.

It occurred to him that Sandy may have gone to his mother's house, but Tony was not about to go over there. Sandy had to come home eventually. He just had to wait it out. He had been there for about an hour when he got a text from Marco.

> **Sandy is here at my house. Quite upset, but okay.**
> **Stay away. U r a shit.**

Tony was very relieved. He had no idea why Sandy opted to go there, but Marco was probably the best person in the world for Sandy to talk to about this. Also, Marco would never betray Tony. They managed to stay friends all these years because Marco understood him. Sometimes he thought that Marco knew him too well. They had attempted to hook up once when they were young, but it wasn't good for either one of them. They both realized then that they were meant to be platonic friends. Tony was more than a little anxious waiting for Sandy to return.

The conversation after Sandy came home went better than Tony thought that it would. He was prepared to beg if he needed to. He had to lie about the sex with Marquise because Sandy would never have forgiven him. Besides, it was Marquise's word against his. There was absolutely no way that he was going to lose Sandy over a minor indiscretion. Marquise was a non-factor. However, he told himself that he had to clean up his act—he definitely didn't want to ever find himself in this predicament again.

That night he wasn't sure how it was going to be with Sandy going forward. It was impossible to tell if Sandy believed him or not. He was quiet for the rest of the evening, but that wasn't that unusual lately. However, there was no tension in the air that he could discern, only awkwardness. Tony thought about going back to his own place rather than staying the night. He was trying to read Sandy because he was too afraid to just come out and ask. He really wasn't sure what to do, but he eventually decided to stay and see what happened. He felt fretful. But when he reached for Sandy during the night, Sandy responded. Only then did he breathe a sigh of relief.

However, the question of what to do about Marquise remained. Tony didn't like the idea of just sitting around and waiting for the other shoe to drop. The next morning, he called his friend Charlie at the Syracuse Police Department. It was unusual for a criminal defense lawyer to have a friend on the police department, but Tony had been friends with Charlie Spence ever since their college days at SUNY Oswego. The two had roomed together first year and still had many mutual friends. Sandy explained the situation to Charlie, who laughed at first.

"Same old Tony Moreno. Thinking with the wrong head again, huh?" Charlie joked.

"Look who's talking, I learned everything I know from you," Tony responded.

"The hell you say, I'm not as pretty as you are, Counsellor. Anyway, how can I help you with the woman scorned? You know that he hasn't committed any crime yet."

"I know," Tony admitted. "But can't you do a drive-by or something before he does? I'm telling you that he is pretty unstable. I tried to scare him myself, but I don't think it worked."

"Yeah, I guess that I could give him a little call. If he's a law student, then he should be afraid of breaking the law and possibly ruining his career before it gets started. Give me the number. But

I have to tell you that sometimes it's better to leave well enough alone," Charlie warned.

"I know, but at this point I can't take that chance, Tony insisted. "Here, I just sent you the number."

"Alright, I will let you know how I make out," Charlie said.

"Thanks, Charlie."

Tony understood that Charlie was right, and he was taking a big chance. Marquise could make a lot of trouble for him. Tony could lose his job if he filed a sexual harassment claim against him at work. Tony was technically in a supervisory role when Marquise was an intern at Legal Aid. Although he was highly thought of among the staff, Tony was very much aware that this sort of thing was taken very seriously by the county and that his supervisor is a real by-the-books kind-of person. Tony was only starting to realize just how big a jam he really was in, and what was ultimately at risk.

The phone rang. Tony picked it up. It was Charlie.

"That was quick," Tony said.

"I called him. I told him that I was following up on a harassment complaint that we received involving a threatening text message. His response was that he hadn't threatened anyone. I then told him that I was not accusing him of anything and that this was only a courtesy call and that our plan for now was just to continue to monitor the situation. I further advised him that if there were any more text messages or phone calls to anyone in Syracuse, that we would pursue an arrest warrant against him and have him brought back to New York for prosecution. He said that he didn't want any problems and that he would not send any more texts. He also said that it was all just a big lie because he was the one being harassed."

"That's awesome," Tony replied. "Charlie, I really appreciate it. I owe you one, Buddy. I feel like I'm fighting for my life here."

"I don't know for sure if it worked. I mean, if he is really as crazy as you say. But he sounded scared. I never said your name."

"I know. But it was worth the try. Thank you. Maybe we can get together sometime for a beer and catch up."

"Yes, let's do that. By the way, I want to meet him," Charlie interjected.

"Who?" Tony asked.

"Your guy. Sandy is his name, right? I want to meet the guy who tamed the great Anthony Moreno."

"I don't know what you're talking about," Tony replied.

"The hell you don't. He must be something really special."

"He is," Tony admitted.

Chapter 22

Sandy was more than ready for the third counseling session. He wanted Gary's opinion about Tony. He was trying his best to keep everything in perspective, but he didn't like the idea that Tony was thinking that he had gotten away clean. That was what his father had done to his mother for all those years. However, he was not his mother.

"So how was your week?" Gary asked.

"I have reason to believe that my boyfriend is cheating on me," Sandy calmly said.

"What kind of reason?"

"The guy sent me this text." Tony showed Gary the text message.

"I'm assuming that Tony is your boyfriend's name."

"Yes."

"How long have you been dating?" Gary asked.

"Three years."

"That's a long time. Do you think he would cheat on you?"

"Yes, I do," Sandy conceded and looked directly at Gary before lowering his gaze.

"Why?" Gary wondered.

"Because I know him. He lives in the moment, which means he can be easily seduced by his desires."

"If you know that about him, then why do you stay in the relationship? I mean, if you can't trust him."

"I love him," Sandy offered.

"Does he love you?"

"I think that he does. At least, to the extent that he is capable of loving anyone. He can be so loving and kind."

"Is that enough for you?" Gary pressed.

"I don't know."

Gary just looked at Sandy, who was deep in thought processing what he had just said.

"Sandy, this is just my opinion, but it is generally very difficult to find fulfillment in a relationship with someone who is either incapable or unwilling to fully commit," Gary persuaded.

"So, what are you saying, that I should break up with him?"

Gary commented, "No, I would never say that. That is not my place. It is entirely your decision who you give your time and heart to. But love is not just something that just happens to us. It is a choice, and it is very important that we choose carefully because life is hard enough, even with the right person."

"My mother stayed with my father even though he wasn't fully committed to their marriage. It wasn't perfect, but she survived. She is still here," Sandy quietly affirmed.

"Is that what you want to do, just survive? All relationships are different. One of the biggest mistakes we can make is to compare ourselves to other people. What might be acceptable to you, might be unthinkable to someone else, and vice versa. The question is, what do you need in a relationship to feel valued and secure?" Gary preached.

"I love him," Sandy redirected.

"I know. You said that."

More prolonged silence.

"Sandy," Gary said speaking in a softer tone. "Excuse me for asking, but did you love your nephew?"

"Yes, I did."

"But your love wasn't enough to save him, was it?" Gary urged.

"No. I didn't even know that he needed me," Sandy's voice trembled, and he began to cry a little. "He was just a boy. A beautiful boy. He had his whole life to live, and I should have been there for him. I let him down. I think he tried to tell me once, but I wasn't listening. I was selfish—and now he's gone."

"You're not any more selfish than any of us," Gary contended. "You were just living your life as best you knew how. It's hard because we're only human, and we don't know it all. That's okay. Had you been aware of what was going on with your sister, you would have acted differently. Deep down you know that you would have done just about anything for him because you loved him that much. Am I right?"

Sandy just nodded his head, unable to speak.

"True love is when we are willing to change our very existence for someone else. That is how you loved your nephew and it sounds to me like that is how you love Tony. I can tell. Hopefully, that is how much Tony loves you too, or you will never be on equal footing."

"He tells me he loves me all the time," Sandy managed to say.

"I'm sure that he does, Gary stated. "But love means different things to people. This is just something to think about… because love is not what we say, it is what we do."

"Tony does more for me than even my own father ever tried to do."

"Can you forgive him if he was seeing someone else?" Gary beseeched. "Do you love him enough to forgive this transgression?"

Sandy whined, "I don't know, I mean, I want to forgive him."

"But you don't want to forgive your father for his failures," Gary incited. "What is the difference?"

Sandy didn't know how to answer that question. He just sat there for what seemed like an eternity, thinking and searching.

"This is a good start. Good for you." After a pause he continued, "Here's another way of looking at it. What if this is just who Tony is? Is it fair to the zebra to expect him to change his stripes? The trick is to find a way to accept him for who he is without losing yourself in the process. That is love too."

"I don't know what to do."

"Talk to him, "Gary encouraged. "Make sure he knows how badly he hurt you. And then just watch to see what his actions reveal about what's truly in his heart."

"I'm afraid," Sandy admitted.

"What are you afraid of?"

"I don't know… I know that you don't like it when I say that, but I really don't know."

"Sandy, I'm just trying to get you to face your feelings. But only you can tell me what those feelings are. If I ask an adult how she feels, she should be able to tell me that she is happy, or sad, or cold or hot, or whatever the case may be. But if I'm asking why she thinks she is sad, then it's okay if she doesn't exactly know why. It's okay that you don't know why you are afraid. However, it is something to think about, isn't it?"

"Yes. I get it."

The whole session went by fast for Sandy. He really did like Gary's no-nonsense style. He never wanted to be coddled in any way. He might not always like the truth, but he always wanted to know the truth. The thing that hurt him the most about "growing up Coleman" was that he was not told the truth or allowed to honestly react. When a child is never permitted to cry it out, he learns to hide a part of himself, even from himself. Sandy knew that he had mastered the art of withdrawing from reality.

Verna called him on Friday night. She wanted to know if he was willing to go to Buffalo to pick up Whitney, who had a doctor's appointment on Monday in Syracuse. Although Verna was doing much better physically, she didn't want to be in the car for that long. Sandy agreed to go. He figured that maybe the drive would do him some good. Plus it would be a chance to spend some time alone with Whitney.

He decided to drive to Buffalo on Sunday. The weather forecast called for a clear day with no rain or snow. It was a straight shot down the New York State Thruway I-90 and should only take him three and-a-half hours to get there if traffic wasn't bad and if the weather cooperated. His goal was to get there by noon. Verna called just as he was leaving to remind him to call her when he got there.

It ended up being an easy drive. In the past, whenever he had to spend that much time alone in the car, he would listen to worship music in an attempt to find new songs for the choir and worship team to sing. This time, he had the radio on an R&B station, although he played it softly and wasn't really listening to it. He found himself lost in deep thought about some of the things that Gary had said at their last session. It was exactly noon when he pulled into the parking lot of Tanya's apartment complex.

His nieces were clearly very glad to see him. As soon as he walked in, they pounced on him and wanted to show him their room and their toys. Sandy played with them while Tanya finished getting lunch ready. He couldn't help but think about Stevie as the girls giggled and jumped around. He wondered what Whitney thought when she looked at them. They were so alive, the way that his nephew had been. Stevie was a little older than Sophia and Gabrielle, but he was always good with them. He would chase after them and even play dolls with them.

Whitney looked better than she did the last time that he saw her, but still not like herself. She had lost a lot of weight and wasn't wearing any makeup. He remembered a time when she wouldn't even answer the doorbell unless she was fully made-up. When he hugged her, she seemed extremely frail, and it made him cringe. For some reason, he had been thinking that she was much further along the road to recovery than she apparently was.

When he spoke to Tanya in private, she said that Whitney was really struggling, and that she was worried. Tanya could hear her crying in her room most nights, and she wasn't eating. Whitney was content to stay in bed all day and had to be coaxed into coming out and participating in activities. She was so depressed that she often didn't even know what day of the week it was. She wouldn't answer her phone or speak to anyone besides Verna. Tanya said that Whitney hadn't mentioned Stevie even once.

"When mom is on the phone, does Whitney actually speak to her, or does she just listen?" Sandy asked under his breath.

"That's the really strange thing to me," Tanya confessed. "She actually carries on a conversation with mother. I must say that I don't really get it, considering how much they used to act like they hated each other most of the time, and I don't know exactly what they are talking about, but it is more than she's willing to say or do with anyone else."

"Really? Well that's good to know. I'll talk to Verna. We have to figure something out," he noted.

"Sandy how are you, really?" she inquired as she picked up the dishes.

"I'm a mess. But I'm determined to make it through."

"Good, because I need you to survive."

"I need you too."

Most of the ride home was in silence. Whitney would only talk in response to his questions, and then only in monosyllables. Sandy had stopped trying by the time they got to Rochester, which is almost halfway, and they drove the last hour without either one speaking a word. Sandy pulled up into his mother's driveway at 4:50 p.m. He carried her bags up to her room and Whitney immediately laid down on the bed.

"How was the drive?" Verna asked.

"She's in pretty bad shape."

"I know. I didn't want to tell you," Verna admitted.

"Why not?" he asked pointedly.

She heard his tone and only looked at him for an instant before diverting her eyes.

"Well, we have to do something before we lose her," he admonished.

"I wanted to talk to you about that," she replied. "I spoke to my sister yesterday. Flo called me to say that the lady in the condo next to her had a stroke last month and they had to move her into a nursing home. She is a very nice person. I've spoken with her several times. Anyway, Flo spoke to the lady's son, and he said that he would rent the condo to me at a really good rate. He will also give me an option to buy it after his mother passes. It's almost too good to be true."

"When would you go?"

"In two weeks...and I'd like to take Whitney with me. I already asked her, and she said that she would go. I think that it would be good for her. Whitney's doctor said that she needs to start all over again. This could be it. She would have me and Flo there to take care of her, and I think that the change will help to jump-start her on the road to recovery."

"It sounds good," Sandy said without sounding convinced.

"But Sandy, I won't do it if you say no. We won't go."

"What? Why?" he asked.

"Because, I feel like we need your blessing to go. This isn't just for Whitney, it's for me too. There's nothing here for me but you. I know you're hurting too, but you're stronger than you know. I raised you, so I know. What do you think? Can we go, please?" She implored.

Without much hesitation, he replied, "Yes, you can go with my blessing, but I need you to promise me something now."

"What is it?"

"Actually, there are two things," he began. "The first is that you have to promise me that you will do everything that you can to push Whitney to be independent again. That means everything you do for her has to be about getting her to the point where she doesn't need you. I mean it."

"What else?" She nervously persisted.

He paused and sucked in his breath before saying, "You have to pray for me every day."

"I promise," she said, now with tears streaming down her face.

Sandy went with Verna and Whitney to the doctor's appointment because he wanted to hear for himself what was going on with her. He also wanted Verna to see that he intended to take an active role in his sister's care. The medical practice that Whitney went to was downtown, not far from the University. Sandy waited in the waiting room alone while Whitney was examined, but they called him in at the end. Dr. Juliette Childs was nice. She was tall with short brown hair and an athletic build. She sat down with the three of them and began by talking directly to Whitney.

"You seem to be doing okay physically. I'm a little worried about your weight loss, and if that continues it could be a problem. You need to eat, even if it's just a little something. I know you say that you're not hungry, but you can get yourself some of those small cans of nutritional shakes or drinks and have those. I think they even make a pudding now, if you like pudding. But you need to keep your strength up before you really get sick. We don't want that, okay?"

Whitney only nodded.

"I also think it's great that you're relocating to Florida. I've never been to Jacksonville, but I've heard great things. You need to get some counseling when you get there, though. If you can't find someone, then just call me, and we will help."

Turning to Sandy and Verna, Dr. Child's said, "She needs to take her medications. I think that they are helping. Once you get a new doctor in Jacksonville, let me know. We can send records.

She is just a little stuck right now, but we can't let it get any worse. Any questions?"

"By counseling, do you mean a regular counselor or a psychiatrist?" Sandy wondered.

"A good counselor or therapist will do. Depression is not a mental illness. It is a coping mechanism. Perhaps someone who specializes in grief counseling would be good. Depression is serious business. What has happened to Whitney is unthinkable. It is understandable that she is a little sad and withdrawn. But we don't want it to get to the point where she becomes a danger to herself. She is young and otherwise healthy. Just getting more sun should help. Baby steps, I say."

"Okay. Thank you," Sandy said.

"Whitney, I hope you feel better soon, Honey," the doctor said. "Drop me a line if you think about it. I would love to know how you're doing."

They drove straight home after the appointment and Whitney went immediately to her room and shut the door. Sandy recognized the similarities between his condition and hers, which was helpful because it gave him an opportunity to see it from the outside looking in. Obviously, what Whitney was experiencing was far worse, in that she had almost completely shut down.

"Mom, when you talk to Whitney on the phone, what is it that you talk about?" he asked.

"She likes to hear about heaven. I think that she's worried about Stephenson and what he might be feeling. It reminds me of when she was a little girl and she wanted to hear the same bedtime story over and over again every night. I just keep telling her that heaven is a perfect place where everybody is happy all of the time and people get to see God face to face every day."

"Does it seem to make her feel better?"

"I can't be sure, Verna admitted. "One time she asked me, 'So my baby is happy?' I told her that he was very happy and that he wants her to get better so that he doesn't have to worry about her."

"Are you concerned that she might be suicidal or something? I mean, all this talk about heaven," Sandy questioned.

"No, I really don't think so. That may come later, I don't know…to some extent, she hasn't moved much past the moment when they first told her that he had died; I mean, in terms of what that really means. She feels guilty and sad, but she isn't focused too much right now on her own pain. She only knows that he is gone, and she will never see him again. Her doctor is right, she's stuck."

"You seem to understand her," he acknowledged.

"I think that I have always understood the way she thinks. Maybe she's more like me than I've been willing to admit."

"So what do you need for me to do, relating to the move?"

"There's really not a lot to be done. My prayer group is going to help me pack our clothes. The condo is furnished, so I don't need to take anything. I have to go to the bank and post office tomorrow. I called Whitney's job last week and they said that she is on extended medical leave with all of her health benefits. I think that means that she can come back if she wants to. The most important thing is that you have to take care of this house and my car, but you already know how to do that. I think we're good."

Chapter 23

Sandy paid Gary the insurance copayment and sat down. While he was not exactly looking forward to his session this time, he had been keeping track in his head of things that he wanted to possibly discuss.

"How did it go this week with Tony?" Gary began.

"Okay. It is business as usual with him," Sandy recounted.

"What do you mean by that?"

"He is acting like nothing ever happened, like he doesn't have a problem in the world," Sandy explained.

"Maybe he doesn't."

"Maybe," Sandy admitted.

"Did you try to talk to him about how you feel?"

"Not yet."

"Why not."

"I really didn't see him much this week at all. I admit that I was a little hesitant to bring it up. Plus, I have a lot going on with my mother and my sister too," Sandy explained.

"But you are still planning to talk to him, correct?"

"Yes, I am."

"It is important that you do," Gary encouraged

"I know."

"Have you been intimate with him since you received the text that day?"

"Yes."

"How did it make you feel?"

"Good. Better than good."

"You didn't feel cheapened in any way?"

"No, I wanted it."

"Why?"

"I told you, I like it," Sandy proclaimed defiantly. He was becoming annoyed.

"But do you think that you may be sending him mixed messages?" Gary asked.

"I don't know what you mean."

"You said that he has gone back to business as usual. But it seems like you have too. What else is he supposed to think?"

"Right," Sandy agreed, but felt judged. He sulked.

"Sandy tell me about your job."

"I work in a warehouse," he stated without emotion.

"No, not that one. The one you had at the church. I'm sorry, I was not clear."

"What do you want to know?" Sandy asked while growing increasingly sullen.

"Do you miss it?" Gary forced.

"Sometimes," Sandy articulated.

"What about it do you miss?"

"I miss the process," Sandy explained. "You know of working on a song to get it right. I miss that feeling of helping people to experience God in a way that is real."

"I'm not sure that I understand." Gary replied.

"Real worship, the kind that touches the heart of God, is not a type of music. And it is not about how well a certain song is presented or how it makes us feel. Rather, it is a place where we can go. It is a place where we meet God."

"Where exactly is this place?"

"It is kind of hard to explain. God is everywhere present, right? He is here with us right now. But we are not in a place of worship. That is a higher place and it is reserved for certain people and him to be together."

"I thought that God wants everyone to worship him," Gary countered.

"He does. But not everyone is capable of it."

"Sounds like you are saying that God favors some people over others."

"He does," Sandy quickly replied.

"So, you believe that God does not love everyone the same?"

"We do not all love him the same. Worship is a sacrifice, meaning that it is something that we choose to give to God. Not every sacrifice is acceptable to him."

"Sandy, you speak so matter-of-fact about this. How do you know all of this?"

"Because I have been to the place."

"When was the last time you were there?" Gary inquired.

"I don't remember."

"Do you miss it? Not being there, I mean?"

"No... Maybe." Sandy voiced.

"What is stopping you from going to this place of worship? Is it not being at the church?"

"No, that's not it at all... I've chosen not to go there anymore."

"Why?"

"Because it costs too much to get there and you can only stay there for so long. We can't live there," Sandy rationalized.

"I'm sorry, but I don't completely follow that."

"I told you that it is hard to explain."

"Do you realize that if what you say is true, then you know God in a way that most of us never get to?" Gary suggested.

"You mean never choose to. You said it yourself during our last session, love is a choice."

There was a long period of silence as the two men entertained their own thoughts for a moment.

"What is going on with your mother and your sister?" Gary asked.

"They are moving to Jacksonville next week. My sister is not getting any better. We are hoping that the change will help her to heal faster."

"Her son was just murdered. She is not supposed to be better."

"Will she ever be?" Sandy wondered aloud.

"Yes, of course she will. There are generally seven stages to dealing with grief. She's at stage one now. She is in shock. It is hard to say how long she will be there. It can be a long road to acceptance and there is no timeline in grief. The next step is typically pain and guilt, which leads to the manifestation of some kind of anger. There are a lot of really good books out there on the subject. I could recommend a few to you if you like."

"Actually, I would like that," Sandy encouraged. "I want to help her as much as I can, and we are kinda worried."

"Okay, I will get that for you."

"Tell me something. What stage do you think I'm at?" Sandy searched.

"I'm hesitant to try to answer that for a number of reasons. Also, I could be wrong. We have only met a few times, but you were already grieving when your nephew died. You were grieving the loss of your job and everything that came with that. It is not that different, you know. We all have to grieve the losses and disappointments in our lives or we can't function properly. I think that you are angry and depressed, which are steps 3 or 4, depending on who you ask. Also, people skip steps and relapse."

"I'm tired of feeling this way," Sandy exclaimed.

"I think that you are making great progress. I really do. You are a pretty strong guy. Clearly, you have learned over the years how to take a hit and keep moving. That is both good and bad because you have also learned how to avoid having to address your true feelings in the process. It is a behavior that frankly you need to unlearn so that you can practice healthy coping skills."

Sandy didn't say anything.

"Are you comfortable with your sexuality?"

"No," he responded without any thought at all."

"Why not."

"Because I have always been taught that homosexuality is a perversion."

"The science does not support that."

"I know. But the Bible clearly teaches that it is wrong," Sandy contended.

"Not everyone believes that the Bible says that either."

"They are wrong," Sandy asserted.

"Again, you sound so certain about that. How can you know for sure?"

"It is hard to explain."

"Please try," Gary encouraged.

"God is a real person. Not just someone we made up like the Easter bunny or Santa Claus. He is a real, live, moving and breathing being. He has likes and dislikes just like you and me. For instance, I don't like tomato soup, so please don't make me tomato soup, not if you want to please me. I know that it is only soup much like any other soup, and some people love it. But I don't like tomato soup. God doesn't like homosexuality."

"But how do you respond to the argument that our understanding of God must evolve over time along with our understanding of the universe and science or God ceases to be relevant?"

"I say, that anyone who thinks that really does not know God at all. It is not about winning an argument based upon human reasoning. It is about knowing him."

"And you think that you know him?" Gary asked.

"Nobody really knows God completely. Only what he chooses to show us."

"Sandy, I think that I understand why you can't sleep at night… Anything else that you want to talk about before we end today?"

"I do have one question… Have you ever counselled or know of anyone who claims to have once been gay and went on to live their life as a straight person?"

"That is an interesting question. Why do you ask?" Gary questioned.

"Because I have never met such a person."

"Well. I'm not sure if I have either," Gary admitted. "There certainly are people who have discovered later in life that they are same sex attracted and who have changed their lives to accommodate their new feelings. But I do not believe in conversion therapy or anything like that, if that is what you are asking."

"No, I know. My question is whether you as a Christian counselor are aware of even one instance where someone who was in the gay lifestyle when he found Jesus and was later delivered from homosexuality to the point where that person is now living as a straight person with a wife and kids and the whole nine yards?"

"I have to admit that I have not counseled anyone like that, but that does not mean that they aren't out there. Because human sexuality is complex, I suspect that there are many people who have experienced some kind of spiritual transformation that greatly influenced their sexual practices and the way they see themselves. Does that answer your question?"

"Yes, it does. Thank you." Sandy said.

Gary just sat there looking at Sandy without saying anything. Sandy had noticed that he had a habit of doing that. Sandy was not sure if that was intentional on Gary's part because he was trying to bring special emphasis to a point, or if he was just at a loss about what to say next. Sandy suspected that it was probably a little of both, but he was never that good with awkward silences. They made him feel tense.

"Sandy, if you don't mind me asking, what do you think about the idea of the importance of getting to the point of loving yourself, flaws and all?" Gary asked.

"Not much. I think that it is probably better to love God because that is where it all starts."

"So, you don't think that people have value outside of their relationship with God?" Gary persisted.

"Um… That is not what I'm saying at all. Just that our lives are not our own and there are more important things that we can do with the little time that we have on this earth than learning to love ourselves."

"Like what?"

"Like trying to know God and worshipping him." Sandy was adamant.

"If you believe that, then how could you possibly leave the church?"

"I didn't leave, I was kicked out," Sandy argued.

"Just go to a different church. There are probably a hundred or so churches in Syracuse alone that would welcome you and your obvious gifts."

"Maybe, I have heard that before, but it is not that easy."

"Tell me why not."

"Because, I should not have to go in through the back door to get into my father's house. Plus, there is a big part of me that doesn't want to go back now and have to live under that kind of judgment. It is easier this way," Sandy proclaimed.

"Is it really?"

"Yup."

"So, what are you going to do?" Gary wondered.

This time it was Sandy who didn't know what to say. He looked at his watch and he was glad that the session was finally over. Usually, the time passed rather quickly, but today it dragged on a little. He was also glad that their meetings were just once a week. He thought it doubtful that he could handle any more than that.

By the time that he had completed his shift, Gary had texted him the titles of four books about dealing with grief. On his way home, he stopped at the bookstore and bought the two that they had in stock. He was looking forward to a quiet evening alone. Tony called while he was leaving the bookstore and they spoke briefly. After that, he spent most of the night reading. Mel sat quietly next to him as he read and both of them eventually fell asleep. Unexpectedly, he ended up sleeping most of the night, but his sleep was anything but restful.

Chapter 24

Verna's friends had an impromptu going away dinner at her house the day before she and Whitney were scheduled to fly out. Rosa Perez made all the food herself. They insisted that he be there, and they invited Tony too. Sandy reluctantly agreed to go and made some excuse as to why Tony would not be able to attend. It turned out to be a nice time. Miss Rosa was an excellent cook and there was enough food to feed a small army. Whitney only made a quick appearance before scampering away. Verna appeared to be in good spirits. It was obvious that, although she would miss her friends, she was looking forward to starting anew.

"I have decided that it would be a shame to let all these good looks I got go to waste. I'm still not too old to find me another husband, a rich one this time," she joked.

They all laughed and shouted words of encouragement. It was times like these when he was most proud of his mother. This woman never lost hope. To look at her, no one could tell how much she had endured. Other than when she was a child growing up in Brooklyn, or perhaps during the early years of her marriage, there had never been a time when she was truly at peace. She deserved to be happy.

Because Whitney had retreated to her room early, Sandy went up and sat with her for a while. They really didn't talk that much because there was not that much to say. Whitney was only a shell of herself. He understood that she was simply refusing to accept what had happened and needed time to fully mourn the loss of her only son.

"Whit, are you hungry? I brought you a little something."

"No," she said.

"Are you sure? It's really good. And you need to eat."

She shook her head and he put the tray that he was carrying on the nightstand.

"Hey, do you remember the time when I was like 4 years old and me and you and Tanya were at the park and that big kid pushed me down and kicked me?" he asked while looking for a place to sit on the bed.

She nodded.

"And like out of nowhere you tackled him and beat his face into the ground."

She nodded again and maybe smiled a little.

"I thought that you were the bravest and strongest girl in the whole world... Well Whit, I still think that. I really do. You know how to fight."

"No, I don't... I can't," she cried.

"Yes, you can. You can do it. If you can't do it for yourself, then do it for me and for mom and Tanya. And do it for Stevie too. He would want you to live."

She started to shake, and he took her in his arms and held her.

He whispered in her ear, "You know, there is basketball in heaven."

The Syracuse airport is relatively small. They were taking the 6:30 a.m. flight out, which meant that they had to be at the airport at 5:00 a.m. They were both up and ready when Sandy arrived at the house at 4:30 a.m. It was a short drive to the airport, only twenty minutes. Most of the people in the check-in line were young kids in military uniforms. Sandy noticed that everyone was quiet, probably because it was so early. The line moved quickly, and Verna and Whitney only had one piece of luggage each to be checked. He walked with them as far as he could go. Sandy kissed Whitney goodbye first.

"Hey big sister. I'm going to be checking in on you all of the time because I love you and I want you to feel better soon. Okay?"

"Okay," was all she said.

Looking into her eyes, he pinched her nose like he used to do when they were kids and she clearly smiled for a second.

"Alright mom… let me know if you need anything," he said.

"I will. Thank you, Sandy, for everything. I will keep you posted on Whitney and I won't forget the promises that I made, and you don't forget yours either," she urged.

"I love you mom."

"I love you too baby. You have always been the love of my life."

"Give my best to Aunt Flo."

"I will."

She pulled him close and they embraced, neither wanting to let go first. She then turned, and the two women walked away. There were tears in Sandy's eyes as he watched the back of them. The truth is that as much as he complained about his mother, she was the only one who had any idea of who he really was. Oftentimes, Tony wanted to tell him what he should think and who he should be. It was very subtle, but he understood that Tony was hoping that he would eventually change in many ways. In contrast, Verna's love for him was unconditional. Nevertheless, he was a grown man now and at this point in his life, he needed Tony's love more.

Chapter 25

D id you get my message with the names of the books on grief counseling?" Gary asked.

Sandy replied, "Yes, I did. Thank you again. I read two of them."

"Really? What did you think?"

"I thought they were good," Sandy confirmed. "It gave me some insight into what my sister is going through."

"What about what you're going through?"

"One of the authors was talking about grieving broken relationships and she said that, 'Life sometimes needs to fall completely apart before it can come back together.' I've never heard that before; do you believe that's true?" Sandy inquired.

"Yes, I do. I think what she was talking about is that we all are inevitably faced with the loss of a relationship at some point in life, be it the death of a loved one, the loss of a job, or a bad break-up, and most people fall completely apart at first and then slowly, over time, the pieces come back together again."

"So I'm normal?" Sandy asked.

"Yes, you are…I'm sorry if you were hoping for a different answer," Gary dryly affirmed.

Both men smiled. Then there was more of that silence that Sandy had grown accustomed to when talking with Gary.

"Have you spoken to Tony yet about how you feel?" Gary posed.

"No, he's at a law conference in Albany this week," Sandy responded. He knew Gary wasn't going to like his answer, but it was the truth.

"What does Tony think of you going to counseling? Is he supportive?"

"Yes, mostly," Sandy replied with apparent hesitation.

"What do you mean?"

"He wanted me to go to a counselor who specializes in LGBTQ issues."

"Oh, I see," Gary said.

"I think he's afraid that a Christian counselor would be too judgmental and not understand what I'm going through."

"So, he's not a believer?"

"No, he's pretty much an atheist. But he was raised Roman Catholic."

"Isn't that a problem for you?" Gary solicited.

"I don't know what you mean."

"Actually, I think you do," Gary insisted.

Taken aback, Sandy confessed, "When I was at the church, he could be a little condescending at times, but that was just because he was jealous of all of the time I spent there."

"Sounds to me like it was more than that."

"Probably," Sandy whispered and bit down on his lower lip.

Gary sat up and asked, "How did you feel when he was being 'condescending'?"

"Not good."

"Did you ever tell him that?" Gary probed.

Insulted, Sandy ranted, "I get the impression that you think that I'm some kind of pushover when it comes to Tony. I'm not! It's just that I've learned that I have to pick my battles with him."

Gary calmly replied, "Sandy, that might be okay as long as you pick the *right* battles. Nobody wants to be dumped on all the time with other people's emotional crap."

"That's not the way it is with us," Sandy insisted.

"Are you afraid that if you say the wrong thing, he will leave you? Gary provoked. "Is that it?"

"Maybe, a little...yes," Sandy answered truthfully.

"Listen, you should be able to say how you really feel about anything to the person you are in a relationship with, and he should be able to say however he feels in response. Healthy relationships are the ones where people feel secure enough to be who they really are."

"I have no experience with that, so I wouldn't know," Sandy conceded.

"Come on, you make your own choices," Gary insisted. "This guy of yours doesn't *make* you do anything. Don't play the victim."

"I'm not blaming Tony, exactly," Sandy defended. "It's just that he's the best thing that has ever happened to me, and I don't want to blow it."

"Just so we're clear, you think that the best thing that *ever* happened to you is a relationship with a man who you believe is or was cheating on you?"

Sandy was seething now. He barked, "You don't know him!"

"You're right; I don't."

There was a moment of silence.

Gary finally spoke up, "Sandy, did you ever think that the real reason Tony doesn't want you talking to someone like me is because maybe he's afraid I might tell you that he's not good for you, maybe he's also afraid that you might leave him?"

"No," Sandy mouthed.

"Think about it."

Although he tried to hide it, Sandy was very angry when he left Gary's office. He felt that Gary was overly critical of his relationship. The last thing he wanted or needed was to have to defend his choices. Everybody who met Tony was impressed by him. Even his mother seemed to like him. Sandy figured that he needed to do a better job of explaining why it is that he and Tony work together. This was not about him settling for anything. Tony could literally have anyone he wanted in the whole world, and yet he chose Sandy. Moreover, they both gave their best to each other. Their relationship was special, no doubt about it.

Sandy was in a sour mood all afternoon. Verna had left him a message on his phone that they had arrived safely and that she would call him later. There was also a message from Ms. Smiley's secretary asking him to call the law office. He decided he would return that call later. He was in no mood to talk about the lawsuit.

On his way home from work, he stopped to get a haircut, which he did twice a month. The barbershop he went to was on South Salina Street in Syracuse, not too far from Mount Moriah. Benny Sanders had been cutting his hair since Sandy was a boy. Reverend Coleman used to take him there on Saturday mornings and they would both get a haircut. Benny was addicted to sports just like his father was, so the two loved to discuss the latest hot topic, which was usually something to do with football. Now a man in his late fifties, the place wasn't that busy on weekdays, probably because most of the young boys preferred a younger and more "hip" barber. Sandy liked that there was rarely a long wait anymore and he could get in and out without much fuss.

There was only one man there besides Benny when Sandy walked in. Benny was giving him a shave. Altogether, there were two barber's chairs and one sink in the shop. The unoccupied chair was always empty these days. Sandy recalled that in years past, there had been another barber who had worked alongside Benny, but he was long gone. Sandy said hello and sat down in one of the mixed-matched chairs for waiting customers. Benny acknowledged Sandy with a nod and then continued his very important conversation about the plight of the black quarterback in the NFL. Sandy smiled to himself and started looking through an old newspaper he found on the chair next to him.

Sandy was there only about ten minutes when Benny completed the shave and the man in the chair got up, paid, and left. Sandy sat in the barber's chair. Benny didn't have to ask about the haircut Sandy wanted because Sandy always got a basic fade cut, low on the sides and back, and a couple of inches on top. He just draped Sandy with the plastic cover and started cutting his hair with an electric clipper. Initially, Benny stayed with the apparent topic of the day. However, at one point he abruptly changed the subject and began to talk about an upcoming medical procedure he needed. He said that a recent MRI revealed that he had a mass on one of his kidneys and that he was scheduled for further testing later in the week. Sandy just listened while he talked. Benny sounded nervous, although he said that he wasn't worried.

It never took Benny very long to cut Sandy's hair and he was done in less than twenty minutes. Sandy got up, took a quick look at his hair in the mirror, and paid him. Benny only charged ten dollars for a fade haircut. Sandy gave him twelve.

"Thank you," Benny said.

"I hope everything works out with your doctor's appointment," Sandy offered.

"Thanks. Like I said, it's probably nothing," he said nervously. "I feel pretty good."

"I'm sure you'll be fine," Sandy encouraged.

"Hey Sandy, will you... pray for me?" Benny asked under his breath.

"Yes, I certainly will."

"No. Will you pray for me right now?" Benny begged. He suddenly looked desperate. He was perspiring and there was moisture under his nose.

Sandy's heart almost stopped. He couldn't remember the last time he had prayed; he didn't even pray when Stevie died, or at the funeral, or in the aftermath. Sandy wanted to explain to Benny that he no longer prayed for anybody or for anything, however, he could see the fear in Benny's eyes and could feel Benny's pain. He simply didn't have the heart to refuse him. He took a deep breath and placed both of Benny's hands in his, closed his eyes, and softly prayed.

"Heavenly Father, as partakers of your amazing grace, we come before you now, standing on your Word and your promises. We know you have all power in your hands and that every good thing comes from you, that healing comes from you. You said in your Word that by the stripes of Jesus we were healed. Father, I pray that you touch Benny's body and take away any and all sickness and disease that may be present in it. Father, I thank you that there is no disease in or near his kidneys, and that the works of the enemy are defeated in his life. Father, we thank you for a good report this week. Praise the name of Jesus and thank you for the blood of Jesus, which has set us free. It is in the name of Jesus that we ask and pray for these things. Amen."

When Sandy opened his eyes, he saw that Benny's eyes were full of tears. Benny thanked him, turned, and walked away. Sandy immediately walked out the door and hurried to his car. As soon as he got in, he burst into tears of his own. He was also shaking uncontrollably and felt dizzy. It was about five or ten minutes before he regained his composure enough to begin the short drive home. The cry made him feel better, the way sick people often feel better after they vomit. He remembered reading in one of the books that he just read about grief, that many people who are grieving a loss or who are experiencing symptoms of depression occasionally have episodes where they completely lose control of their emotions. Honestly, he much preferred this to having panic attacks.

Sandy was not paying attention when he drove away and he ended up driving right past Mount Moriah. He slowed down and took a hard look at the structure. Reverend Coleman was so proud of the church that he had built. One of the biggest problems in the black churches that no one wants to talk about, is how the pastors were all in competition with one another over matters like whose church was the biggest and who had the best choir. Many secretly desired to be recognized by local officials, such as the mayor or the police department, as one of the key leaders of influence in the community. Even though his own father may not have always had the best motives when it came to church growth and development, Reverend Coleman always worked hard and acted in the best interest of his congregation. He literally gave his last breath to them, which is one of the reasons that Sandy had so many fond memories of growing up in the church.

***

Tony called at 11:00 p.m. He sounded like he had been drinking. Sandy could always tell when Tony was drinking by how loudly he spoke.

"Where are you?" Sandy asked.

"I'm at Shorty's. A group of us went out for a few after work. What are you doing?"

"I'm watching the news."

"How was your day? How was your counseling session?" Tony shouted.

"It's a long story."

"Do you want me to come by later?"

"No, "Sandy admitted. "You need to be careful driving home tonight."

"I think I can make it there. It's not that far," Tony insisted.

"It's far enough. Why take the chance? We can see each other tomorrow night."

"Sandy, don't you miss me?" Tony inquired.

"Yes, of course I do. I just don't want anything bad to happen to you."

"Yeah, I guess...maybe I will see you tomorrow then," Tony said.

"Goodnight," Sandy said softly.

"Goodnight, Sandy Baby. I love you."

"Me too," Sandy replied.

The truth is that Sandy really wanted to be alone. He felt pretty beat down and he didn't want to have to pretend otherwise. He needed time to think—and frankly, to feel sorry for himself. Tony's presence just complicated matters. Reverend Coleman used to talk about couples being "unequally yoked." His father thought that it was a mistake for a Christian to marry or to "join with" an unbeliever because their goals and foundational bases are not the same. He would say, "You cannot tie a strong ox with a weak one because they just go around and around in circles and the field never gets plowed." For some reason, that description always made sense to Sandy, although he had no experience with farming. However, he and Tony were not married, and he never thought about being "yoked" to him. Still, Sandy could not deny that Tony tended to put down everything Christian at every opportunity, and that Sandy felt disrespected every time that he did it.

He slept soundly, considering all he had been through that day. He only woke up once during the night and was able to fall right back into a light sleep until 5 a.m. He had forgotten to return the call to Ms. Smiley's office yesterday and made a mental reminder to do so today. Sandy was very much aware that he needed to come up with more activities to fill his day. The problem was that he had no interest in anything. Taking that class at the community college didn't help. When he was employed at the church, there was always something that should have been done yesterday, and he had thrived on that kind of energy. All this down time was killing him. He thought it was odd that Gary never said anything about that.

Sandy was on his way to work when his phone rang. He answered without checking to see who it was.

"Hello."

"Hey Sandy, did you hear the news?" Tony asked.

"What news?"

"About Julio. He's dead."

"Dead?"

"Yes, they found him in some crack house in Baltimore. Someone shot him and another guy too. It looks like some kind of drug deal gone bad or something. It was on the news."

"Are they sure?" Sandy asked.

"Sounds like it. What are you going to do? Are you going to tell your sister?"

"Yes, I think that I would need to tell her that her husband is dead, don't you? Good thing she's not here. I'm honestly not sure what kind of response this will trigger in her."

"How about you? You okay?" Tony asked.

"Yes. I'm good," Sandy replied.

"Call if you need something."

Sandy smiled and said, "Okay. Thanks. Have a good day."

"You too," Tony echoed.

Sandy wasn't quite sure what to make of this turn of events. As far as he knew, no one in his family was ever that preoccupied with finding Julio. At least, they hadn't spoken about it. The important thing was just getting through this loss as a family. A part of Sandy wanted Julio to suffer for what he did to Stevie, and death seemed too easy a way out for him. That anyone could be that evil was incomprehensible.

He had to wait until his break to call his mother. She hadn't heard anything, but she, too, just accepted the information for what it was worth. Apparently, they had found a counselor for Whitney and her first appointment was scheduled for next week. Verna thought it best to ask the counselor what they should say to Whitney. That made sense to Sandy because the last thing that he wanted to do was to push his sister over the edge. Obviously, she needed to be told, but there didn't seem to be any pressing reason to do it right now.

There was so much going on inside of his head. The good thing was that his job was stress-free and the work often helped him to think. He still hadn't made any effort to get to know any of his coworkers. He was friendly enough, but he hadn't befriended any one of them. That is one of the reasons that he was genuinely surprised when so many of them showed up at the calling hours. He laughed at their jokes and pretended to be interested when the conversation turned to sports or something worse, but normally he just ate his lunch alone or with whoever happened to be sitting at the same table as him.

At the conclusion of his shift, he was handed a flyer by one of the managers. It was for a retirement party for Tim Money, his direct supervisor. Tim was a good guy and was the one who had hired Sandy. He had also come to the calling hours. Sandy knew that there was probably no way he could get out of going. The party was being held at a small Italian restaurant on the east side of Syracuse on Sunday at 7:00 p.m. The cost was forty dollars dollars, which included the collective gift that the team was giving to Tim. Too bad that he couldn't just donate without having to attend the event. He resigned himself to the fact that he was just going to have to suck it up and go.

Just as Sandy was getting into his car to go home, Tony called again.

"What's for dinner, Honey?" Tony joked.

"I don't know. What are you cooking?"

Tony laughed, "I was thinking pizza and wings."

"That works."

When Tony arrived at 7:30 p.m., Sandy was in the shower. Tony was waiting for him on the bed when he came out. As a result, dinner was delayed. As he lay there afterward, Sandy thought about what Gary had said about talking to Tony about his feelings. Sandy finally admitted to himself that he didn't really want to raise the issue again. He just didn't see the point. After all, what was done was done. Tony obviously knew that he wasn't happy about the situation. While he knew in his heart that Tony had been unfaithful, he also believed that Tony was sincerely remorseful. Tony was nothing like Reverend Coleman. Sandy concluded that he was going to have to tell Gary that he had decided to just let sleeping dogs lie.

Chapter 26

M s. Smiley wanted Sandy to come into the office. She said it was important and that he might want to bring Tony. Sandy was a little offended that she thought he needed help making sound decisions about his case. Regardless, he knew Tony was not available. Sandy still wasn't fond of going to his lawyer's office and he had to talk himself up just to get himself to walk through the front door. She agreed to meet with him after hours and he drove there directly from work. She said that it wouldn't take too long. The office was closed when he arrived, but the door was open and the lights were on.

"Sandy, come on in," she called out.

"Hi," he said as he walked through the door.

"Hi. Have a seat. How are you?"

"I'm good," he said. He was nervous.

"Sandy, do you recall the last time we spoke, and I told you that the church had made a motion to have our lawsuit dismissed?"

"Yes, I remember."

"Well, last week I put in an opposition to their motion. It usually takes months, sometimes up to a year or so, before the magistrate decides these motions. But I got a call this week from

David Smith, the church's lawyer. He said that the church would be willing to make us an offer of settlement right now."

"What kind of settlement?" he asked.

"They are willing to offer you two years' salary plus attorney's fees. Of, course there will be no reinstatement to your former position."

"I don't want to go back there," Sandy blurted out.

"I know."

"Why do they want to settle now?" He asked.

"I don't really know the answer to that," she admitted. "I would like to say that it's because my opposition papers were so good that they are running scared, but I really don't think that's it. Sandy, there are many reasons why people choose to settle, and not all of them have anything to do with who ultimately has the best chance of winning the case. Most of the time, it simply comes down to costs. Litigation costs run high, so often it's about finding the cheapest and most cost-efficient way to get rid of the case."

"So, what do you think we should do?" he asked.

"Well that really is your call," she articulated.

"I know, but what do you think I should do?"

She signed heavily and moved her chair closer to him.

She began slowly, "I believe that I mentioned to you that the church has a pretty good defense. No court is going to tell any church that they have to hire or retain someone in a ministerial position who the church thinks is not qualified for moral reasons. In response to the motion, I argued essentially that you were not a "minister" in the true sense of the word, but I'm not sure that the court will buy that. And even if the court denies the church's motion and sets this down for a jury trial, there still is a good chance that we could lose with a jury. In this district, juries are very unpredictable. People who live outside of Syracuse, say in Oswego county or Binghamton, are very conservative and might not be overly sympathetic to a gay man who hid his sexuality from his employer, a church."

"Sounds to me like you think we should settle," Sandy asserted.

"I'm just trying to be realistic so you can make the best decision. I'm willing to take our chances if you are, but you have to recognize that there is a risk. I believe both you and your mother are terrific people and I think that I can get the jury to see that, but that alone might not be enough to win the case."

"Well—" he hesitated.

"Sandy, I have to be honest with you," she interrupted. "When I first met you, I looked at it this case as being about discrimination. But the truth is that that is only a small part of it. This case has more of the feel of a divorce. Please don't take this the wrong way, but you and this Reverend Glenn act much like a couple who are divorcing, and divorces are usually messy. I watched the two of you at the depositions and it is clear that you both have hurt feelings and there is plenty of anger because trust was broken. But it is also readily apparent that the two of you are family and you will always have that connection, regardless of whether you like it or not. This is not my typical wrongful termination case. When this case is all over, no matter how it goes, the two of you—meaning you and him or you and your church—are going to have to find some common ground going forward. Otherwise, the dysfunction will eat away at you both."

"I really do want this to be over," he conceded.

"I know you do," she sympathized. "I always knew that your heart was not in this litigation. You have good reason to be angry, but no one is going to think less of you if you just walk away now."

"I think that is what I want to do," he said boldly.

"I also should tell you that you also have the option of making a counteroffer if you think that this is not enough money. Maybe I can get them to come up a little."

"No, I don't want you to do that."

She added, "They also want you to sign a confidentiality agreement, in which you agree to keep the terms of the settlement confidential."

"That's not a problem," he said.

"Sandy, do you have any other questions?"

"No, I don't think so."

"Okay, you can call me later if you do. Would you like some time to think about it?'

"No, I don't need any time."

"Then I will call Dave tomorrow and tell him that we have a deal, alright?"

"Yes," he said and exhaled loudly.

"For what it's worth, I think you are doing the right thing," she offered.

"Thank you for everything," he said.

"You are very welcome."

Sandy hurried to his car. He felt relieved. Was this really over? He really needed to move on with his life and he was glad that he no longer had to worry about having to testify in open court about his private life. Just the thought of it terrified him and kept him up at night. He really hoped that Tony saw it the way that Ms. Smiley did. The fact is that Tony was very invested in this lawsuit now for reasons of his own, and Sandy didn't want to let him down.

Nevertheless, the decision was his to make and he really didn't want to be challenged on his reasons for wanting the case settled. Had it not been for Tony, he probably wouldn't have sued Mount Moriah in the first place. Not that he was blaming Tony, because he was not. He realized that Tony was only looking out for him. However, the entire process was weighing on him heavily, and at this point he needed to be free to focus his energies on something more positive.

He called Tony from the car. They agreed to meet for dinner downtown near the campus at this little place that they liked called Coco's. Tony and Marco knew the owner and his husband. The food was basic American cuisine and frankly, it wasn't that good. Nonetheless, the atmosphere often made it worth the price of admission. One night, the entire restaurant spontaneously erupted into a medley of Madonna songs.

Sandy arrived first and got a table. There were only two other people in the whole place, and both men were seated together. He noticed that one of them was somewhat attractive, although he was heavily tattooed. Sandy wasn't a fan of tattoos on most people, and this guy had one on the side of his face just below his right ear. He preferred the clean-cut all-American look. The guy, who appeared to be in his mid-twenties, smiled at Sandy a couple of times. Sandy didn't think much of it and just figured that he was probably a graduate student or something, trying to flirt behind his boyfriend's back.

Tony walked in fifteen minutes later and ordered a beer as soon as he sat down. Sandy told him about his meeting with Ms. Smiley. Tony listened without expression and asked a couple of questions about the motion that Sandy could not answer. At first it seemed like Tony was critical of the church's offer, but Sandy was relieved when he said that he agreed with Ms. Smiley that the settlement was probably for the best.

"It just bothers me that these people are never held accountable for their actions," Tony argued.

"What do you mean? They are going to pay me, not the other way around."

"I know. But they still think that they were right, and that it's open season on gays."

"I don't think that's true at all," Sandy protested. "They don't want me leading worship, which in the end is their call."

"And you're okay with that?" Tony snapped.

"It's not my decision; it's not my church," Sandy shot back.

"Not anymore—they made sure of that," Tony pronounced and took a big gulp of his beer.

Sandy whispered, "Even Ms. Smiley said that they had a good chance of winning in court."

"Well, maybe so, but that's one of the reasons this country is lagging behind the rest of the world; shallow thinking by ignorant people."

"You judge others so harshly while objecting when you feel judged," Sandy countered.

"I'm sorry, but I'm not the one who believes that we should live our lives according to a book written over two thousand years ago by people who believed that the earth was flat and that a man could live inside of the belly of a whale."

Sandy was offended.

He quickly decided that he wasn't going to say anything else on the subject. As kind and as loving as Tony could be, it scared Sandy that he continued to be oblivious to the hurt he caused with his words. It wasn't worth it either to try to make him see it, because he only dug his heels in deeper when he was pushed. Sandy wasn't bothered by the fact that he and Tony had a difference of opinion on a matter, but Tony showed such disdain for anyone who dared to disagree with him. It was becoming more and more apparent that Tony didn't respect him as an equal.

Several people came into the restaurant while they ate their dinner and Tony knew a few of them. At one point during the evening, he struck up a conversation with one of the other patrons about the problems with absentee landlords and college students, and Sandy just pretended to listen to their exchange. The night ended with Sandy saying that he didn't feel well and that he was going home. Tony wanted to finish his beer. He gave Sandy a brief kiss goodbye and turned away quickly as Sandy headed for the front door. By the time that he reached the exit, Tony was already talking to someone else.

Chapter 27

Sandy arrived for the retirement party right at 7:00 p.m. and the parking lot was almost completely full. He took one of the few parking spots that were left. He had never been to this restaurant before, although he had driven past it a thousand times. From the outside it looked small, but turned out to be much larger inside than it appeared.

The main door of the restaurant opened to the bar. There was loud music playing as well as the sound of people talking and laughing over the television. A waitress crossed in front of him carrying a tray of drinks, and he asked her for the location of the retirement party. She directed him to a back room, which meant that he had to walk through the crowd at the bar. Obviously, Sandy was never a bar person, so he couldn't quite understand why anyone would want to stand around in a crowded room and shout at each other in order to be heard.

As he was walking through, one of the men standing at the bar said "hi" to him. Although he looked familiar, Sandy didn't recognize him, and he just said "hi" back in response and kept moving. The room where the party was to take place was only halfway full. Servers were still setting up and bringing in food for a buffet. There were ten round tables covered with tablecloths with place settings and flowered centerpieces. Up front was another table that was clearly the head table with a podium next to it.

Sandy took the first open seat that he saw in the back. There was no one else sitting at the table. He felt a little uncomfortable at first, but two coworkers from the warehouse came in just a few minutes after he did, and they sat with him. The table eventually filled up, as did the rest of the room. The conversation was light, and Sandy became more at ease. Tim, the guest of honor, and his wife came in last, and everyone stood and applauded as they walked to their table.

It ended up being a nice celebration, and Sandy had a good time. The food was good, and all the speakers were entertaining; except for Tim, who spoke too long and told too many inside jokes that most people there couldn't possibly appreciate. One of the guys sitting next to Sandy was very funny and Sandy laughed so hard a couple of times that he almost lost his breath. It felt good to laugh and not think about how screwed up his life was.

The party officially ended a little after nine, but Sandy stayed longer because no one sitting at his table had left yet. Tim and his wife had relocated themselves to the next table, and the fun continued while the servers cleaned up around them.

Tony had texted him once, wanting to know where he was, and Sandy quickly responded to his inquiry. It was not until almost ten that everyone decided to break it up and head home.

Sandy needed to go to the men's room before driving home. There were several people still sitting at the bar, but most had already left. There was no one in the bathroom and he was standing at the urinal when he heard the door open. After he finished, he turned to see a guy standing there looking at him. It was the same guy who had said hello to him at the bar earlier when he first walked into the restaurant. Sandy still wasn't sure who he was.

"Hi," the young man said.

"Hi."

The man walked over and opened the door to one of the two stalls that was there.

"You coming?" he asked provocatively.

"What?"

"Come on," he said as he raised both of his eyebrows and gestured to the inside of the stall.

Without much hesitation, Sandy walked toward the stall. The guy pulled him inside, closed the door behind them and immediately pushed Sandy's back up against the wall. He then pressed the front of his body up against Sandy's and using his right hand he easily brought Sandy to a state of arousal. He then dropped to his knees. Altogether, they were in the stall for about ten to fifteen minutes. They never spoke, and the guy left first. Sandy kept his eyes closed and barely looked at him, but he did recognize the tattoo on the right side of his face.

When Sandy came out of the stall, the guy was gone. He walked over to the mirror and stared at his reflection for about a minute before leaving.

He drove home without giving any thought at all to what he had just done. He was calm and controlled. He didn't plan for that to happen, and what was done was done. People experiment sexually all the time, and he dismissed this as nothing more than an aberration. Maybe he was finally starting to grow up.

Mel didn't greet him at the door when he arrived home, but he just figured that the cat was sleeping somewhere. He immediately went into the bathroom, turned on the shower, took off his clothes and got in. The water felt good and it relaxed him even more. He hated having to get out. After getting dressed, he got into bed and turned the light off. He fell asleep almost immediately and slept the entire night through.

Chapter 28

Sandy was in a pretty good mood when he arrived for his counseling appointment. However, after what happened in his last session, he had decided that he would no longer allow Gary to criticize or judge his relationship with Tony. On this subject, he was not willing to compromise. Although he didn't have all the answers, a life without Tony in it was unimaginable. Simply stated, he was not going to allow Gary—or anyone else for that matter—to put doubts in his head.

"How was your week?" Gary began.

"Good," he replied, trying to sound upbeat.

"How are you sleeping? And how is it going with the medication?"

"I'm definitely sleeping better. I'm still taking the medication, but I'm starting to think that I don't need it anymore."

"Really? What makes you think that?" Gary asked.

"I guess because I'm sleeping better. I just feel more in control."

"In what way?" Gary probed.

"Looks like my lawsuit is going to settle, so at least I don't have to worry about a trial. That's such a big relief. I can't tell you how much of a relief that is. And I have pretty much accepted everything that has happened, and I just want to move on."

"I heard on the news that they found the man who murdered your nephew. How do you feel about that?"

"I'm glad about it, I guess. I never knew Julio, so I'm just relived that he is out of my sister's life for good and we don't have to worry about him anymore," Sandy asserted.

"Do you think about it in terms of justice for your nephew?"

Sandy responded without hesitation, "No, I don't. I don't even know what 'justice' is anymore."

"I just meant, did you want to see him punished for what he did? Many people in your shoes would want him to suffer."

"I'm human, so I guess that a part of me did want him to really suffer...but like I said, I'm just glad he's gone forever."

"You just mentioned that you settled your lawsuit, are you happy with the settlement, or are you just glad that you won't be called to testify?"

"Both. It's not a lot of money, but this was never about the money for me anyway."

"What was it about?"

"Discrimination," Sandy stated.

"Do you feel vindicated?"

"I wouldn't say that exactly. It's more like I feel less victimized."

Gary nodded his head in agreement. He was thinking and sat motionless for a few seconds.

"What is the name of this church again?" Gary wondered.

"Mount Moriah Baptist," Sandy answered.

"Is that Bobby Jones' church?"

"No, that's United Love."

"Mount Moriah? What is the significance of that? Isn't that the name of the mountain in Jerusalem, right?"

Sandy explained, "Yes, it's the place where the Temple was located in the Old Testament and also the place where God supposedly told Abraham to sacrifice his son Isaac."

"Ah, that's right. That's always been one of the stories in the Bible that has baffled me. The idea that God would ask Abraham to sacrifice his beloved son seems out of character for God. I understand that the point is to show the importance of having faith, but you must wonder about a God who would ask such a thing. I don't think that many people today could do what Abraham did. That is probably one of the reasons that human sacrifices are later condemned in the Bible. It seems contradictory."

"No, I get it," Sandy replied. "That was the Old Testament. Today we are supposed to offer our own bodies to God as a sacrifice. That's why we can't do whatever we want with our bodies."

"I don't believe I know what you mean," Gary said.

"See, God demands our obedience. He means what he says, and it's no joke. Abraham was obedient to do what God told him to do, even though he didn't understand it because he was afraid of what would happen if he disobeyed God. As a result, God rewarded his fear by sparing Isaac in the end. But nobody fears God today. Many people love him, or at least the idea of God, but few actually fear him."

"That's really interesting. I have to think about that," Gary acknowledged. "I generally think of the idea of fearing God as having reverence for him, not actually being afraid of what he might do to us. I probably need to go back and read the story again," he mused.

"Do you mind if I ask you whether you have forgiven the folks at the church for what they did to you now that the case is over?" Gary raised and shifted in his seat.

Sandy shook his head and explained, "I don't know. No one has asked for my forgiveness."

"I don't believe that's how it works, do you?" Gary asked.

"I know," Sandy conceded.

"What about your father?"

"What about him?"

"You still haven't gotten to the place where you can forgive him for the way he was with you, have you?"

Sandy rolled his eyes and coolly responded, "No, so what?"

"Why not?"

"Because he didn't ask me to either," Sandy laughed to himself.

"You do know that it is not good to hold grudges against people. Unforgiveness is like cancer to you, not to them. It is *your* issue to be faced."

"I know..." Sandy hesitated, "look, I loved my father, but I really didn't like him very much," Sandy stated and searched his heart. He paused in thought again before answering. "I guess that I just never understood him. I wish that it could have been different between us. I don't know what else you want me to say."

"No, I get it," Gary interjected. "What about Tony? Have you forgiven him?"

"There is nothing to forgive him for," Sandy snarled.

"Really? That's very generous of you. Most people have a real problem with their partner's infidelity," Gary contended. "Have you spoken to him like we talked about?"

"No, I didn't. Everybody makes mistakes, including me. I know how he feels about me. That's all that really matters. Can we just drop it, please?"

"You sound like a high school girl who just found out that her boyfriend kissed a cheerleader under the bleachers after the football game just before the big homecoming dance," Gary said in a dismissive manner.

"I don't think that's fair," Sandy protested.

"Fair?" Gary exclaimed. "What kind of mistakes have *you* made?"

"Never mind...you'd be surprised."

"Try me," Gary dared.

"No. I'm not playing this game," Sandy insisted.

"It's not a game. You brought it up, not me"

"Why do you care?" Sandy resisted.

"Why are you so afraid of the truth?" Gary taunted.

"I had sex with a stranger," Sandy divulged.

"When?" Gary asked in disbelief.

"Last night."

"What?" Gary sat up in his chair, his face suddenly flush. "Are you just saying this to make a point? How did this happen?"

"It was only oral sex and it just happened," Sandy explained and looked away.

"How does something like that just happen?"

"We were together in the bathroom at a restaurant and—"

"Are you kidding me? You picked up a guy in a public bathroom?"

Sandy didn't say anything. He could not believe that he even told Gary what he did. It sounded gross and he was suddenly embarrassed.

"Why did you do it?" Gary demanded.

"I don't know why."

"Come on Sandy, we both know that's not true. Tell me why."

"I said I don't know why...I don't know what you want me to say!" Sandy yelled.

"I want you to tell me the truth. You had to know that you were being extremely childish and reckless. Was it some kind of a death wish or were you just trying to get back at Tony?"

"You don't understand...you can't possibly understand!"

"Explain it to me then," Gary insisted.

"No," Sandy shouted.

"Are you proud of what you did? You sure managed to get even with Tony, didn't you? Did you enjoy it? Tell me, who did who in that bathroom?" Gary mocked.

"No. Stop it! That's not it at all. What kind of counselor are you anyway? You're awful! I thought that you were supposed to be helping me!"

Sandy was seething inside.

"Tell me. Just say it. Be man enough to just say it," Gary persisted. "Why did you do it?"

"Because...because... he won't let me go!" Sandy shouted. "He won't do it! I just want to go! I made my decision and he lost! He lost! But he won't leave me alone! I don't want him anymore. It's not fair! Everybody else gets to have what they want and who they want and live however they want, but not me!"

Sandy was shaking uncontrollably.

"Who are you talking about? Tony? What do you mean he won't let you go?"

"No, I'm talking about God! I can't do what he wants. I can't. I tried, but I can't do it! I can't sacrifice who I am. Not even for him. And I don't want to. I won't! The world is full of people who are much better than me. But he keeps coming back to me. Why not just go after one of them and leave me alone?"

Sandy suddenly dropped from his chair to his knees. He covered his face with his hands and cried loudly.

Gary remained in his seat and let Sandy cry it out for about a minute. Finally, he dropped down on his knees right next to Sandy.

"Sandy, listen to me," he whispered. "All this time you have been running from God because you are afraid of him. Don't you see, you cannot truly know God without fearing him? You know him…you know him."

Sandy suddenly opened his eyes and stared at Gary. Then he lowered his head again and sobbed. Gary put his arms around him. They stayed like that until the end of the session.

Chapter 29

Reverend Glenn wasn't happy at all about the settlement with Sandy. He had let everyone on the board of trustees talk him into it. Even his own wife thought that he wasn't being reasonable. Their lawyer had informed them at a board meeting that the insurance company for the church wanted the lawsuit resolved now and that they didn't want to spend any more money defending the case. For them, it was all about the economics, but for Reverend Glenn, it was much more than that. He felt that he was being asked to compromise his principles. It seemed to him that everyone had rights except Christians.

The wake and funeral for Sandy's nephew had been hard for him too. Not that anyone had said anything out of line to him, but he felt out of place, like he didn't belong there. The whole Coleman family was understandably devastated, and he genuinely felt bad for them, especially Sandy's sister. He had never seen her before all of this happened, but he could tell that she was a very beautiful woman. It was also clear that her grief—and perhaps her guilt too—had drained all the life out of her. One of the things he had come to notice recently is that funerals today are often not quite as awful affairs as they used to be. For instance, he remembered going to the funeral of a woman in his building when he was a boy and how traumatic it was for everyone. People were screaming, wailing, and trying to take the body out of the coffin.

Things like that simply don't happen as much anymore, and he really was not sure how to account for the change. Regardless, funerals for children remained extremely taxing and emotional in most instances, especially for the parents. As a result, he disliked them immensely.

Mercy was quiet during the drive home after the calling hours. Initially, he just thought that she was feeling bad for the family. One of the things that he loved most about his wife was that she had such a caring heart. Her name suited her well. However, later that night he noticed that he was getting the cold shoulder. She barely looked his way after they got home.

"Honey, is something wrong?" he asked.

"What do you think?" was her terse response.

"Well, I don't know, which is why I asked."

"What did you say to Sandy tonight?" She demanded.

"I don't know what you're talking about."

"Yes, you do. I saw the whole thing. Whatever you said to him, you hurt his feelings. He ran out of there so fast trying to get away from you."

"Look, I didn't say anything," he protested. "He was just upset. You saw what happened when he almost fainted at the casket. That all had nothing to do with me."

"I don't believe you, so you had better listen to me, Mister," she railed. "One thing that you have never been is a mean person. Only a monster would kick someone when they're down. I'm going to continue to believe that you would never intentionally do that. I know you're angry with Sandy about the lawsuit, but don't forget who you are, and that you represent Jesus himself to a hurting world. That boy is in so much pain that I can barely look at him. It breaks my heart. He needs to feel God's love in the worse way about now, and not your judgment or your anger."

He didn't say anything, and she turned abruptly and walked away. He had learned early in their marriage that when she used that tone with him, the best thing to do was to be quiet and wait for the storm to pass. While he still didn't think that he had said anything inappropriate to Sandy, he knew she had a point. He was angry. Sandy's lawyer was a snake, and she had made him feel like he was the one on trial when he was only trying to protect his congregation. Sandy made his decision when he chose his secret lifestyle, one that is inherently incompatible with what the Bible teaches.

Although he would never admit it, he was very glad that Sandy had decided not to play the piano at the funeral. When Sister Coleman asked him about it at the funeral home, he was hardly in the position to say no. However, the other daughter had a good voice and maintained her composure well, so it was all for the best. There was no denying that many of the people there really wanted to hear Sandy play, but that would have been like fingernails on a chalkboard to him. It also would have been a slap in the face—and certainly not something that would have been pleasing to God.

He didn't personally know any gay person who was openly living a gay lifestyle. Of course, there were gay and lesbian men and women in the projects in Rochester when he was growing up, but most people made fun of them, at least behind their backs. When he was in the army, people who had those kinds of feelings knew to keep them to themselves. He understood that times were changing, but that didn't mean that all change was good. As he said at his deposition, the world is a dark place and has been corrupted by lust. In his opinion, homosexuality is a sin primarily because it is rebellion against God. Scripture is clear that the unrighteous will not inherent the kingdom of God.

Honestly, a big part of it for him, too, was that the idea of two men being together in that way was extremely distasteful to him. Nevertheless, on some level, he probably did get it. The desires of the flesh are powerful, and our bodies tend to crave what we give it. The more we eat fast food, the more we want it. To some extent, our carnal desires are the enemy. In the end, sex is sex, and forbidden fruit is always sweet. That is one of the reasons the Bible teaches that we must crucify our flesh, meaning bring it into submission to the Word of God.

It would probably have come as a surprise to many of his members to learn that he was not exactly opposed to gay marriage, at least not in the abstract. In his view, one of God's greatest gifts to humanity is freewill, and all adults should be able to live their lives however they choose, if doing so doesn't infringe upon the rights of others. He never believed in legislating morality. The church is called to be light in the darkness, not out campaigning to force nonbelievers to act and live the way that we believe they should. Everyone has the right to reject the gospel and its truths. In his opinion, this is where many Christians are missing it.

Indeed, he had heard many people make the comparison of the struggles of blacks in this country—which led to the civil rights movement of the 1960s—to the current plight of homosexuals. The contention is that we should be the first to sympathize with their predicament, having been oppressed ourselves; however, what they don't understand is that the black church in America will never entirely embrace the gay agenda, because to do so is an affront to the God who loved us first and set us free from bondage. Our fight and our struggles are not the same as their battles.

As the senior pastor, he understood that his voice has great influence in the lives of his members, so he was trying hard not to be too alarmed by all the hostility in the world being directed at Christians today. He wished that he could have said he was surprised by it, but he really wasn't. History clearly sets forth how much the early church was despised and persecuted. It only made sense that it was all coming back around again, and believers should expect persecution for the sake of the gospel. However, many so called "religious right," have so spiritualized their politics that they have almost completely lost their humanity. God is not registered democrat or republican, nor is he liberal or conservative. God is God, and his thoughts and ways are so much higher than ours.

The one thing that Glenn was most certain of was that God is love, and that means he loves everyone—including the homosexual. The way he saw it, all men are born with a sinful nature. However, Jesus said that he didn't come into the world to condemn anyone, and that his heart's desire is for all men to be saved. Therefore, he fully recognized that the church must have a merciful attitude toward all sinners, including those who are homosexual. Nevertheless, sin should never be overlooked, especially in the lives of the men and women who are called to lead in the church.

Just prior to their explosive meeting when Sandy was let go, Glenn honestly expected that Sandy would just go away without much of a fuss, knowing that his sin had been exposed. There was nothing malicious on his part. He didn't intentionally go to work that morning looking for a fight. Truthfully, he had been dreading it. The only thing that he would change if he could, was that he had become so angry. Unfortunately, when Sandy challenged him, he lost his temper, and the whole thing escalated rapidly to a place he never had intended it to go. It was never in his heart to condemn Sandy or to hurt him. For that, he was ashamed and truly sorry.

Only a few of his members had been bold enough to ask him directly about what had happened with Sandy. His response was always that Sandy had decided to resign for personal reasons. The problem was that he had never instructed his staff as to how to answer that question. It just never occurred to him. As a result, word got out quickly and there was a bit of a fallout afterward because most of the congregation really loved Sandy and his father, especially the music people. Therefore, he had to admit that he hadn't handled that part of it as well as he would have liked to.

When Sandy first sued the church, it was the talk of the congregation for months. Understandably, most of the older members, especially those in leadership, saw Sandy's actions as an act of betrayal and they circled around their pastor. He had considered addressing the subject from the pulpit or publicly in some manner, but he thought better of it. There were still many people who were loyal to both Sandy and his mother, and he didn't want anything that he said to offend them—or worse—to be used against him in court.

Recently, he had been having dreams where he was testifying in court, and the judge and the jury were all laughing at him. In the dreams, the more that he answered questions coming from Sandy's lawyer, the harder they laughed. He had the same dream several times, and each time he was covered in sweat when he woke up. He was hopeful that now that the case had been settled, maybe the nightmares would stop.

Fortunately, Mount Moriah weathered the loss of Sandy Coleman quite nicely after all, as he knew that it would. Clearly, the worship at the church took a couple of steps backward, but he was confident that they could get it back to where it was under Sandy. The way he saw it, God always has a ram in the bush. The new kid seemed to be growing a little every week. God's word was more important than the music anyway.

He had just learned that Sister Coleman left the church and moved to Florida with her daughter. She never mentioned to him or to Mercy that she was leaving Syracuse, but he was not particularly offended by that. The talk was that the daughter was still struggling greatly, and that they needed to get her to some kind of specialist as soon as possible. Hopefully the move will be good for both of them. Obviously, he wasn't at all sorry to see Sister Coleman go. Her presence had been divisive from the beginning, whether she intended it to be or not. However, his heart did go out to her and he continued to pray for their entire family.

Glenn was also trying to expand his own horizons a little. Unlike his predecessor, he had never had any interest in preaching away from his home church. It just made him too nervous. Some ministers were called to just be a pastor of a local church, and there was nothing wrong with that. However, two months ago he was invited to speak at a church in the Rochester area, and he had reluctantly accepted. To his complete surprise, he was very well received. He was so encouraged afterward that he accepted another invitation from an old classmate to preach at a church in Toledo, Ohio.

The problem was that the engagement was scheduled for the upcoming weekend and he still hadn't finished writing his message, and it was already Tuesday. He had been planning to rework a message that he had preached at Mount Moriah several months back, but he needed to add to it. He had been so busy lately that he kept putting off working on it. He promised himself that he would go back to the church that night after dinner when no one was else was there and work in his office until he had finished it.

Chapter 30

S andy was still sad, but this was different. Gone was the feeling of hopelessness. Oddly, he had more hope than he had had in a long time. Hope for exactly what, however, he was unsure. He was a mess when he left Gary's office after his last counseling session. So much of a mess that Gary asked him if he was okay to drive. He was clearly in no condition to go to work, so he called-in sick. For some reason, he drove to his mother's house instead of going to his apartment.

It was so quiet there. This was the first time he had been in the house since Verna and Whitney left. The truth is that, as unhappy as he had been there at times during his youth, he had always felt safe there. That was mostly due to Verna, who kept him grounded. The problem was that he had never needed her the way that she wanted to be needed. That is, she wanted to be involved in every aspect of his life so she could protect him from any and every harm. However, that was just way too much Verna for anyone. Rather, he just needed to know that she was there if he needed her. It had always been his desire to test the waters of life on his own. She never seemed to have understood that about him and had interpreted his resistance to be rejection. He hoped that there was still time for them.

He slowly walked up the stairs to his old room. It was still mostly the same as it was when he had left to move into his own apartment years ago. It smelled the same too, not like him exactly, but like the stuff his mother used for cleaning furniture. He took in a big whiff. He opened the closet door and wasn't surprised to see that some of his old clothes still hung there. Even one of his costumes from when he was in the high school play was still there. He smiled to himself because he remembered it like it was yesterday. Verna was so proud of him that she could hardly contain herself. As he recalled, even Reverend Coleman seemed pleased.

As he sat down on the bed, so many memories rushed through his mind. He had felt so alone as a teenager, but the truth was that he never really was. Once we give our lives to Christ, we are never alone; and we can never just walk away from God either. That is, either we stay or we die; those are the only choices. He could see that clearly now.

His existence was never as tortured as he had thought. He certainly was better off than most of the people he knew, especially his sisters. Sadly, he was just so blinded, and because of that, he had spent so many wasted hours lying on his bed feeling sorry for himself. He used to wish that his life could be different. Now he only wished that he could go back somehow.

Perhaps for the first time in his entire life, he was not afraid of what was in store for him in the future. He knew beyond a shadow of a doubt that God had a plan for him and he didn't have to figure it out. He just needed to be obedient. In this regard, he knew what he had to do next— and just the idea of it cut him to the core. He had to accept the fact that this whole thing was his fault. Instinctively, he began to pray. However, he didn't pray for his own strength or for courage, or even for Jesus to intervene on his behalf and change his circumstances. Rather, from the very depths of his heart, he prayed for Tony.

He spent the rest of the day at his mother's house. He didn't want to leave. Somehow he managed to take a two-hour nap and he felt better when he woke up. Back at his apartment, he decided to pack up all of Tony's things. There wasn't much, some toiletries, underwear, a pair of jeans, a couple of shirts, and a sweater. There were also some work papers that Tony had left lying around. He put all of them in a box. After he finished, he called Tony.

"Hi, what's up?" Tony answered.

"Nothing. How are you?"

"I'm good."

"Am I going to see you tonight?" Sandy asked.

"I'm sorry, Babe, but I can't. Working late again. How about tomorrow night?"

"Okay. How about I make you dinner at your place."

"My place?"

"Yeah, I have to be downtown anyway. I could just go there afterward."

"That's okay with me, but you know it's not clean," Tony replied.

"Yes, I know. Any idea what time you'll get home?"

"Probably around seven, is that okay?"

"Perfect. I'll see you then," Sandy uttered with feigned optimism.

"Sandy, are you okay?"

"Yes, why?"

"I don't know. You just sound different."

"No. I'm good. See you tomorrow."

"Okay. Goodnight, Sandy Baby."

"Goodnight." Sandy hung up. He could literally feel his heart breaking inside of his chest and he cried on and off for the rest of the night.

He was pretty much a zombie at work the next day. He probably should have called in sick again, but he really didn't have any more sick time to use. He tried to stay focused on the work but he simply couldn't think straight. The day seemed to drag along. Twice he had to be redirected, and he forgot to sign out at the end of the day and had to go back to do that. Everything seemed to be moving in slow motion, even traffic. Finally he arrived at Tony's apartment at 5:45 p.m. He had to make two trips from the car because, in addition to the bag of groceries that he had purchased on his way to work that morning, he also had the box with Tony's stuff in it. He put the box in the hall closet where Tony wouldn't see it right away and cleaned the kitchen before starting dinner. He also gathered up his own possessions from the bathroom, put them in a bag, and carried it out to his car. Tony walked through the door at 7:15 p.m.

"Honey, I'm home."

"Hi," Sandy said. They kissed.

"Spaghetti? Did you get the sauce I like?" Tony asked.

"What do you think?" Sandy asked playfully.

"What did you have to do downtown?"

"What?" Sandy responded.

"You said that you had to be downtown today for something,"

"Oh, I needed to go to the health food store," Sandy lied.

Tony went into the bedroom, presumably to change his clothes and to freshen up. Sandy told himself that he needed to settle down. It was important that this evening be special. He realized that Tony would get suspicious if he acted too much out of the ordinary. When Tony came back, he had changed into a t-shirt and jeans. He sat down at the table and immediately began to talk about his most recent case. Sandy gave him a beer and tried to listen as he continued to set the table.

Dinner went well. Tony complimented him on the food and he seemed to be in a good mood. Sandy almost broke when Tony brought up again the subject of them taking a vacation to the Caribbean. He just promised to look into it and continued eating. After dinner, Tony insisted on cleaning the kitchen by himself so Sandy went into the bedroom and turned on the television. Later, Tony came in and cuddled up next to him as they watched a movie.

The lovemaking that night was wonderful, but they had always been good together. Sandy had never felt that connected to another person before, and that was a large part of it for him. As much as he was an introvert and a loner, he hated that feeling of being all by himself in the world. He desperately desired to be fully known and accepted by another person, and Tony filled that void mostly. He was going to miss this. The physical connection was undeniable; being with Tony seemed so natural, so right. As he drifted off to sleep, a part of him was hoping that he would never wake back up again.

When he opened his eyes, the clock on the nightstand read 3:00 a.m. He laid there for several minutes listening to the sound of Tony breathing. There was a small amount of light in the room coming from the streetlight just outside the window. Tony was slightly snoring. Then Sandy got out of bed slowly and went into the bathroom to get dressed. There were no words to express exactly how he felt. His body was infirmed. His brain was numb.

Tony was still in a deep sleep when he returned, and Sandy hated to have to wake him. He sat down on the bed and just watched Tony sleep. He looked so peaceful, almost childlike. Then he pulled back the covers so he could see all of his lover's naked body. He couldn't help himself and he took the opportunity to study every curve, every detail of every muscle. He breathed in the smell of him and gently touched his back. This was probably a mistake, and he knew it, but he didn't really care. He wanted to be able to remember—he needed to remember for now.

"Tony?" he whispered. "Tony?"

"Yea, what's wrong?" he asked while rubbing his eyes.

"Nothing's wrong," Sandy said with tears streaming down his face. "This is goodbye. I love you, but we can't be together anymore. I'm so sorry. I hope you can forgive me one day."

"What? What are you talking about?" Tony mumbled and sat up, still dazed.

"I have to go now. Please try to understand."

Sandy started to walk away. He had been hoping to get away without a scene and without Tony trying to talk him out of leaving. But he wasn't fast enough, and Tony caught up to him before he reached the front door and grabbed him by the arm. A slight struggle ensued.

"Wait! Sandy, I don't understand. Did something happen?"

"No, nothing happened. I just know now that I made a big mistake being with you. I have to go," Sandy cried.

"What? This is crazy. What are you talking about?"

"I'm so sorry," Sandy sobbed.

"Did you really think I was going to just let you leave like that?" Tony shouted.

"All I am is broken pieces. Please just let me go. I can't breathe!" Sandy begged and tried to walk away again.

"Sandy, please…can't we just try to get to the bottom of this?" Tony pleaded. "I know that you're upset, but can't we just talk?"

"I don't want to talk. I just want to leave. If you love me, then you'll let me go."

"I do love you and I will never let you go. We belong together!"

"No, can't you see that I'm dying here, bit by bit?" Sandy appealed. "Every day, there is a little less of me. If I don't leave now while I can, I'm going to die. Is that what you want? For me to die? I know you see it. I know that you do! Tony, please just let me go!"

"No, I won't let you go. I won't do it. What is this, some kind of Jesus nonsense or something? That's it, isn't it? Can't you see that those people don't care anything about you? It's all a lie! There is no God…and if there is, he doesn't care anything about you or me."

"That's the lie. You don't know him!" Sandy erupted.

"Oh, really. They fired you and outed you without as much as a second thought. They are weak-minded, controlling people who thrive on feeling superior to other people. Please don't let them tear us apart. Hurting yourself by denying who you really are and what you want is not going to change anything. It won't bring Stevie back, and it won't satisfy them. What kind of God can't accept our love? It just doesn't make sense!"

"Tony, I'm sorry, I really am. But you will find someone else better for you than me." Sandy turned and opened the door. "I love you."

"No! No!" Tony followed him onto the front porch. "I don't want anyone else. Please don't leave me. You don't have to do this. Sandy, I'm begging you. Is this what you want? For me to beg? I'm standing on this porch bare-assed to the world and begging you not to go."

Tony was both crying and huffing. His hair was wind-swept, and he looked lost.

"Sandy! Sandy! Please, Baby! Please!"

"I can't. I can't," Sandy cried out hysterically as he ran from Tony.

Suddenly, it was as if he had somehow stepped outside of his body and was elevated above. He was watching the whole scene from a few feet away. He watched as he ran to his car, opened the door and got in. He put the key in the ignition and it immediately started. He pulled away without looking back. His heart was pounding hard inside his chest and his breathing was becoming more and more labored. He was certain that he was having a heart attack or a stroke. He was driving erratically because he was crying so hard that he could barely see the road. It was painful for him to watch, but he couldn't turn away. He was certain that he was dying. Was his entire life all in vain? If only there was a way to start all over again. At that moment he heard, almost imperceptibly, the quiet cry of his heart:

"Lord, I'm sorry. I want to live. I repent before you. Please don't let me die. I recommit my life to you!"

Immediately, he came to himself, slammed on the brakes and shifted the car into park. Then he jumped out of the car just as he began to projectile vomit. Everything inside of him was coming out of both his mouth and his nostrils. It lasted for about a minute. Once he had completely emptied himself, he then started to dry-heave. Just then, another car pulled up next to him.

"Hey buddy, you okay?" the driver shouted out of the window.

Sandy couldn't speak or even raise his head. Somehow he managed to wave the person on.

"You know, drunk driving is against the law. You're going to kill somebody!" the driver shouted before he spun off.

Sandy just stood there for what seemed like an eternity. His mind was racing. Slowly, he got back in his car and drove away. He felt better and much more in control of his senses, but he was also very drained and weak. Both his throat and chest hurt too.

Fortunately, it took less than ten minutes to get there, or else he probably would not have made it. He parked his car and immediately exited. At first, he moved very slowly. However, his gait began to gain momentum gradually and before he knew it, he was running. There was a sense of excitement and expectation that came over him just as he reached the door. He punched in his four-digit code. It worked, and he pulled the door open. Using the flashlight on his phone, he maneuvered his way through the sanctuary doors, down the aisle, and to the altar. Immediately, he dropped to his knees and began to pray. He offered to the Lord a sacrifice of praise and thanksgiving. He offered up his own life and he felt safe again in his father's house.

And the glory of the Lord filled the temple.

Chapter 31

Reverend Glenn slowly opened his eyes. Startled, he sat straight up in his chair. Initially, he had no idea exactly where he was. It took a couple of seconds before he realized that he had fallen asleep at his desk. He looked at his watch and was surprised to learn that it was 4:50 a.m. Apparently, he had been sleeping for almost three hours. He thought that it was odd that Mercy hadn't called him. She had always claimed that she could not fall into a deep sleep without him lying next to her. He felt as though he should call her, but waking her up now seemed unnecessary. Maybe if he could somehow manage to get home and into bed without waking her, she would never know how late he had stayed out and he wouldn't have to endure her scolding.

Both his neck and his back were hurting, and he needed to take a muscle relaxer, painkiller—or something—before the muscles in his back start to tighten up. His body was simply too old to be trying to pull an all-nighter like an eighteen-year-old college student. No doubt he would pay the price for this lapse in judgment. The strange thing was that he didn't recall feeling that tired while he worked. Maybe he was so intent on completing his sermon that he completely ignored what his body was trying to tell him. It wasn't like him to black out like that.

He walked out of his office toward the bathroom. He had apparently reached that age when men cannot sleep through the night without needing to empty their bladder. However, if it weren't for that, he might have slept the entire night at his desk. The need to go was suddenly more urgent, and he walked faster. Oddly, he thought he heard music playing. It sounded like the piano. It was faint, but it seemed to be coming from inside the church. Perhaps it was just a phone that someone accidentally left behind. He continued to the bathroom and after relieving himself, he stared at himself in the mirror as he washed his hands. He thought that he looked old. He felt old.

They kept the aspirin in a cabinet in the lunchroom. He managed to find some extra-strength pain reliever and returned to his office. His desk was a mess. There were books and papers covering every square inch of it. He took the two tablets that were in his hand, put them in his mouth, and swallowed them both along with some leftover cold coffee from the cup on his desk. He was still drowsy and needed to go home to bed. He wasn't too thrilled either at the prospect of having to go out into the cold morning air.

He quickly read what he had written. At least he was able to finish the draft of his sermon. It still needed some tweaking. He had felt impressed to make more changes to his original message than he had first anticipated, but he was pleased with it. It sounded good. One of his professors in Bible college had stressed the importance of keeping one's message fresh because people can always tell when they were being served something that was stale. He believed that the Holy Spirit always provides exactly what is needed in this hour, and it was a big relief to not have to worry about getting it done any more. He read the title again: "Let God's love be perfected in you."

Next, he gathered up his belongings and straightened up his desk a little before heading down the stairs toward the side door exit. He told himself that he would only work a half-day today and that he would try to come in around noon. That's when he heard the music again, only it was louder now. Out of curiosity, he decided to see if he could figure out where it was coming from. He turned on the light next to the door, which only illuminated a portion of the hallway. He started walking into the darkness in the direction of the sanctuary. The music got louder with every step. Even before he reached the sanctuary doors, however, he knew that the music was coming from inside. The hairs on the back of his neck stood up.

Though he could not really see anything, he felt a gentle breeze brush his face as he opened the sanctuary door. He managed to take one step inside before he was forced to drop to his knees. It was as if someone or something had pushed him down, and the weight of it held him down. At the same time, it was electric, and he knew in an instant that he was in the presence of the Lord God Almighty. Immediately fear gripped him and he wanted to get up and run away. However, he couldn't offer any resistance.

There was a small light coming from the floor just beneath the altar, and he could only make out the shadow of what appeared to be an angel sitting at the piano and playing the most beautiful song that he had ever heard. Every note touched the very heart of him and echoed in his spirit. Each chord progression probed deeper into the memory senses of his brain and created vivid pictures in his head. There were bright colors—red, gold, yellow, and purple. The melody contained hidden meaning being revealed. His fear slowly began to subside and gave way to a sense of euphoria unlike anything he had ever known. The rhythm of the music somehow perfectly matched the natural rhythm of his body. He wanted to dance and he felt like he could fly. He was suddenly aware of a new way to express love for God. A heaviness saturated the room and it was a struggle just to think straight. He was now lying prostrate on the floor, face down. He held on as long as he could before he lost consciousness.

When he opened his eyes, someone was standing over him and trying to help him up. He had no idea how long he had laid there. The music was gone, and his first thought was how much he missed it already. It was hard for him to focus and it was a couple of seconds before he recognized Sandy. When he did, his eyes suddenly got big and an unexpected rush of emotion filled him. He began to cry as he was immediately overcome with guilt and shame.

"God, I'm sorry. I'm so sorry. I didn't know. I didn't mean it," he sobbed without restraint.

Without saying a word, Sandy pulled him to his feet. The two men held on to each other for dear life while the Spirit of God restored their souls.

Epilogue

Sandy was pacing back and forth and talking to himself. He didn't understand it. She knew that he hated to be late for church, and yet here they were again. Even worse still, in the year-and-a-half that they had attended Grace Union Baptist Church, he had never been this late before. If she made him miss the whole worship service, he was going to make her pay—and pay big time.

"Get out here this second or I'm going to leave you!" he shouted.

Suddenly she appeared, "How do I look?" Whitney asked as she spun around in her dress.

"Terrible!" he replied. "You look terrible!"

Mel just stared at him disapprovingly.

"You just be quiet," she said.

"I don't understand why you can't be on time. Don't nobody care how you look anyway."

"We both know that's not true," she said and smirked.

"It is true. Solomon Grey doesn't count."

"Why not? His new restaurant is doing really well. Everyone in Jacksonville is talking about it."

"Just come on! I don't want to waste any more time talking about your old tired boyfriend."

"Reverend Grey is not tired, and he is not my boyfriend," she disputed. "I told you that we're just friends."

"Whatever. All I know is that we need to hurry."

Sandy drove as fast as he could. Good thing they only lived a few miles from the church. The music ministry at Grace Union was outstanding, and he especially loved listening to the sister on the piano. She had the same spirit that he did. Nobody there even knew that he played the piano, and he was perfectly content to just be a regular member and allow the Holy Spirit to be his guide. Maybe he would never again play the piano in a church service, but that didn't really matter. Things just have a way of working out if we are obedient. It was all in God's hands now.

When he and Whitney first moved into their apartment, Verna bought him a new piano as a gift. He loved it and played it all the time. His life was a testimony to how much God loves his children, as well as to the undeniable truth that although God will, in fact, pass judgment on the unrighteous one day, he also is committed to rescuing his own people here and now. Since leaving Syracuse, Sandy had grown considerably in his relationship with God.

And on those rare occasions when regret and loneliness seeped into his consciousness and he found himself longing for what once was—or perhaps what might have been—and he could not seem to find his rest, he sat himself down at his piano and under the veil of darkness, played his love songs before the Lord until his heart was full again and his joy was renewed.

Note from the Author

Dear Reader,

To those of you experiencing same-sex attraction in any one of its various forms, first, it is important that you know that you are not alone. Every Christian struggles with the desires of his or her flesh in some fashion. The truth is that you are wonderfully made, dearly loved, and precious in the sight of our heavenly father. Secondly, if you have ever confessed Jesus as your personal Lord and Savior, then you have right standing before God right now. The spirit of the born-again believer, which is who we really are, is neither gay or straight. Third, you should endeavor to find and join a church that teaches the uncompromised Word of God in love. And when you get there, you should make every effort to meaningfully connect with at least one brother or sister who regularly builds your faith and affirms who you are in Christ. Beloved, it is my sincere prayer for you that the Holy Spirit will strengthen you daily as you walk out your salvation and grow up in Him.

Reverend Ed

About the Author

Ed Thompson is a lay minister at Abundant Life Christian Center, East Syracuse, New York. He is also a trial attorney in New York, having practiced law in Syracuse for more than twenty-five years. He is a former federal prosecutor and a former assistant public defender. Additionally, Ed will receive a master's degree in biblical studies from Alliance Theological Seminary of Nyack College in May 2020. Presently, he resides in Baldwinsville, New York, with his wife and daughter. *Piano in the Dark* is his first book.

Ed can be contacted at ethompson.esq@gmail.com.

CPSIA information can be obtained
at www.ICGtesting.com
Printed in the USA
LVHW082154100320
649693LV00015B/1233